D1112760

THE DEAD
CALLER FROM
CHICAGO

ALSO BY JACK FREDRICKSON

Hunting Sweetie Rose
Honestly, Dearest, You're Dead
A Safe Place for Dying

THE DEAD CALLER FROM CHICAGO

Jack Fredrickson

MINOTAUR BOOKS

NEW YORK

A THOMAS DUNNE BOOK FOR MINOTAUR BOOKS.
An imprint of St. Martin's Publishing Group.

THE DEAD CALLER FROM CHICAGO. Copyright © 2013 by Jack Fredrickson. All rights reserved. Printed in the United States of America. For information, address St. Martin's Press, 175 Fifth Avenue, New York, N.Y. 10010.

www.thomasdunnebooks.com
www.minotaurbooks.com

ISBN 978-0-312-60527-8 (hardcover)
ISBN 978-1-250-02098-7 (e-book)

Minotaur books may be purchased for educational, business, or promotional use. For information on bulk purchases, please contact Macmillan Corporate and Premium Sales Department at 1-800-221-7945 extension 5442 or write specialmarkets@macmillan.com.

First Edition: April 2013

10 9 8 7 6 5 4 3 2 1

For Mildred Kohout Fredrickson,
who always, always believed

ACKNOWLEDGMENTS

Once again,

    Mary Anne Bigane, Joe Bigane, Patrick Riley, and Marcia Markland prod me into doing better,

    India Cooper polishes a thousand things,

    Kat Brzozowski keeps track of it all, with grace,

    Jack and Lori give me meaning,

    and Susan gives me wonder.

THE DEAD
CALLER FROM
CHICAGO

Prologue

It was March, well past midnight, and it was cold. The only light came dimly from the streetlamp at the far corner.

The blurred shape of the bundled-up man moved low through the shadows of the fronts of the darkened houses. His feet crunched loudly on the crusted snow. The noise would sound no alarm. It was late. No one would be about.

Except this night. Another man followed fifty yards behind, tight to the same dark buildings. His shadow, too, was formless and indistinct. This man dared to make no sound at all.

Suddenly, the bundled-up man in front froze, then in the next instant rose from his crouch to look behind. In that moment, he was backlit by the pale milky light at the corner, a man wrapped so thickly against the cold he appeared more square than tall. He strained, listening.

There was nothing, only the wind moving restlessly up the street.

The shadowing man had melded into the darkness, invisible.

The bundled-up man dropped back into his crouch and ran on, down to the last house before the gap torn in the row, and disappeared up the stairs into the darkness of the brick arch.

The shadowing man charged at a dead run, his feet loud on the hard snow. He ran up the stairs and slammed open the door.

For an instant, there was nothing. Then bright flashes of blue-white fire lit the front windows, one, two, three. Gunshots, muffled by thick plaster and old glass.

An instant passed, and then another, and then the door banged open again.

The man in the center of the room, a faint ghost in the acrid gunpowder haze made yellow by the light of the streetlamp, turned without haste at the new intrusion. The revolver dangled heavy in his right hand.

Behind him, a man lay with his back against the wall that faced the dining room, where a piano topped with graduation pictures and perhaps a flower in a vase might have once stood. His eyes were still open, and still surprised. Three little holes surrounded by irregular spots showed dark on the wall above him. Through-shots; blood splatters.

The man in the center of the room raised his gun. "You're here for your friend?" he asked softly.

"Of course."

He shrugged. His knuckles bulged as he squeezed the trigger.

One

By my adjusted new standard, I'd become almost rich, and I felt myself swelling with optimism as Lester Lance Leamington, astute television advertiser, allowed as to how he could make me even richer. All I had to do was follow his advice, conveniently presented in a five-disc DVD series enticingly entitled *Making Millions from Molehills*. Though his features were blurry on my elderly analog four-inch television, its reception now modified by a government-mandated digital converter that dangled from it like an anchor on a chain, there was nothing fuzzy about his latest achievement. Lester Lance Leamington had hit the big time. He'd moved from late-night commercials jammed between spots for fast juicers and miracle scratch removers up to midday infomercials. If that wasn't testament to his financial acuity, I couldn't imagine what was. No more would he be talking to stupored, drowsy people; Lester Lance Leamington had risen into the clarity of sunlight. Now, for only twenty-nine ninety-nine, including shipping, he was going to show folks how to ascend just like him.

"All it takes is attitude," he was saying as I squinted in rapt attention, for on my tiny TV, he was only an inch tall. "Embrace your future. Call our toll-free line today. If you're not completely satisfied, we'll refund your money immediately; less, of course, the modest eighteen ninety-nine for processing, shipping, and handling."

Miraculous though it sounded, I was not yet ready to embrace my financial destiny. My new money, almost three thousand dollars from a tiny insurance company that promised more work, was already budgeted for past-due utility bills, a paydown on the lone credit card that hadn't canceled me, and wood, lots of the good oak I needed to continue trimming out my turret. There was the complication, too, that I had no DVD player, nor plans to buy one. My eyes were set on affording a furnace, ductwork, and a gas line to set it all to humming. It was early March, I lived in an unheated stone turret set beside a frozen river just west of Chicago, and the notion of warmth was constantly on my mind.

There was one final concern, I supposed. I watch television while semireclining in an electric blue La-Z-Boy that I acquired, well used, in an alley, perching the set on my breadbasket. Balancing a DVD player wired to a converter box wired to a television seemed like an awful lot of precariousness, just to get rich.

My cell phone rang, saving me from having to ponder the dilemma further.

"You doing anything worthwhile?" Leo Brumsky inquired.

"I'm being advised by Lester Lance Leamington."

"That TV lunatic with the red hair and green suit?"

"I don't know; my television is black-and-white. What matters is I am on the road to wealth."

"That insurance job up north?"

"My new client is delighted with the photographs I took of their insured, he of the broken back, up on a ladder, cleaning his gutters. They're talking about putting me on retainer."

"How much?"

"The company saved two hundred grand, easy."

"No, I meant you. What was your take?"

"Twenty-eight hundred and fifty-three dollars," I said. Then, to maximize the impact, I added, "Plus change."

"Ordinarily, I wouldn't intrude on a man burdened by such weighty considerations, but I have need of your brawn. I'll be right over."

I did not protest. His car had a fine heater.

Ten minutes later, a white Ford Econoline van rattled up to the turret where, since evicting the pigeons, I've lived alone. I'd been expecting a Porsche cabriolet, but the flash of a too-large orange traffic officer's jacket and purple pants, bright as beacons even at fifty feet, confirmed it was Leo.

He gave my own outerwear the fisheye as I got in. Hypocrisy, especially concerning clothing, was one of his most pronounced traits.

"A rented van?" I asked.

"Two coats?" he dodged, still round-eying my duds.

My blue blazer was longer than my peacoat, so it wasn't like he'd experienced a moment of deductive brilliance.

"I'm wearing my blazer in case Lester Lance Leamington drops by to give me personalized investment advice. Word of my newfound wealth is sure to spread." I aimed the heater vents to blast directly at my face.

A smile full of big white teeth split his narrow bald head, topped as it was, preposterously, by a chartreuse knit hat adorned with a purple pom. "You're wearing two coats because your limestone monstrosity retains cold like the arctic," he said, pulling us away from the curb.

I loosened the collar of my peacoat to more fully absorb the truck's free heat and asked where we were going.

"Once again, I'm branching out beyond my usual realm of expertise," he said.

Leo's usual realm of expertise was establishing provenance. The big auction houses in Chicago and on both coasts paid him in excess of half a million dollars a year to establish the lineage and authenticity of the pieces they offered to bidders.

"How far outside your realm?" I asked, as he swung northbound onto the Tollway.

The rented van shuddered its way up to sixty miles an hour. "Medical frontier," he said, grinning. "I've come up with a cure for aging baby boomers who suffer reduced physical and mental dexterity. Soon all will rejoice at the sound of my name. The visage of me, Leo Brumsky, the man who saved them from decrepitude, will adorn parks everywhere. They'll erect statues, bronze if not solid gold, of the Great Brumsky—"

"As targets for pigeons?" I myself had become an expert on pigeons, or at least their eviction.

"All will hail the name Brumsky, the genius who discovered the cure."

I pressed him no further. Silence would be the only way to drive him crazy.

His eyes remained fixed on the road. "Nonsplits," he offered up, after a moment.

I stared ahead, as silent as would be any bronzed Brumsky.

He lasted less than another hundred silent yards. "Aren't you curious about nonsplits?"

"Sundaes without bananas," I threw out, quite nonchalantly.

"Ah," he said, squeezing the wheel with his chartreuse-mittened hands to keep from blurting out anything more. It was to be a stand-off between us.

After fifteen minutes of absolute silence, he left the tollway, turned into an industrial park, and backed into a loading dock of the Great Prairie Nut Company.

"I'm sure they don't need another nut," I said.

"Stay here." He got out.

Ten minutes later, two men bounced a tall barrel into the back. They secured it with the yellow web straps lying on the floor and slammed the tin doors.

"I thought you needed my brawn, heroic as it is," I said, when Leo got back in.

He said nothing, easing the truck up the dock incline as though the barrel contained eggs. The game was still afoot.

It was too much. "OK. What are we hauling that must be so carefully secured?"

"Spent fuel rods. I'm converting your turret into a storage facility."

"I do investigations, and have deduced you've bought a barrel of nuts."

"Not mere nuts: nonsplits, the gateway to a more flexible life."

"And Brumskys, bronzed, will adorn parks across the land?"

"The world will rejoice." Once again we lapsed into silence, until we got to his street.

I turned my head to look out the side window, shocked. "What's going on?" A backhoe and a bulldozer were demolishing two bungalows toward the end of his block.

"Amazing, huh?" He sounded not at all happy.

"New homes? Here?" It was stunning news. Rivertown, the greasiest of the empty factory wastelands stuck like barnacles to the edge of Chicago, hadn't seen new construction in decades.

"Rumor has it there's to be only one, a McMansion on three lots. The bungalow just to the west is also coming down." He shook his head. "It's going to ruin the neighborhood."

His block, like almost all the residential blocks in town, was built solid of brick bungalows put up before the Great Depression for workingmen when manufacturing, instead of stripping women and stripping cars, was what pulsed in Rivertown.

"Who's building it?" I asked.

"No doubt some fool egoist, anxious to set himself above respectable, working-class neighbors."

"Be still, my lusting heart." Unlike Leo, who held the past dear, I had mixed emotions. The grit of Rivertown was deep under my skin, too; I was comfortable with solid lower-middle-class. Yet, if there was interest in redeveloping the crooked old burg, then my five-story turret might attract someone with lots of money and a crazed need to live in a tube. I could move up, like Lester Lance Leamington, to a place with central heat.

"I suppose you should see a lawyer about your zoning again," Leo said, turning up the alley.

There was the rub. The turret, built by my lunatic bootlegger grandfather as the beginning of a castle, had sat empty and ignored following his death at the start of the Great Depression. That changed at the end of World War II, when the town's fathers—an especially shameless lot of lizards, even by Illinois standards—sought to build a new city hall. They seized most of my grandfather's land along the Willahock River, and his mountain of unused limestone blocks, and erected a magnificent city hall of huge private offices and tiny public rooms. They'd had no need for the turret, though, and it continued to languish empty, racking up property taxes no one in my mother's family thought to pay. Sixty more years passed, and then the children and grandchildren lizards now running things thought to invite development, with its prospect of big-time bribes for construction and operating permits. For that, they needed to perfume the city's corrupt, tank-town image. They announced a new era, terming it the Rivertown Renaissance, and decided to use the turret on the Willahock River as an icon to plaster on their trucks, stationery, and the porta-potty in the town's one park. The lizards offered up a greasy deal: My aunt, the churlish bull-headed woman who'd inherited sole ownership of the turret after her sisters died, would get decades of unpaid property taxes wiped away. In exchange, the turret would remain in my family's hands, but it would be rezoned as a municipal structure, making it unsalable and thereby ensuring the city could use it forever as its new symbol. My aunt was elated . . . and cunning. To make sure her children would never suffer responsibility for the turret's upkeep, she willed the place to me on her deathbed, as a sort of grand last flush as she exited the planet.

Being of reasonable mind, I ignored her munificence at first. Then, disgraced by a scandal not of my making, and emotionally trashed by behavior that was, I got tossed out of my ex-wife's gated community. Drunk and utterly broke, I needed a roof. The turret had that, though it leaked. It also had pigeons, and no heat. Still, it was indoor living, of a fashion, and offered the faint hope that I might convert it into a residence to sell.

Right after moving in, I began petitioning to get the turret's zoning changed back to residential. Elvis Derbil, nephew of the mayor and the town's building and zoning commissioner, always refused. The turret was the city's icon; they'd invested too much in splattering its image all over town.

I had no money for a long-term legal battle, so I retreated. Even after Elvis resigned because of a scandal of his own—he'd altered freshness and fat-content labels on truckloads of stale salad oil—I hung back. My income from researching insurance claims and photographing accident scenes was little more than what I needed for materials to rehab the turret; I'd fight the zoning battle after the turret had been fixed up. However, if upscale yups were now about to charge Rivertown, bent on pushing over bungalows to build McMansions, times were changing faster than I'd dared hope. My future needed to be embraced, pronto. That meant reigniting my zoning battle.

Leo turned into the alley and stopped at his garage. Though the bungalows in Rivertown were built of the same dark brown brick, the colors of their frame garages varied within a subdued palette of whites, beiges, and grays. Not Leo's. His was a particularly vibrant shade of yellow, trimmed in neon green. Ma Brumsky loved her only child.

He got out, opened the big door, and disappeared behind his late father's ancient brown Ford LTD. Pa Brumsky had been dead for years, and his mother didn't drive, but Leo still kept the old beast in its usual spot and in prime running order. He respected the totems of his past.

He came out wheeling a dolly, and together we muscled the barrel out of the van, along the narrow walk, and up into the screened rear porch. Like all the neighborhood women who had enclosed back porches, Ma Brumsky used hers as a walk-in pantry. Leo had created a space for the barrel between cases of Diet Mountain Dew, bagged prunes, and All-Bran.

"This is going to improve flexibility how?" I asked.

"It might even cure the 'Zheimers," he said. He undid the clips on the barrel and lifted the lid so I could see inside.

"Pistachio nuts," I said.

He jabbed a hand into the nuts and withdrew a few as if he were cradling tiny torpedoes of gold. "Look closer; behold the miracle."

I took one from his palm. "A most ordinary pistachio," I said, having keen observational skills.

"How would you open it?"

It had not burst open. There was no seam."Nonsplits," I said, at last understanding his earlier use of the term—and not.

A Home Depot plastic bag lay on the case of All-Bran. He smiled, reached inside, and pulled out a pair of needle-nose pliers. *"Comprende?"* Sometimes he switches to Spanish, though never for very long, because he does not know the language.

"Oui," I answered in flawless high school French. "Ma and her lady friends will have to use pliers to open the pistachios, thereby strengthening their motor and mental skills. Thus the world will be saved, bronze Brumskys will be erected, and pigeons everywhere will have something appropriate to aim at."

"Genius, huh?"

"Drive me home." I had no time to dawdle. Yups were coming.

Five minutes later, he pulled up to the turret. "Come over tomorrow, and behold the beginnings of the new age."

As I climbed out of his rental van, I told him I would bet every one of my newfound twenty-eight hundred and fifty-three dollars that nothing but good was on the horizon for us both.

I will remember that moment for as long as I live.

Two

I awoke the next morning early and optimistic. I shrugged into my three sweatshirts, XL, XXL, and XXXL, and fairly raced down to the second-floor kitchen to make coffee. I was anxious to embrace the day and all the yups it brought forth, exactly as Lester Lance advised.

Burbling along with Mr. Coffee, I looked around with new satisfaction. I'd learned finish carpentry and cabinetmaking in that kitchen and thought the new oak cabinets, moldings, and trims looked fine indeed. True, the badly dented microwave offered a discordant note, presenting as it did the tiny potential of glow-in-the-dark aftereffects, and the rusty avocado-colored refrigerator I'd found in an alley worked well enough in the winter but was not at all reliable in the summer. No matter; they'd be gone soon. Only high-end stainless steel appliances would impress yups, and those were on the horizon. I had a new client, talking retainer.

Mr. Coffee gasped at last, and I took my coffee across the hall. As on each of the five floors, a huge fireplace was set into the southwest curve. It had been used only once, to share a fire with a woman reporter whom I'd never quite gotten to know.

I pulled the plastic garbage bag down over my desktop computer, covered my card table desk with a bedsheet, and began cutting thin strips of oak molding to surround the slit windows.

Architecturally, the narrow windows were historically accurate, ideal for archers to repel attacking marauders. Because they were set into rough stone, trimming them was fussy, slow work. By one o'clock, I'd only finished two and was ready for a break.

I went into the kitchen, drank the last burned dregs of the coffee, and ate half a cup of Cheerios, dry. Drinking burned coffee was a longtime habit. Dry Cheerios, though, were new. I'd had the happy yellow box since my divorce, but I'd used it simply as a cabinet divider to separate the small mounds of Twinkies and Ho Hos that were my ordinary staples. I'd been inspired to a wider view when, simultaneously, Lester Lance Leamington moved up into the daylight and I acquired a generous client. Change was in the wind for sure, and I reasoned I should improve my nutritional life as well. I began supplementing the Twinkies and Ho Hos with small test doses of Cheerios, administered one half-cup at a time. It had been almost a week, and I'd experienced no ill effects from the little sawdust-colored circles. In fact, that day I thought I noticed more spring in my step as I bounded up to the third-floor bedroom, where I keep my clothes piled on a chair next to my bed. I changed into unstained khakis and my least wrinkled blue button-down shirt, slipped on my blue blazer and peacoat, and walked my new health and optimism down the street to city hall.

The Building and Zoning Department was in the basement, the darkest floor of all. Unlike the mayor's first-floor office, where the big bundles from pimps, bookies, and tavern operators were counted out behind thick mahogany and closed drapes, the windowless basement offices were for collecting ordinary, day-to-day gratuities for permits that in any other suburb wouldn't require a bribe at all. I hadn't been down there since before Elvis Derbil had been perp-walked out by federal agents.

His door had been changed only slightly. The opaque glass now read J. J. DERBIL, BUILDING AND ZONING COMMISSIONER. Only the first name had changed. Official positions were passed along through families in Rivertown like genetic disorders.

The secretary in the outer office hurried out another door when she saw me. That had been her habit since the first time I'd come to scream at Elvis.

"Ahem," I said, clearing my throat behind the counter in the now empty outer office.

"Do you have an appointment?" a woman's voice called from inside Elvis's old private office.

"Purely an introductory call," I called through the door.

"You are?"

"Dek Elstrom."

"Oh, Christ."

"We've met?"

"You're the pain in the ass that lives in that limestone toilet-paper tube. Go away."

"I'm a taxpayer. You work for me." I laughed. Even I saw that as ludicrous.

"Make an appointment, Elstrom."

"Who are you?"

"The building and zoning commissioner, you idiot."

"I meant your name."

"Derbil."

"I meant your first name."

"Make an appointment," she said for the second time. She certainly had Elvis's communication skills, though my nose told me she didn't use his coconut-scented hair spray.

"I want you to rezone my property from municipal to residential."

She laughed. I left, thinking that to stay longer might jeopardize our budding relationship.

Since I was all dressed up, I drove to Leo's. I needed humor, and good coffee to wash away the dregs I'd just had at home, and heat, in which to enjoy them both.

I parked in front. As always, his walk and steps were immaculate, despite the snow that seemed to have fallen every day since November. Oddly, Leo's old aluminum baseball bat lay on the snow next to the walk.

The sound of a vacuum cleaner came through the front door. As did a sort of pinging, as though gravel were ricocheting inside, against the walls and windows. I had to knock loudly for almost a minute before the vacuuming stopped and Leo opened the door. Though he was dressed with his usual absurd cheeriness, in a too-large aqua-colored Hawaiian shirt festooned with monkeys riding balloons, and red cargo pants, he was not smiling. His normally pale face was flushed dark, perhaps from exertion.

"Vacuuming, Leo?" I asked, affably enough.

"With a normal vacuum cleaner, not a Shop-Vac like others must use," he said, trying for a smirk. On a head so pale and thin, a smirk was always an interesting contortion, because it made his thick black eyebrows look like they were trying to mate.

"I'm here for coffee," I said.

"First we clean." Leo never gets sidetracked. He thinks and lives sequentially. He is not like me.

I stepped inside. The living room had been shelled, literally. Splintered beige pistachio shells and crumbly bits of yellowish green nut meat lay on the carpet, the tops of the picture frames, the windowsills, and the yellowed plastic slipcovers that had protected every piece of upholstered furniture since Leo was an infant.

Two vacuum cleaners sat in the middle of the floor. One was an upright, the other a canister on wheels. A broom and a dustpan were set against the big-screen television. Shells crunched beneath my shoes as I took another step into the room.

The needle-nosed pliers Leo had bought for Ma and her friends to manipulate their minds and hands into better mental and motor health lay loosely spilled out of the Home Depot bag, apparently untouched. More interestingly, different, heavier tools—three wood-handled hammers, a handsaw, two silver adjustable wrenches, even Pa Brumsky's huge pipe wrench—were scattered all over the floor.

Several twisted, smashed-in tray tables were propped against the wall, ruined.

I understood why Leo's short aluminum baseball bat was lying on the snow outside. It was another tool, grabbed from the basement.

"Ma and her lady friends decided heavier implements would be more efficient?" I asked, summoning up my own smirk as I imagined the sounds such heavy weaponry must have made, whacking at tiny nonsplit nuts.

He ignored me. Pointing to the two vacuum cleaners, he asked, "Upright or canister?"

I took the upright, since it required less bending.

Even though the front room was tiny, it took a full twenty minutes because the two vacuum cleaners kept sending bits of shells and meat zinging in new directions. Finally, he shut off his vacuum and took a last look around. Leo's five-six, and that day he looked every bit the perfect miniature of a general surveying the field of an earlier, disastrous battle.

"Movie night?" I asked.

"Movie night," he agreed sadly, picking up an empty quart of vodka that had been kicked under a chair.

It had taken her less than a month, once Leo bought Ma the big-screen television, to discover soft cable porn. Only days after that, she found the harder, pay-per-view stuff. I could well imagine the rapid-fire chattering, in Polish, as Ma called her friends, all but one widows, with news of what could be summoned into her front room.

Gone was bingo at the church. Gone were rotating weekly bridge evenings. Mondays, Wednesdays, and Saturdays were now for new adventures, as Ma's circle of septuagenarians and octogenarians tottered over to Casa Brumsky to witness the slicked contortions on Ma's new TV.

I'd stumbled into one of those movie nights the previous summer. Eight old ladies sat primly in front of tray tables, sipping vodka from water glasses, munching from bowls of bridge mix, fried Wheat Chex, and prunes, staring at things on television they'd never previously dared discuss, in Polish, English, or any other language.

They'd looked up, red faced, when I knocked on the open screen door. The three that had walkers began banging their wheels on the floor, summoning Leo up from his basement office, where he'd taken to hiding on the nights when the girls came over. He charged up the gangway from the back of the house and yanked me off the front porch like I was explosive. He told me it was best to call before coming over; the girls liked privacy on movie nights.

"I still believe cracking the pistachios will spark them up a bit," Leo said now.

"Don't movie nights do that?"

He shook his head at my lack of vision. "I figured by the time they worked through the barrel of pistachios, they'd have improved their finger dexterity, loosened their shoulders and necks, and be thinking at warp speed."

I gestured at the heavy tools lying on the sculpted brown carpet. "They thought faster than you, for sure."

"Ma even got her meat tenderizer, the big square one she used to use on whole sides of beef. And someone messed up the garage, looking for Pa's tire iron."

"Your old baseball bat, too. It's lying on the snow outside."

"Jeez, you should have heard them, Dek. They sounded like a highway crew jackhammering a road." He sighed. "Let's bring coffee down to my office. Ma will be too embarrassed to show herself with you around."

Leo's office was directly under the living room. It must have been deafening, beneath a loud cloud of moaning porn stars, banging walkers, and falling wrenches.

Leo read my mind as always. "I couldn't stand it and spent the night at Endora's." Endora was his girlfriend. An ex-model and current Newberry Library researcher, she was a head taller than he was, though both their heads possessed the same oversized IQ. She lived in a condo, downtown.

His office was furnished with mismatched furniture, files, and equipment and was always orderly and neat. He sat behind the ancient wood desk, and I took the huge green upholstered chair his father had died in, all those years before.

"Tell me about this new client that's going to make you rich." He took a yellow wood pencil from the cup on his desk and leaned back. Leo was amazingly dexterous and often walked a pencil up and down between his fingers.

"Offices in ten states. They've hinted that the twenty-eight hundred was just for openers, that there will be a retainer coming for a lot more work. Maybe I've hit a golden confluence—"

"Confluence?" he interrupted.

"Confluence. It means a joining of two or more streams, like—"

"I know what a confluence is, you jackass. I just can't let you throw around such words as though they're part of your regular vocabulary."

"Confluence," I went on. "Maybe I'll have the dough to finish the turret and get my zoning changed just as yups are a-gathering right here in Rivertown—"

His landline phone rang. "Leo Brumsky," he said, holding the receiver with his left hand as his right kept finger-walking the pencil.

I tuned him out and looked around the office. As always, there was no sign of any current project, but I knew there had to be several. Leo Brumsky was highly regarded in the auction world.

On display, though, was Bo Derek. The movie goddess from the late seventies looked back at me from a poster above the light table. She sat in the surf and wore only a thin blouse, mostly unbuttoned. The blouse was wet. It was why Leo bought the poster when he was in high school. It was still the only work in his, an art examiner's, office. Even as adults, we agreed, it was all the art he needed.

The soft tap of his pencil hitting the tiled floor caught my ear.

"Snark?" His voice was higher than I'd ever heard.

I kept my eyes on Bo. The office had gone absolutely silent, except for Leo's breathing. It had quickened.

A moment passed, then another. Then he spoke, in a voice that was disbelieving. "Speak up, will you? You're whispering."

I had to look. His normally pale face had gone absolutely white. He was staring at the blank place on the wall above his four-drawer file cabinets, seeing nothing.

"No. I ran into Tebbins, and he told me about you, and all, so I threw it out; I didn't figure you'd want—" he said, his own voice now barely above a whisper. "I tell you: It's gone."

His free hand reached for another pencil. It snapped in his fist.

He mumbled something that I couldn't make out and hung up the phone.

"Who was that?"

His head didn't move.

"Leo?" I said, louder.

He looked up at me, slowly, like his neck hurt.

"That first summer you were gone," he said softly. "After first year of college . . ." His voice trailed away, and he again turned to look at the blank spot above the filing cabinets.

I remembered that summer. I'd left Rivertown at the end of the summer before, to begin college in Chicago, but really to get as far from Rivertown as I could afford. After freshman year, I stayed in the city because I had nowhere else to go. I took an early-morning summer session class, worked three part-time jobs, and waited for the memories to fade. A girl I'd known had died. For a time, I'd been suspected of killing her.

I'd never wanted to summon back those times, but now I realized Leo had never mentioned that summer, either, other than once he'd said he'd worked at the city's municipal garage.

"Who called, Leo?"

His eyes were glass, unblinking, as he turned back to look at me.

"A dead man," he said.

Three

To my shame, I forgot about the strange call Leo had received. My new client called, offering a seventeen-hundred-dollar fee to document a fraudulent insurance claim in Cedar Rapids. I was packed and gone first thing the next morning, certain it wasn't Iowa I was headed for but Fat City.

Leo phoned a day later. I was in a meeting with two of my client's agents. The call went to message but he hadn't left any words, and I forgot about that as well. It was like that with Leo and me. When one of us—almost always Leo—got busy, calls didn't get returned, unless someone yelled "Important." He hadn't.

I'd been back in Rivertown for two days, typing up reports, before I drove over to his neighborhood just before dusk. Even then, it wasn't Leo I was anxious to see, but rather that harbinger of coming good times, the new construction sprouting on his street.

They'd made good progress, in spite of the fact that it snowed three inches right after I'd left for Iowa. A huge hole had been cut square into the ground for a foundation sizable enough for what would surely be the largest house in Rivertown. I supposed the third lot, where the bungalow slated for demolition still stood empty, would be used for a side yard, and perhaps a detached garage.

I imagined some of the neighbors, good solid blue-collar types with sensible values, were appalled at what was sure to be a monument to an arrogant ego being plopped down smack in the middle of their neighborhood. I suspected more would be excited, like me, at the prospect of finally making out financially in a grub town like Rivertown.

I continued on down the block, thinking that if Leo were home, I'd blow off about having been traveling, as he so often did, on professional business, as he invariably did, and about how my professional life was just like his, except he had multiple clients, made huge money, and was generally well regarded in his profession. Since my business, and my life, had been trashed in a falsified document scheme some time back, that kind of talk would be good for half a laugh.

I coasted to a stop at his curb, surprised.

His house was dark, his sidewalk and front steps still covered with the three inches of new snow. For some people, uncleared snow didn't matter, and they took their time shoveling it away. Not so Leo Brumsky. He was fastidious to a fault about keeping his walks clean for Ma and her movie-loving friends, and he always attacked the task swiftly. When he was out of town, he had a standing deal with a snow removal service, paying them extra to put his bungalow first on their work list.

Snow lying on a walk, several days after it fell, was never allowed.

I trudged up the front steps and rang the bell. When there was no answer, I knocked, loudly. No one came.

I high-stepped across the tiny lawn to the gangway between his house and the neighbor's. Leo's office window, like all the basement windows, was barred. I knelt down. His office was dark, like every other room in the house.

Someone tapped on glass high behind me. I stood up. The gray-haired neighbor babushka looked down from her side window. She jabbed a finger toward the front. I walked back up the gangway.

"You're awful late," she said, leaning out past her wood storm door.

"What?"

"I seen you enough since you were a kid to know you're Leo's friend. Get shoveling."

"I just stopped by."

"Leo's got to be more careful with his arrangements. We got three more inches."

"No one's home. Did he take his mother someplace?" I was worried he'd rushed her to the hospital. Nothing else would explain snow sitting for so long.

"That's no excuse for not taking care of things so others won't fall. I use that sidewalk to get to the grocery. Now I have to walk clear around—"

I cut her off. "Is Mrs. Brumsky all ri—?"

Now it was her turn to cut me off. "They're away, but that's still no excuse. It always snows in Chicago in March, for pity's sake. Somebody needs to clear it off."

"Away? Both of them?" I could only think there'd been a sudden emergency, though Leo had never spoken of a relative out of town.

"Vacation, for pity's sake."

My mouth went dry. "Leo told you they went on vacation?"

"Fort Lauderdale, I think. Or maybe Miami Beach. Florida, for sure. Or maybe it was . . ." She scratched her head, confusion descending like a veil.

"You're sure: Leo took his mother on vacation?" I asked again, damning myself for not returning Leo's call when I was in Iowa.

"Of course I'm sure. They left right before all that snow came down. You going to shovel, or what?"

Something was wrong. Ma Brumsky's idea of a vacation was to cruise a shopping cart at Walmart. Even before she'd become tethered to her front room by the wonders of big-screen television, I'd never known her to want to travel. Leo, of course, took vacations, but only with Endora. They went to exotic spots like Gstaad or St. Barts. Leo was an obedient, loving son, but he'd never expressed any tolerance for vacationing with Ma Brumsky.

Then there was the uncleared snow. Leo was a meticulous planner. His removal service would have come around while he was away.

Unless he'd not thought to tell them they would be away.

I had my cell phone out before the neighbor slammed her door.

Leo's voice answered, telling me to leave a message. I did. "This is Dek. Snow has accumulated all over your sidewalk. I'm going to shovel, but Lester Lance Leamington is advising me to embrace greed, not menial labor. I expect payment of at least a thousand dollars, along with a phone call explaining what's gotten into Ma, abandoning television to take off on vacation."

I clicked off. Cracking wise hadn't made me feel any better.

A snow shovel leaned against the back porch. As I pushed the snow through the gangway to the front, I paused to look up and smile winningly at the neighbor's window. The curtain fluttered.

I cleaned the sidewalk and the front steps and returned the shovel to the back of the house. Even with the exercise, even wearing two coats, I'd begun to shiver. Something was wrong.

I started the Jeep, turned the heater on high, and called Endora's cell phone. I got routed to voice mail. I called her office at the Newberry and got her machine. Finally, I tried the library's main number. The operator said Endora wasn't in. She wouldn't tell me anything else.

I drove back to the turret, drank coffee, and tried trimming out a window. After ruining five pieces of wood, I gave it up and left three more messages on Leo's cell phone and two on Endora's. By now it was well past dinnertime. I microwaved something pictured on its box as looking beige. It came out green. I took it to my electric blue La-Z-Boy and switched on my tiny television with its dangling converter. Though it was just past ten, Lester Lance Leamington appeared, untroubled, optimistic, and chock full of the same crap he'd been spewing late-night and midday.

I carefully resealed the green food in its microwavable container, threw it across the room, and went upstairs to bed.

Four

The next morning, I grabbed for my cell phone before I got out of bed, even though I'd left the ringer on. None of my calls to Leo or Endora had been returned.

I dressed quickly and drove down Leo's street. Workers were unloading a huge pile of cement forms in front of the new excavation. They were going to be pouring a big basement.

I parked in front of Leo's bungalow and got out carrying my tool bag, like I'd come to fix something. It was true enough. I hoped to repair my peace of mind.

Even though it was cold, right at freezing, and early, the neighbor woman was out in the snow in her backyard, wearing galoshes and a black down coat. She was hanging laundry. The array on her line, large ladies' undergarments all, showed that she lived alone. I supposed the wet things would freeze quickly and make sounds like huge thunderclaps when they cracked, should the wind pick up.

"Get hold of Leo?" she shouted through the wood clothespins in her mouth.

"There might be a problem with the hot water heater," I said, to explain the tools.

"Then why are you going to the garage?"

"Just checking everything," I said.

"You tell Leo how it's dangerous to walk around unshoveled walks?"

"He was mortified."

Her eyes and nose followed me as I walked to the garage. Turning my back to hide my hands, I rummaged in my tool bag for my thinnest putty knife and slipped it between the service door and the jamb. The door popped open on something I hadn't expected to see.

Leo's purple convertible was inside. He rarely kept his Porsches longer than two years and always kept them immaculate. No longer. A foot-long scrape of brown paint had been cut into the rear fender on the passenger's side.

Pa Brumsky's monstrous old Ford LTD, painted that same brown, was gone. It had been backed out for the first time in a decade, hurriedly enough to scrape the Porsche.

I slammed the service door shut and quickly walked to the house.

The flimsy porch door was unlocked, as usual. Ma didn't worry about thieves coming for her Diet Dew, prunes, and All-Bran. The barrel of nonsplits rested where Leo and I had dropped it, the object of one of the last laughs we'd shared.

The thick back door was locked. Again the thin putty knife worked fast magic. I stepped inside.

My shoes crunched on pistachio shells. A sparse trail of them had been dragged all the way back from the front room. There'd been another movie night since Leo and I had vacuumed, but this time, impossibly, no one had cleaned up. The trail of shells fit with the scraped Porsche. Leo and his mother had been in a panic to get away from Rivertown.

Leo's bedroom was at the back. I went in, ducking under the plastic airplane dangling from the ceiling. There'd once been a whole squadron suspended there, painted in psychedelic variations of yellow, purple, green, and pink. Even as a child, Leo had seen the world brightly. Now only one remained, a World War II Spitfire he'd painted in orange and green stripes.

His bed was made, but that meant nothing; he spent most of his nights downtown with Endora. I checked his closet. The same startling mix of pants and Hawaiian shirts was nestled in with the plain white shirts and conservative two-thousand-dollar designer suits he wore for work. I couldn't tell if anything was missing. He could have packed little to nothing if he was in the kind of hurry that caused him to trash his Porsche.

The kitchen was a mess. The sink was piled with supper dishes, and more pistachio shells lay on the wax-yellowed linoleum. The door of one cabinet was open. It was the low, easily reachable one that Leo kept stocked with the tiny, airline-sized bottles of whiskey, gin, and vodka that he thought would slow Ma's drinking. The shelf had been swept clear. It was a good sign. Ma had been in a hurry, but she'd been lucid. She hadn't left her booze.

I opened the refrigerator. It was full, as always stocked with store goods and a dozen of Ma's scratched, opaque Tupperware containers. Two unopened gallons of milk rested on the top shelf. Even after he'd stopped growing at five foot six, Ma always insisted that Leo drink two glasses a day.

Ma's bedroom opened off the dining room. Her bed was unmade, and two of her dresser drawers had been pulled out. She'd packed fast.

Christ on the cross, her only decoration on the dark papered walls, was slightly askew. It could have happened when she'd jerked open the closet door beside it.

In the front room, cocktail glasses and bowls of bridge mix and prunes lay on brand-new tray tables facing the big-screen television. Leo must have hid the big tools; only the Home Depot pliers lay on the new tables. Not surprisingly, the pistachio shells were the thickest on the front-room carpet.

Shells on the floors, dirty dishes, swept-away booze bottles, pulled-open dresser drawers, and one swiftly scraped Porsche all pointed to a fast escape.

Ma and Leo had fled.

My footsteps drummed on the old wood steps as I went down to the basement. Not many months before, Ma asked Leo to clear it out so she and her friends could exercise. Ever the positive thinker, he'd dragged the clutter to self-storage.

When she specified shiny dance poles, dimmable lighting, and the red velvet walls of a strip club, he remained optimistic. Anything that fought the arthritis was fine. He even kept a smile pasted on his face when she requested a new big-screen television to play the special high-bass, heavy-drum videos that one of her ancient friends found in a dirty-movies store downtown. When the ladies began sewing costumes of beads and pull-away Velcro, he began to pray for release.

It came, with pain. First, one of Ma's most imaginative octogenarian friends, Mrs. Roshiska, was carted off to the hospital with a slipped disc. Another of the girls then damaged a rotator cuff, the result of tugging too exuberantly on the pole. Finally, Ma herself took to bed with sciatica.

Leo acted fast. He brought everything back from self-storage: the tiny artificial Christmas tree they used to shake off and put on top of the rabbit-eared television, before Ma got the big screen; the model railroad layout I'd helped Leo set up in seventh grade; the dozen boxes of drugstore china Ma liberated when she'd been young and there'd been such a thing as drugstore lunch counters. In no time flat, Leo restored the artifacts of the lives Brumsky to the same mounded mess they'd been in since I was a kid and would have given anything to live in a place so cluttered with memories of good family times.

That day, though, the pile in the middle of the basement had the musty smell of stuff that would never be needed again. Leo and his mother were gone and unreachable, as though they'd been sucked off the planet, and that made no sense at all.

Leo's office looked neat and orderly and waiting for work, as always.

I sat behind his desk. The coffee cup of sharpened pencils rested where it had always been. I'd had a cup just like it, festooned with the name of some fool who'd dared to run against one of the lizards for water commissioner. Mine had gotten lost in one of the monthly moves I'd had to make as a kid, shuffling from one aunt to the next. Leo, though, still had his cup, like everything else from his youth. Once he owned something, he kept it for life.

Like me, as his friend.

The last time I'd been in that room, Leo had snapped a pencil he was taking from that cup. He'd gotten a phone call that drained the blood from his face. He'd called the man Snark.

He'd whispered, "But you're dead," disbelieving, into the phone.

He'd said something else I didn't understand, about throwing something out because he thought it was a joke, and he'd mentioned someone named . . . what was it . . . Teddings.

I'd asked him about his caller, Snark. He hadn't answered at first. He'd paused for a long moment and then, in a soft daze, mumbled something about the summer after I'd left Rivertown. I asked him again who'd called.

"A dead man," he finally said.

I looked across the office. The very wet Bo Derek, sitting in the surf, smiled back. We'd been high school freshmen when he found that particular piece of art rolled up in a big can at the Discount Den. We still joked that was the moment we discovered love, or at least a sufficiently wet and excited approximation of it.

I leaned forward. A picture I'd never noticed before hung above the row of mismatched filing cabinets, barely visible behind the tall art reference books. It was a pastoral scene of a lavender barn and two pink, green-spotted cows against a background of rolling orange hills and leafy red trees, signed with a big "Leo B." in the corner. He must have done it in fifth or sixth grade. Leo was forever resurrecting stuff from the massive pile in the center of the basement floor.

I rummaged through his desk. Pens and notepads and checkbook and envelopes and green Pendaflex file folders. Everything looked normal.

I went up the stairs thinking that I should bring out the vacuum and the broom and the dustpan. The Brumskys, Ma and Leo, kept their modest place neat. To see it a mess seemed somehow a sacrilege.

A thought then stabbed: There might be a need for cops and forensics people to see things exactly as they were now.

I went out the back way and tried to lock the door tight against that kind of thinking.

Five

Besides the caller, Snark, the other name Leo had mentioned during the phone call was Teddings. It sounded as though Leo had known them both, that first summer of college.

The city's maintenance garage was a cinder-block building, two blocks south of the bars along Thompson Avenue. A man in blue overalls was inside, toweling a black stretch Cadillac Escalade. Another two Escalades were inside, along with a Cadillac Seville, waiting to be washed. Rivertown might have been the greasiest town stuck to the west side of Chicago, but it could never be said that its Cadillacs were allowed to get as dirty as its reputation.

"Is there a man named Teddings here?" I asked the man wiping down the Escalade.

He pointed to a man working beneath the open hood of a dark green city pickup truck. The image of my turret was emblazoned on the truck's door, there in exchange for the forgiveness of old tax bills and a sleazy bit of rezoning.

"Is Teddings here?" I asked the mechanic.

He kept his head under the hood of the truck. "You mean Tebbins."

"OK," I said. "Is he here?"

"He's a building inspector now. Try city hall."

I drove back to the turret, parked, and walked down the street to city hall. I'd never liked living close to where the lizards scuttled, but an advantage was that the street was always immaculate during snow months. I supposed that was because lizards moved close to the ground and didn't like ice rubbing their swollen bellies.

The building inspectors were at the end of the hall, just past J. J. Derbil's office. The name on the glass said a man named Bruno Robinson was the chief inspector. The department secretary was also named Robinson. She looked up from the *National Enquirer* spread out on her desk. At least three years of back issues were piled on a low bookcase next to her. I asked for Tebbins. She asked if I had an appointment. I said no. She pointed to a private office and told me to go right in. As I passed her desk, I saw that she was reading a report of aliens taking over the Pentagon. I wanted to hope that Rivertown would not be next but feared I was several decades too late.

Tebbins was in his late sixties. Officeholders don't retire in Rivertown; they collect both salaries and pensions until they drop in their offices from the greasy weight of doing too little for too long. Like the department secretary, he read, too, to pass the time. The day's *Sun-Times,* open to the sports section, was on his desk. Apparently, he was not worried about aliens.

His mouth turned down when I told him my name. "Elstrom . . . Elstrom . . . the name is familiar . . ." He snapped his fat fingers in recognition. "Aren't you that nut that lives in the turret across the lawn?"

"The very same," I said, preening. "I'm here about someone named Snark."

A flash of recognition raised his fat chin for a second before he made his face go blank. "Snark who?"

"Snark somebody; I don't have a last name. I think he used to work for you at the city garage. Leo Brumsky worked there that same summer."

"Leo I remember," he said, his face brightening. "Odd little guy, but conscientious, the way he used to climb up on those trucks." He leaned back. "We didn't often get good help to wash trucks."

"And cars?"

"What?"

"Lots of kids are needed to wash all those Cadillacs?"

"I don't know what you mean."

Sure he did. He knew about Cadillacs, like he knew about someone named Snark, whoever he was.

I started to turn, then stopped with a thought. "Good news about that new house going up, right?"

"What the hell does that mean?" Rivertown's building inspector asked, of the only new construction begun in years.

I named Leo's street. "Big one, too. Got to be a million dollars going up on that property."

His face darkened. "I can't help you, Elstrom."

I passed a larger private office on my way out. According to the nameplate next to the door, it belonged to Chief Inspector Robinson. His desk had a newspaper, too, but he acted a lot friendlier, giving me a smile and a wave as I walked by.

I'd walked halfway back to the turret when a burgundy Escalade passed by. I couldn't see the driver behind the dark tinted glass, but the Cadillac was dirty. Odds were good he was headed to the garage for a wash.

I'd struck out at the garage and struck out at city hall. I decided to try the garage one more time.

I had to laugh as I pulled up. The burgundy Escalade that had passed me on the road was indeed parked in front of one of the wash racks. The chief building inspector was just getting out.

"Get what you need from Tebbins?" he asked.

"Robinson, right?"

He stuck out his hand. "Call me Bruno. You didn't look happy, leaving our office."

"Tebbins dusted me off about someone he might have known when he worked here."

He smiled. "Try me. I was in charge of the garage back then."

"I'm looking for someone named Snark."

"Snark Evans?"

"I don't have a last name."

"How many Snarks can there be? He worked here, part of one summer, years ago."

"You remember him, even though it's been a long time."

"Not just because of the name. He was a punk. Why the interest?"

"A friend of mine knew him."

"And that friend would be . . . ?"

I'd already decided I had to play some things openly to explain my interest. "Leo Brumsky."

He grinned. "Now there was a good kid. Skinny, couldn't have weighed a hundred and fifty pounds. Worked hard every minute. It was lousy work, too, washing trucks. It was before we had the power wash equipment. How is old Leo?"

"Still lives in Rivertown. He's a provenance specialist—"

"A what?"

"Someone who authenticates things for auction houses."

"Figures. He was real smart. He was here at the same time as Snark. They weren't exactly friends, I don't think, but they ate lunch together most every day, out back. You here asking on your own, or for Leo?"

"It's complicated."

"I would have thought Leo had heard, but maybe not." He scratched his chin. "Come to think of it, Leo left early that summer, too."

"Heard what?"

"Snark Evans died, late that summer."

The shock in Leo's voice, when I asked who'd called, came back: *A dead man,* he'd said.

"What did Evans die of?"

"No idea. Evans left here around the middle of July, and that I remember only because I had no chance to find another kid in a hurry. They were all working other summer jobs. With Leo already gone with mononucleosis. I was screwed. That summer, city vehicles stayed dirty. Anyway, later on, someone said Snarky was dead. Probably killed in some dumb-ass robbery."

"Snark was a thief?"

"Like I said, a real punk. We had a master key for all the lockers—well, let me just put it to you this way: Tebbins found out Snarky was selling stuff out of his locker."

"Hot stuff?"

"Earrings, and other ladies' jewelry, and men's watches. I figured he was breaking into cars or shoplifting stores. We figured the law was on him, the way he quit sudden."

"Then he was killed?"

"Not until after he was gone a month or two. Someone saw a newspaper clipping saying he'd died out of state somewhere. Why would a nice guy like Leo be interested in that greaseball after all these years?"

"Leo never forgets the past. He remembers people and gets curious about what's happened to them."

"So he hired you to indulge that curiosity?" He'd cocked an eyebrow, too smart to buy the lie. "I wouldn't have thought he had any real fondness for Snarky," he went on. "Nobody did. Whatever is on Leo's mind, you tell him to be careful about Snarky. The kid's no good, even dead."

I asked him some of the same questions again, and he gave me the same answers again. He didn't know much.

Then he said, "Heard you stopped in to see the big boss, J. J."

"Word gets around?"

"Some folks in city hall got nothing to do but talk."

"I need to get my zoning changed."

He laughed. "Good luck on that. City thinks of your place as its own."

"We're not done, J. J. and I."

"Best you mind yourself there. She's smart, not like Elvis, that brother of hers. Word is, J. J.'s going to be mayor, and soon. Don't trifle with her."

I had one more thought. "Leo's leaving had nothing to do with Snark Evans, right?"

His eyes were steady on mine, knowing there was plenty I was wasn't saying. "Not to my knowledge, but maybe you should ask your good buddy Leo that."

"I will."

He shook his head. "It was a bad summer, all around."

Walking back to the Jeep, I had the thought that perhaps that bad summer had come around again.

Six

The Newberry Library had sat a few blocks north of the Chicago River for over a century, half of what it was meant to be. According to legend, it was planned to be Chicago's main library, but its benefactor, Mr. Newberry, expired en route to Europe before it could be built. No sooner had he been returned to Chicago and rolled up the hill to the cemetery, still in the same barrel of rum in which he'd been preserved aboard ship, than his wife and daughters began squabbling over his financial remains. By all accounts a parsimonious lot, they ultimately agreed to fund only half the proposed construction. Chicago's city fathers, already exhibiting the sensibilities that would make them famous for centuries, grabbed what they could—and then built half a library. The front facade was erected as specified, but the sides were stopped exactly halfway back, and the rear was sided with cheap common brick. Instantly unsuitable as a central library, the quirky building became a repository for obscure old manuscripts, periodicals, and maps. And Leo's girlfriend, Endora.

Though never quite a superstar, she'd been a popular model from the time she was eighteen and had appeared frequently between the covers of most of the major national magazines. Her brains matched her beauty. During her modeling years, she was a top student at North-western, earning bachelor's and master's degrees in history.

When the fashion assignments slowed to a trickle, Endora quit modeling, used a fraction of her cash to buy an upscale condo, and took a low-paying job as a researcher at the Newberry. It was there that she met Leo. She towered over him physically, but their massive intellects and slanted views of the world were perfectly paired. If she'd thought to hang model airplanes from her bedroom ceiling, she'd have painted them with psychedelic brightness, too.

I was Leo's best friend, but Endora was his life. If anyone knew where Leo had gone, it was she.

But she wasn't answering her phones.

As I climbed the wide stairs into the Newberry, I thought of when, just a few years before, I'd gone to that library to hide from the press. My reputation was trashed, my marriage was collapsing. All I could think to do was to hide out in the deep quiet of one of the upstairs reading rooms and look at old maps of places that no longer were. It helped to calm my pounding head.

She'd watched over me those days, checking on me frequently, bringing me up to the employees' rooms for lunch and coffee. She'd showed me her cramped little cubicle and introduced me to her boss. He weighed over three hundred pounds and shook all of it when he laughed, which as I remembered was quite often.

He remembered me but was guarded. "Tell me why you're looking for her?"

I was guarded, too. "I called here yesterday. They said she wasn't in. I tried again today. They said she wasn't in. I thought I'd swing by, hoping she'd returned."

"You also tried her cell and home numbers?"

"Of course."

"And without her having returned your numerous calls, you still thought stopping by would be productive?"

I tried giving that a shrug.

"Cut the crap, Dek."

"I'm trying to find Leo. A neighbor told me he's on vacation, with his mother. His mother doesn't vacation. Leo does, with Endora. Nobody's around; not Leo, not his mother, not Endora."

He studied my face for a long moment and said, "She phoned a few days ago, saying she needed personal time. She didn't mention anything about a vacation."

"You found that odd," I said.

"Endora has never asked for personal time."

"Have you noticed anything else strange going on with her?"

"That call, so sudden, was enough. She's got a major exhibit starting in two weeks, and this is absolutely the worst time she could take off. Endora is never vague about anything. She's precise, factual, and succinct. But the day she called, she was vague as hell about everything, including when she'd be back. Obviously there was something going on in her life, but since she's never asked for anything before, I let it alone."

"She mentioned once she had family in northern Michigan. A mother, I think."

"The Newberry never releases personal information about its employees."

"No need. You can find some pretext to call her mother to make sure Endora is safe."

He kept his face blank, noncommittal.

"You're a research man, right?" I asked.

"This is the Newberry, dear sir."

"This morning, I tried researching a name on the Internet: Snark Evans. I found nothing on the criminal background and general sites. That was no surprise; Evans is a common name, and for sure Snark is an earned name, not a given one."

"Who is he?"

"A small-time punk, a burglar, who died years ago."

"How does this concern Endora?"

"Someone calling himself Snark Evans upset Leo with a phone call, right before he and his mother and Endora disappeared."

He said he could promise nothing.

Like the builders of the Newberry, I said I would take what I could get.

It had started to snow. I stepped out of the Newberry into great sticky clumps of it, coming down as though some maniac upstairs were sitting in the dark, shredding wet white felt. March was like that in Chicago. It teased with sun and a warming day, promising spring, and then slammed down a sticky blanket so wet and thick people could only think winter would never end. On such days, everyone plodded. Traffic crawled; pedestrians dragged themselves across intersections like they were shouldering lead. It took me an hour to get south to the expressway, another to get to Leo's block. By that time, it was dark.

Two men were getting into pickups at the big hole between the houses. The pile of cement forms at the front of the excavation didn't look any smaller. They'd made no better progress than I had, that day.

Leo's house was another big hole between bungalows lit against the night. I pulled to the curb and shut off the engine, thinking of the lights that weren't there. There'd been no time to set lamps on timers. Absolutely, they'd run.

A pair of headlamps came down the street behind me. One of the pickups passed by. The second followed a moment later.

A third pair of headlamps switched on, back at the construction site, and the vehicle started coming down the street. Halfway to Leo's, it swung sharply to the curb and its lights were switched off.

Someone had stopped to make a call, perhaps, or check directions, or simply to park closer to a house. I rolled down my window to catch the sound of a car door slamming as someone got out. I heard nothing. I waited in the dark, watching the rearview mirror for five minutes, maybe ten. No door slammed. No headlamps came back on.

I started my engine and pulled out. Turning right at the corner, I saw the headlamps start up behind me. It didn't have to mean anything.

I pulled onto the bright carnival that was Thompson Avenue, and for a moment, there were all kinds of headlamps behind me, slow-cruising gents checking out the meat winking through the snow. I turned off onto the side street, then onto my street. Getting out, I looked back. A car had pulled off onto the side street that led to mine and stopped. Men used that stub of a street sometimes, with the less demanding of the girls that worked the curbs.

Invariably, though, the johns cut their headlamps. Not so the car that had pulled off Thompson. Its headlamps remained on.

I stepped into the cold that was the turret, but I didn't turn on any lights. I found my way up the wrought-iron stairs and turned past the kitchen to the slit window that most directly faced the street. The headlamps were moving toward the turret. The snow was too thick to see what kind of car it was.

It stopped in front of the turret. Its lights went out. I swore at myself for not turning on the outside light. It would have helped me see.

Nothing happened for two or three minutes. Then the car door opened and was shut quickly. I couldn't make out anything in the brief flash of the car's inside light.

I waited at the top of the second-floor landing.

Someone started beating on my door.

Seven

The figure stood in the dark, outside my door.

"Jenny Galecki," I said.

"Jennifer Gale, underappreciated media personality," she corrected, raising her chin, sniffing, a parody of arrogant celebrity.

We stood as awkward as kids fixed up for a prom until I found the wit to say, "You followed me from Leo's block?"

Dark haired, slim everywhere except a bit north of her waist, she was every bit as beautiful as I remembered.

"Leo lives there?" she asked, seemingly surprised. With Jenny, things were often seemingly; usually she knew way more than she let on. Then, "You're going out again?"

"Again?" I asked, dumb as a brick.

"You didn't turn on any lights when you got home, and you're wearing your blazer and your peacoat. So, are you going out again?"

"You've never been to my turret in the cold months. In winter, I wear two coats indoors, especially in March."

"You never got heat?"

"There's a small space heater, but bigger things are in store. I'm embracing my future."

She laughed, perhaps at the ice that was breaking. "Lester Lance Leamington? He advertises on Channel 8." It had been her station, until she moved out to San Francisco several months before.

Thinking, as I'd been, at glacial speed, I suddenly became aware we were still in my open doorway. "Let's go out for dinner. We'll ask each other inconvenient questions."

"Where?"

"Someplace with heat," I said smoothly.

She drove us in her Prius, because as she put it, she'd already been in my Jeep. She'd also been upstairs, in the turret. We'd used the fireplace on the second floor, after an especially chilling day in the heat of summer. I think we both thought we might go higher, to the third floor, where there was another fireplace. And a bed. Instead she'd left for San Francisco.

She drove to a barbecue joint just inside the Chicago line. It had black walls and a skull-and-bones painted on its door. Proper gourmet dining was at last coming to the city.

"This place is dark and looks to have many small rooms," I observed aloud, as we stepped into the foyer. Jennifer Gale, former features reporter for Channel 8, attracted attention wherever she went.

"I like it because it's dark and has many small rooms." She smiled. We were definitely thawing.

The waitress parked us in a booth at the back of a particularly dark room. We ordered Cokes and pulled pork from a waitress who didn't give Jenny a second glance.

"So, what brings you back to Rivertown, other than the chance to bump into me?" I asked.

"I've been back for two weeks."

Trying to hide surprise, curiosity, and more than a little disappointment, I said, "That explains why I haven't called."

"Huh?" she said, and we both laughed.

"Are you permanently back?"

"I'm not sure." She turned to look away, across the room. I recognized the gesture. It wasn't that she and I had lied to each other in the past. It was more that sometimes we'd worked too hard at avoiding truths.

"Why are you staking out that new house that's going up?"

"Interesting, such a house in such a town."

"Enough to return from San Francisco to check out?"

She smiled, said nothing. She wasn't going to tell me a thing.

"Who's building it?" I asked.

"I've been seeing your Jeep on that block quite a bit lately."

"Around one particular house, and yet you didn't think to find out who lives there?"

She laughed. "Maybe I did find out it was Leo's, though it doesn't appear that he's around."

"He's away. I'm looking after things," I said.

"Doing a most thorough job of it, too. Tonight, you stopped outside his bungalow, turned off your lights, and just sat, looking after things."

"You could have come up and said hello."

"That's what I'm doing now." She smiled. It was a wonderful smile, articulated by slight lines around her mouth that were hidden by makeup for television. She reached across the table to touch my wrist. It was like fire. "Just like old times?"

"Comfortable, for sure." Except it wasn't. Leo Brumsky was missing from the same block that had drawn Jenny back to Rivertown, and until I knew what he was up to, and she was up to, I couldn't say much at all.

Our pulled pork sandwiches came. "Saved by pork," she said.

"I've always wondered what 'pulled' means," I said, playing along. "I keep envisioning a frantic tug-of-war between a butcher and a screaming pig, with the butcher always winning. Then the image gets too gruesome to think about further, and I let it go."

"Same old Dek," she said.

She talked a careful little about San Francisco and the vagaries of network news reporting. We agreed they were like the vagaries that seemed to afflict everything, except the opinions of addle-headed experts. Nobody honest knew anything about the future, not anymore.

The waitress took away our plates, and Jenny asked, "Why didn't you call after you got back from Indiana?"

"Actually, I did," I said. "I just clicked off before sending the call through."

"I wouldn't have pressed," she said.

We'd both been hunting the same woman. She could have been talking about that. Or she might have been referring to my relationship with Amanda, my ex-wife.

"The papers said you pushed to get transferred," I said, not ready to press, either.

"It seemed an opportune move. Fewer features, more investigative reporting." She said it with a smile, but there might have been a bit of hurt behind her eyes. My not calling wasn't the major reason she went to San Francisco, but it still made me an ass.

"Remember the night we lit my fireplace?"

"We took a warming romantic possibility and invited in our ghosts to cool things down."

"Your husband, my ex-wife, and us. It was crowded."

"We weren't ready."

"I've needed the months since last fall to understand that."

"Now you're embracing your future?" Her face had relaxed to its loveliest.

"One that's looking considerably warmer. I've got a new client, two assignments so far. Soon there might be central heat."

"What a shame. You have such fine fireplaces."

I let that thought hang in the air for a long moment, then asked, "Your ghost?" Her husband, a newsman, had been killed in Iraq.

"He's not coming back." Her eyes were clear and unblinking. "And yours?"

"I've not spoken to Amanda in weeks." Even now, the finality of the words about my ex-wife startled me. I headed for safer ground. "Speaking of ghosts," I said, "the stories you were chasing in Rivertown about Elvis's salad oil scheme and the lizard relatives collecting unearned expenses and travel reimbursements? Channel 8 has reported nothing since you left."

"I kept my notes. How's Leo?" She'd met Leo the previous summer. Like everyone, she'd been charmed in an instant.

"You mean in general?"

"Why does his house need watching by a man sitting in the dark?"

"As I said, he's away."

She laughed. I laughed. At least we were being honest with each other, about not being totally honest with each other.

We left and drove back to the turret in silence. I wondered if she, like me, was going over things we could have said at dinner, or even before that.

She pulled to a stop in front of the turret. "Well, we've established you should have come charging back from Indiana, intent on seeing me." She smiled, hugely. "I forgive you, and so you can see me again, and soon."

For that, and for everything else I wanted to fix with her, I reached over and kissed her, quickly, before I got out of her car and went up to the turret.

Eight

I switched on my computer first thing the next morning. Endora's boss had e-mailed at 3:17 A.M., probably about the time I finally found sleep:

> *Dek, It's too damned late, or too damned early, to be sending e-mails. I'm still in my office. For the last hour, I've done nothing but sit. And think. And now, at last, I've summoned a vague conclusion that begs for another conclusion, which will be up to you to provide.*
>
> *I combed every newspaper, television, and law-enforcement Internet archive available to us here at the Newberry. As you can imagine, I found numerous citations for men named Evans— under almost every given name you can think of. There were thousands!*
>
> *And now, I think I found him in a regional summary of tiny newspaper clips from central Illinois. Attached is the death notice from the* Center Bridge Bugle. *It reports that Edwin G. "Snark" Evans, of that town, died many years ago.*
>
> *Center Bridge is two hundred miles southwest of Chicago. It has fallen on hard times since the John Deere assembly plant,*

*fifteen miles away, closed. The local funeral home and a num-
ber of Center Bridge's businesses have also folded, along with
the* Center Bridge Bugle, *presumably, since I can find no other
references to it. I would imagine many of the town's inhabitants
have moved away, though someone might remain who remembers your Mr. Evans.*

*Now, as to that conclusion that begs for another conclusion:
Though the death notice appears to be straightforward, something about it feels wrong. And that's what's kept me up until
this late (or early) hour.*

*First, who would use the nickname "Snark" in a death notice?
Certainly, nicknames appear in news reports and in obits, but
they're more of the garden variety—a "Bud" or a "Bob" or a
"Skip." To me, something about the nickname "Snark" seems,
well . . . a little "snarky," if you'll allow my joke. The nickname
seems pejorative, a little distasteful.*

*I consulted an online dictionary and found the term was
coined by Lewis Carrol in 1874, to refer to an imaginary animal.
Certainly, there's nothing distasteful about that. Still, the nickname bothers me.*

*Then there's that lack of detail in the obit. Contrary to cus-
tom, the death notice does not report how he died, only that he
was survived by a sister, whose whereabouts are not mentioned.
Nor is there any mention of a wake, service, or funeral, or where
he was buried. Again, I got my information from a summary,
so perhaps that's their practice. Still, it feels bothersome.*

Finally, there's the Center Bridge Bugle *itself. As I've written, I could find no other mention of that newspaper itself. It's
not listed in any of the reference sites for defunct Illinois news-
papers. That's more than odd, and it's triggered an outrageous
thought: Was Snark Evans's the only death they ever reported?*

*I told you: It's late (or early) and I'm probably making no
sense at all.*

*If it weren't for worry about Endora's safety (and of course
Leo's, and his mother's), I would have enjoyed my little sleuth-*

ing assignment. One enjoys a challenge away from Chaucer, my current project. Sorry I didn't find out more.

I stared at the screen. He'd uncovered almost nothing . . . and perhaps so much more.

Fifteen minutes later, I was pointed downstate. The sky was dark, the wind was strong, and the Internet weatherman offered the likelihood that more snow was headed right across my path. Still, I figured the first hundred of the miles to Center Bridge would be an easy cruise, since it was an interstate.

I figured wrong. The wind advancing ahead of the snow was too riled. A hard wind can test patience in any car, but in a Jeep, it can summon frothing lunacy. Jeeps present a stubborn, flat wall to the road; there's nothing aerodynamic to part the wind around them. Add a semitattered vinyl top that's been poorly patched with silver tape, and a Jeep becomes a bucking, flapping mess, akin to a sailing ship in a hurricane the moment the sheets give way. The noise was deafening; the cold coming in, freezing; and the wind resistance so strong that I couldn't get above forty-five miles an hour. I endured it only by tucking in behind several semitrailer rigs as they came up to pass me. I was relieved when I finally got off the interstate south of Champaign.

I figured wrong on that, too. The second leg was two lanes of bad asphalt, cratered by potholes and sheeted in the smooth spots by invisible black ice. The storm had found full strength by then, raining down fine bits of semisleet and hail the size of tiny marbles. Even in four-wheel drive, I was Barishnikov at the ballet, gliding and occasionally pirouetting toward the west.

Single pairs of headlamps popped up behind me now and again, but they quickly disappeared. No one had need, that day, to go to Center Bridge. Nor did any lights at all come toward me. I wondered if that meant that those who'd intended to leave had done so, years before.

That seemed all the more likely when I finally arrived, at three fifteen, a full five hours after I'd left Rivertown.

The business district, both blocks, had been vaporized by hard times. One car and four pickups were angle-parked along its main street. A tavern and, strangely, a Salvation Army resale shop were the only places showing light. The rest of the storefronts were dark, or boarded up.

I went into the tavern. The bartender and his two patrons looked up.

I ordered a Diet Coke and asked, "Any of you know Snark Evans?"

"He's dead," the bartender said.

"Good riddance," one of the patrons on the stools said.

"Never finished high school," the other patron said. "Took off freshman, sophomore year. Folks were surprised he even bothered to start."

"What do you want to know for, anyway?" the bartender asked.

I handed him one of my cards. "A minor insurance policy was taken out a long time ago. One of their managers heard I'd be driving past Center Bridge and asked me to stop in to update his records."

"How big is the policy?"

"That's not my department. Any of Snark's relatives around?"

All six of their shoulders shrugged. "None of that damned family is left," said the second patron.

"They was all bad apples," the bartender said. "The father got killed in a bar fight in Champaign, early on. The daughter was trashy, strutting herself while she was still in grammar school. The mother, she just plain wore out and died."

"The girl is gone?"

"Finished high school, at least. But then she took off, pregnant, most likely."

"Snark was bad news?" I asked the bartender.

"Burglaring, breaking into cars and houses. Everybody knew him and disliked him."

The second patron stood up quickly and went to the window. The sound of a car engine came from outside. "Damn fool, running without lights," he said.

The first man got up and went to join his friend. "I can't see who it is," he said, peering out the window.

"Damn fool, that's who it is. He'll get run up on, if he doesn't turn on his lights."

The engine noise moved on and disappeared.

"The funeral home is closed?" I asked the bartender.

"Why do you want to know that?"

"Official death record, for the file."

"Never was no funeral home in Center Bridge. Closest one was ten miles north, but it closed in the nineties," the bartender said. "Now we got to get shipped almost to Champaign upon expiration."

"Don't matter. He didn't die here," the bartender said.

"Somewheres out west, or down south," the first patron said.

The other two men laughed at that, moving back to the bar.

"The newspaper's gone, too?" I asked, when the mirth subsided. "*The Center Bridge Bugle*?"

"The what?" the first patron asked.

"It might have been that ad sheet down at the Super Food," the bartender said. "It folded ten years ago, with the Super Food."

There was nothing left to ask. I went out into the snow.

Before starting the Jeep, I called Jenny. "I need a favor. I'd like you to call your police contacts, see if anyone has anything on an Edwin G. 'Snark' Evans."

"Why?"

"Because I'm striking out on something I'm looking into."

"Does this have something to do with why you're keeping an eye on Leo's place?"

"Haste will be appreciated," I said.

The wind and the sleet were endurable for five miles, and then a key piece of silver tape gave way, freeing my vinyl top to billow like a brake chute on a dragster. I pulled off to the shoulder on a side road, cut the engine and the lights, and got out with one of the rolls of duct tape I carry.

I'd just stepped up on the doorsill when I heard an engine sound above the wind. A vehicle passed on the highway. It was running without lights, and I couldn't see it for the storm. It was heading east,

though, and I had the chilling thought its driver might have been
hoping to run unseen behind the lights of a red Jeep.

I took my time retaping the roof, straining for the sound of the
engine returning. There was only the wind, swirling around me. After a decent amount of time had passed, I drove back up onto the
road.

I'd poked at a nerve, picked up a tail.

Nine

I slept until early afternoon, and awoke shaky. I tried telling myself that my muscle trembles came from fighting the Jeep against the wind, five hours down to Center Bridge, more than that back. I didn't believe myself. The trembles came from knowing Leo and his mother and Endora were in a bad place, hiding, held captive, or worse, and someone willing to drive blind in a snowstorm had taken an interest in my interest in that.

I pushed out from under my blankets, slipped fast into frigid jeans and sweatshirts, and stomped to the window, as much to warm my legs as to see outside. Rivertown was whiter, but barely. The snowstorm had deposited little more than a new dusting on the old, dirty snow before moving on to the more worthy suburbs in the west.

Down the road along the river, almost out of sight from the turret and farther still from city hall, the hood of a bronze-colored car stood out stark against the new snow. A car tucked in at the end of the river road didn't need to belong to someone who might have tailed me down to Center Bridge. Daytimes, lots of men used that spot, like they used the side road leading to the turret, to enjoy the services of the girls who worked Thompson Avenue or the back of the bowling alley.

I went down to the kitchen, added water to the previous day's grounds, and ignited Mr. Coffee. I had no Twinkies, I had no Ho Hos, so I shook out a handful of my old Cheerios. I supposed they'd lost some of their taste to age, but the little circles had certainly kept up their robust circularity. Not a one gave in to dust the instant it hit my tongue, and I had the hope that my own old age, still decades into the future, would also be accompanied by such comforting rigidity.

I thought about what little I knew. Leo had gotten a phone call from Snark Evans, someone he'd thought was dead. It had triggered panic. Leo had run, taking along those he loved. He'd tried to call me, to tell me what was going on—but only once.

It nagged, his calling only once. He should have called again, and again, if he were in trouble. Unless, of course, he couldn't call.

I pushed the thought away; it would bring scenarios of forced abductions, and I couldn't give in to those. I considered again, for perhaps the thousandth time, whether I should report Leo missing. Not in Rivertown, where the cops were as bent and lazy as the river, but in Chicago, where I could lie and say Leo and his mother and his girlfriend had been abducted, say, from Endora's condo. That would make it a Chicago crime, and that would bring in better, or at least less crooked, brains.

Except the case would be dropped as soon as the cops questioned Leo's neighbor and learned he'd said he was going on a vacation.

I got up to check the window. The bronze car was still at the end of the road. It had been there longer than was required for a curbside quickie.

I called Endora's boss. "Did you get in touch with Endora's mother?"

"I left three messages yesterday afternoon, and one just now. All contained variations of the word 'Urgent.' She's returned none of them." Then, "I trust you went to Center Bridge?"

"Dead or not, Snark and kin are long gone. Leo's in trouble. So's his mother. So's Endora. I need to talk to Endora's mother."

He didn't hesitate. "Her name is Theodea Wilson. She lives in Blenton, in northern Michigan." He gave me the phone number and address.

I tried the phone number. It rang and rang without cutting to an answering machine.

The bronze car was still down the street, and the mild twinge of paranoia about that was still in my gut. I skipped the duffel bag, put my change of clothes and shaving kit into a paper shopping bag, and went out hoping I looked like I was off to return something to a store.

I drove west, watching the rearview. There were too many cars behind me to tell if one was bronze. Two miles up, I had an inspiration. A traffic light was turning yellow. I slowed, as would any law-abiding driver, but then I punched the Jeep through the intersection just as the light turned red.

There was silence for an instant. Then horns honked behind me. The bronze sedan had followed me through on the red.

I drove on sedately, giving him time to slip back out of my sight, behind other cars. I passed increasingly wider lots and houses of affluence, then got to the weed-choked rubble that was Crystal Waters, the once-gilded, gated subdivision where things had gone so horribly wrong. Amanda and I had lived there during our marriage, in the house she'd bought from her father. She'd never much cared for the place, but walls and a gatehouse surrounded the grounds, and the house had a state-of-the-art security system. It was good for protecting the eleven million dollars' worth of art she'd inherited from her grandfather's estate. Her house and her art, like our marriage, were no longer there.

As I'd told Jenny, Amanda and I hadn't spoken in months, and those last conversations had taken on the sounds of last gasps. She'd given up the last vestige of her former life, teaching at the Art Institute, to head her father's philanthropy. I saw her mostly in the society pages of the Chicago papers now, a glittering brown-eyed vixen, usually on the arm of one particularly distinguished-looking silver-haired bastard. Looking happy to have gotten past the sort of fumbler who would live in a turret.

Leo had helped me through all of that.

I pulled into the parking lot of a Home Depot, went in, and watched from behind the door glass. The bronze car, an older Chevy

Malibu, had pulled in to park between two panel vans, three rows from where I'd left the Jeep. I bought a box of finish nails to have something to carry out, got into the Jeep, and turned north.

A mile up, there was a huge shopping center that must have been designed by an angry architect. It had a particularly vexing layout, consisting of six octagonal clusters of stores separated by green spaces with small trees. And speed bumps. The crazy quilt of interconnected parking lots had tons of speed bumps.

Amanda and I had gone there several times during our marriage. It was a place of high-end chain stores and old ladies, driving slowly because speed bumps can loosen old teeth or new dentures. They approached the asphalt mounds as though they were scaling Everest in a blinding blow, slowly, evaluating every twitch of the steering wheel. Traffic coagulated.

Narrow little unloading alleys had been cut through to the centers of the clusters, for trucks to access the receiving docks behind the stores. The alleys were difficult to see. More important for me, it was easy to presume that the trucks exited the same way they went in. They did not. The trucks went out the opposite side of the cluster, onto an unseen side street.

The bronze Malibu followed me toward one of the store clusters. I darted into one of the parking lots and drove down, as though looking for an empty space. He turned into the lot, too, though two rows back.

I came back up the adjacent aisle, as though I were still looking for a parking place. Then I left the lot and butted into the line of cars in front of the stores. The Malibu had no choice but to do the same, though by now he was well behind me.

It came my turn to take a shallow turn to the left, toward a new store cluster, and I became unseen to anyone more than five cars back. I swung sharply into a loading alley, drove all the way through, and came out onto the access road. Twenty minutes later, I was eastbound on the Illinois Tollway, headed toward Indiana.

I scanned the rearview now and again, but no bronze Malibu could have followed me. Still, to be doubly safe, I got off at Route 12 and followed that beneath the curve of Lake Michigan until I got into Michigan and could pick up the interstate again. For two hours, I passed increasingly bigger pines and smaller towns until I ran out of daylight and interstate and had to cut over to side roads where I could see not much of anything at all.

Downtown Blenton, a forlorn, block-long strip that looked only marginally more prosperous than Center Bridge, appeared an hour later. Theodea Wilson lived in a cottage set well away from the other three houses on her street. Her place was dark.

It was too late to bang on doors in the neighborhood, so I headed back to a Super 8 motel I'd passed a mile earlier. It sat next to a restaurant that had a stuffed deer's head encased in glass and lit up on its roof, as though to keep an eye out for the hunter who'd dispatched it to an afterlife of riding a roof without legs and a torso. The 8 had two pickups in its parking lot. One was rusty and red; the other was rusty and green. Combined with the vigilant Rudolph high across the lot, the compound had a sort of perverted-Christmas air.

I checked into the 8 and walked over to the restaurant. Three Harley-Davidson motorcycles were parked by the door. The knotty-pine interior was decorated with broken Detroit Red Wings hockey sticks, a large electric Jack Daniel's sign, lit up, and three ample blond women in tight, low-riding jeans sitting on stools at the bar. All three swiveled in unison as I walked in, making me feel like two hundred pounds of fresh meat being wheeled to a buffet. I took a table by a window so I could be the first to see if any more motorcycle women showed up.

When the waitress brought a menu, I couldn't help but glance past her at the three women at the bar. Their tight low-riding jeans had ridden even lower, displaying three identical Harley tattoos above the beginnings of three identically deep great divides. I should have taken that view as added incentive for continuing to forsake Twinkies and Ho Hos for aged Cheerios, but I was tired. I ordered a burger, fries, and, after the briefest of hesitations, the house specialty, maple apple pie. I promised myself to rectify it all by eating twice as many Cheerios the next day.

The burger was good, the fries were crisp, but it was the maple-flavored apples encased so lovingly in crusted lard that set my mind to reminiscing. I'd had instances where good pie had accompanied revelations. There'd been an exceptional key lime in Bodega Bay that foreshadowed my tracking down a woman who had a fondness for bombs. More recently, a fine apple, topped with Velveeta, had come along with the discovery of a satisfactory-enough development in the case of a missing woman. I liked harbingers, especially if they were pies, and there was no reason to think that a maple apple pie, up in piney country, would not lead to finding my best friend alive and well.

I bid a silent adios to the tattooed backsides at the bar and tumbled off to my room at the 8, sure to sleep well and safe.

Clever me.

Ten

"She ain't been home for two, three days," Theodea Wilson's nearest neighbor told me the next morning. "School's probably out for Easter break. She might be gone to her summer place."

I was holding my shopping bag of clothes like I was trying to make a delivery. "Man, they must have gotten things screwed up down at the store."

"What store?"

"Hardware," I said vaguely. I didn't know any of the nearby stores.

"It's mighty cold for that right now."

"Hardware?"

"Eustace," she said loudly.

"Eustace?"

"Eustace!" she yelled, like I was hard of hearing. "This time, she screwed up. She didn't stop her mail. I been pushing it through the slot and watching out for packages. I can take your bag." She held out a hand.

"It's OK," I said. "I'll have the boss call her in a few days."

"I suppose you could try that," she said and closed the door.

I had a Michigan map in the glove box but could find no town named Eustace. I drove to the BP station on the highway, filled up, and asked how I could get to Eustace.

"Not very easily," the sour-faced woman behind the counter said.

"It's not nearby?"

"It's close enough, less than thirty miles, but it's not a town. It's an island off Mackinaw City, like Mackinac Island. But Eustace is not open to sightseers."

"Why not?"

"No sights."

"I know a woman who lives there."

She cocked her head, seeing a lie. "How'd she tell you to get there, then?"

"She didn't."

She nodded, her suspicions about me, and perhaps all of mankind, confirmed. "Best you try to call first, if you can."

"Cell phone reception up there is spotty?"

"Only on good days." She frowned at another customer walking in and told me to take the highway straight north until the land ended.

I passed much deeper snow than was in Chicago, and more white birches. Big pines were everywhere, including one growing up through the shattered windshield of the burned-out shell of a car. Roadside places sold firewood, stained glass, and deer food. Twenty-five Harleys were parked outside a barbecue restaurant, though I didn't know Harleys well enough to tell whether any belonged to the tattooed, bifurcated ladies from the night before.

There were billboards, too, for gun dealers and places to stay on Mackinac Island. Two touted the Grand Hotel, a place that promised the longest porch I'd ever seen.

The road ended in Mackinaw City. I'd heard of it, of course, like I'd heard of the big island, Mackinac, out on the water. Expensive sailboats raced there from Chicago every summer—manned, I imagined, by taut tanned fellows in pink knit gator shirts and waterproof moccasins, for whom Cheerios meant not just good health but a whole way of life.

Mackinaw City was no city, but rather several blocks of gift stores, resort clothing shops, and trendy bars lining both sides of a wide center ribbon of mostly empty parking spaces. I drove up and down the long main street, checking out the few cars. None were familiar.

I checked out the parking lot for the ferry operation that serviced Mackinac Island, then cruised the side streets. Pa Brumsky's brown LTD was parked beside a peeling tan-painted house four blocks in. I knocked at the front door. A teenaged boy wearing a tousled T-shirt and rumpled jeans answered.

"I've been looking for a big old Ford like yours," I said. "Is it for sale?"

The kid shook his head. "We just rent parking for people going to Mackinac."

"But do you know if it's for sale?" I said, to keep him talking.

"You could leave a note on the windshield, with your name and phone number." He started to close the door.

"Did the owner say when he'd be back?"

A pouty blond girl came into partial view, running her fingers through her own hair because the young man's was too far away. She wore a tousled T-shirt and rumpled jeans, too.

"Leave a note," the kid said, shutting the door.

I envied him. There are points in every life when tousling and rumpling must proceed without distraction. I felt ancient, as though it had been centuries since I'd last been properly tousled and rumpled.

I drove back to the ferry service. Past a row of outdoor restrooms and a gift shop, small whitecaps crashed against a white-fenced dock ramp. Farther out, a ferry was churning the rough water, heading in. Beyond that were two bumps, one large, one small, faint against the gray. Mackinac and Eustace.

No one was around except a man in a white wood ticket booth. "Does that go to Eustace Island?" I asked, pointing at the approaching ferry.

"Nothing goes direct to Eustace. Got to go to the big island, then catch a ride to Eustace."

"I need to go straight to Eustace."

"What the hell for? Nothing there but one old hotel, thirty rooms, built by some moron thinking to compete with the Grand on Mackinac. He went bust in short time. Other fools came along, thinking to compete, too. Busto, every one of them. Only seasonals use it now, green cards mostly, and most of them won't be here for another month."

"A woman I know has a cottage there."

"There are those," he allowed, "a few places that rent to idiots with little money and fewer brains. It's a dismal rock, Eustace."

"Will your ferry take me if I pay extra?"

"Ferry's too big. Docks on Eustace are rickety things, only good for small craft." He pointed to the whitecaps. "Won't be anybody going to Eustace today except the first crew working at the Grand. Best I can say, if you're hell-bent, take our ferry to Mackinac, ask who'll run to Eustace tomorrow, and huddle up at a bed-and-breakfast if you can find one open this early."

The approaching ferry pivoted in a tight arc, reversed its engines, and backed up alongside the ramp. A hardy-looking couple, tanned even in March, wheeled bicycles down the ramp and rode off. Cheerios people.

"When's it leave?" I asked the ticket seller.

"Twenty minutes."

"Even if I'm the only passenger?"

"It's in the contract. We run on schedule, rain, snow, or empty."

I boarded and went up to the open top deck. The day had darkened even further, smudging the horizon into the waterline. Mackinac Island and its tiny sister, Eustace, were lost in the gloom.

The diesel engines rumbled louder below decks, and the ferry pulled away from the dock. No one else had gotten on board.

I looked back at the shore.

A bulky figure was standing alongside the ticket shack. His hands were jammed in the pockets of his black trench coat, against the cold. He looked square and dark and evil. He was looking right at me.

I turned a little, pretending to look up the shore. I could still see the ticket shack out of the corner of my eye.

The bulky man passed something to the ticket taker. It might have been money for the next ferry, but it could have been money to talk. "Why, Eustace," the ticket seller could be saying. "The damned fool wants to go to Eustace, though there's nothing there this time of year but a few seasonals, and lots of rocks."

Impossible, I said to the thought. I'd lost the bronze Malibu back in Illinois.

It started to rain, a little. I went belowdecks, where I'd be dry and less cold.

Where I wouldn't be seen by the bulky man's eyes.

Eleven

A hundred yards out from the shore, the water began kicking harder, making whitecaps two feet high. The ferry was big, but the roil in the water was stronger. The ferry bobbed like a small boat.

I went up to the wheelhouse. The captain was talking casually to the deckhand. They both turned, smiling. They were used to angry water.

"Got work on Mackinac?" the captain asked.

"I've got a friend on Eustace Island."

He winced. "Hell to pay, if that's your destination."

"Can you take me? I'll pay large."

He shook his head. "We'd crash on the rocks."

"How do I get there, then?"

"Arnie Pine," the deckhand said. "Keeps his boat on the next dock over from ours. The *Rabbit*. He's adept."

"Even in this kind of weather?"

"Depends on his lunch," the deckhand said. They both laughed at the inside joke.

We docked on Mackinac Island fifteen queasy minutes later. I stepped onto the wide plank pier, and for a second I just stood in the soft rain, sucking air and enjoying the unyielding steadiness of the wood below my feet.

As promised, the *Rabbit* bobbed at the next dock. It was a swaybacked thing and seemed to groan under the weight of a weathered white cabin that looked too long and tall for its narrow deck. There were deep gashes, some grayed, some fresh, cut into its green hull. No one was on board.

Farther down, a man knelt on the pier, ready to pull a small motor out of a rowboat heaving in the chop. The water rose and he lunged, grabbed the motor, and set it down with a thud onto the pier. "Bad damned water today," he called across, standing up.

"Is Arnie Pine around?"

"He'll be back just before his four o'clock run to Eustace."

I looked down at the water crashing into the pilings next to him. "Isn't it too rough?"

"For everyone else, maybe, but Arnie takes his little ferrying income serious. And," he added, "he'll have had lunch."

"Lunch?" The ferryboat captain and his deckhand had mentioned Pine's lunch, too.

He wiped the mist of rain from his forehead. "Arnie takes his lunch serious," he said. "Especially in rough weather." He lifted his motor and started down the pier.

I had three hours to kill. I walked up the incline to what must have been the main trap for tourists. A few blocks of businesses sat on a gently curving street. Every third or fourth one appeared to be selling fudge. Or would shortly, when the vacationers started coming. For now, everything appeared to be closed.

The Grand Hotel loomed enormous and white above the winding street, easily visible through the leafless trees. Amanda and I had talked once about spending a weekend there. We'd talked about doing all sorts of things like that in the beginning, before my life short-circuited ours.

I wondered, then, if Jenny and I could ever talk of such things, and whether new beginnings were possible at all. It was a gloomy day all around.

I walked up the hill. A cast-metal sign announced that gentlemen were expected to wear coats and ties on the hotel grounds after 6:00 P.M.

A man in a yellow paisley scarf and long wool coat approached me. "We're not yet open for the season."

"I'm just looking around, you know, like for the future," I said.

"Indeed." He glanced pointedly at the inch of blazer that drooped below the hem of my peacoat. His nose was rather pointed, too, and long.

"How much?" I asked.

"They start at a little over four hundred," he said, raising the prominent nose as though he knew I'd come north in a duct-taped Jeep, with my duds in a paper bag.

"For a week?" I asked, snooting right back at him.

"Per night, of course. Good day, sir." He touched the brim of an imaginary top hat in salute and walked away.

Though thick snow covered its sunken terraces and broad expanses of lawn, I could imagine the hotel in full bloom. In a month, maybe two, a hundred white rocking chairs would be set out for the sorts of semiembalmed butts that would be only too happy to shell out four hundred a night to enjoy the view. I was inspired, then, as to how I might amuse myself in such a place. I'd park myself at one end of the long porch, instruct a white-coated waiter to bring me a mint julep, then proceed to work my way slowly down the long expanse, taking the tiniest sip as I tried each available rocker. The objective would be to see how many rockers I could traverse before either the julep ran out or I got ejected, accused of lunacy.

Certainly such a stunt seemed no crazier than spending four hundred bucks just to sleep in such a place for only one night.

Two dozen young men came out from behind the hotel and began walking down the hill toward the tiny fudge town. I checked my watch. It was 3:45. I fell in behind them as they made the turn toward the piers. By now, the whitecaps had swelled higher and were sloshing onto the tops of the piers. One by one, they walked through the puddles and climbed down into the oversized wood cabin of the bobbing *Rabbit*.

Nothing happened for another fifteen minutes, and then a man came down the incline. He had white hair and white stubble on his chin, and he wore an ancient ski jacket and a black watch cap and one glove. There was a decided roll to his gait that had nothing to do with the downward slope of the ground.

"Arnie Pine?" I inquired, when he stepped onto the dock.

He stopped and stared at me for a moment with rheumy, shifting eyes. No doubt, he was seeing me blurred. Arnie Pine had had his lunch.

"I need a ride to Eustace Island," I said.

"The lake's a tad ripply," he said through the booze sloshing in his gullet, of the water sloshing on the dock.

I pointed to the workers sitting on the benches in the boat. "They're going."

He nodded, sensing truth, and squinted at me. "Fifty, for the two of you."

I gave him two twenties and a ten and followed him on board. Several of the workers looked at me, disbelieving, when I went to stand at the open space at the back of the boat. My paranoia had returned, remembering the bulky man at the ticket shack back in Mackinaw City. I wanted to keep an eye on the water, for other boats.

Pine fired the engine, banged the *Rabbit* hard enough against the pier to carve a new gash, and headed out to open water. We'd only gone a fraction of a nautical mile, whatever distance that might have been, when suddenly the sky opened up and began hurling down sheets of hard rain. The lake kicked up even more then, sending great scoops of water crashing into the open back, almost knocking me down. I scrambled into the long, narrow shelter and grabbed onto a stanchion supporting the roof. It wiggled, loose in my hand. In front of us, Arnie Pine was whistling, unconcerned within the haze he'd acquired from lunch.

We plowed on, or prowed on, or whatever one does when one is in a boat bobbing like an empty gin bottle on a heaving lake. I could see nothing, but I felt it all, the pounding rain and the spraying lake, beating in sideways, frigid and wet and clamping onto my bones as thick as dissolving wool. No one made a sound, except one or two of the young workers, who were crying. And Arnie, whistling, still lubricated from lunch.

The small granite cliffs of Eustace Island rose up suddenly in the boat's spotlight, not fifty feet ahead. Pine made no move to cut back the engine. He kept right on whistling, perhaps because he couldn't see the rock for his lunch. I scuttled back out of the shelter into the full force of the rain, certain we were going to crash into the shore. By now the spotlight had swept away from the dock and onto ground that was more granite than green.

A dock appeared in the sleet, a barely visible spindly contraption that looked to have been built of scrap lumber by mumblers with dull hatchets. One hard bump would surely splinter it into kindling. Only thirty feet separated us now.

Yet Pine whistled on, at least for another few seconds, until at last he spun the wheel sharply to cut the boat's trajectory. Only then did he turn the spotlight toward the dock.

The boat barely grazed the thin posts as the lake heaved us up three feet higher than the dock. Two of the young men, no doubt veterans of earlier passages, jumped off with ropes. Faster than snake handlers, they looped the ropes around the spindly posts and pulled the pitching boat close to the dock, leaving slack for the roiling water. Jumping off would only be possible on the rise, and even then, mistiming it by even one second would mean tumbling into the lake and getting crushed between the hull and the rocks.

The other young workers had done it before. One by one, agile as cats on a fence, they jumped perfectly off the bucking boat.

Then there was only me, alone with the whistling, insane Arnie Pine. He'd turned his head to look at me, impatient, I supposed, for the two of us to be off. I took my hand off the scarred top rail. The boat rose. I jumped and fell more than landed on the slick dock. Strong hands seized my arms and legs before I could slide off and pulled me up. I staggered, steadying, and lunged to grab one of the spindly posts.

Two of the workers tossed the ropes back onto the *Rabbit,* and Arnie gunned the boat around. I heard him whistling, above the diesels and the shriek of the wind, as he disappeared into the darkness.

The young men started up the hill, single file, their heads bowed against the storm raging down on them. Lightning flashed, and a monstrous shape of peeling gray wood and dangling shutters appeared at the top of the hill. It was the old hotel, converted now to cheap rental rooms for young men who could find no better work.

I shivered in the rain, waiting, for I'd seen no houses. Another bolt of lightning tore through the sky, and in its brief glare I saw a string of cottages strung loosely along the bluff to my left. All looked to be perched on rock; no trees or lawns had found foothold around them. All were as dark as the old hotel. I wondered if I was alone on the island, except for the seasonals, trudging up the hill.

The granite was slick. I slipped and fell twice, hurrying up to the first cottage. Plywood, secured by wing nuts, covered the front windows. The house was still closed for the winter. I knocked anyway. There was no answer.

The second cottage was not boarded up, but no one responded there, either. An elderly man answered at the third place. I started to ask if he knew a Mrs. Wilson. He slammed the door. I would have, too, if a drenched stranger had come out of such a storm to bang on my door.

The windows of the fourth cottage were boarded over, like the first. I barely heard my fist on the door, for the rage of the water below.

No one answered. By now, my shivers had turned to shakes. I was soaked clear through, frozen colder than anything I'd felt on the boat.

Dark spots moved in a paper-thin ribbon of light that showed at the bottom of the door. Someone was home and had come to the other side of the door. I beat on it again, yelling, "It's Dek Elstrom, damn it. If you know me, let me in before I die."

The door opened, and a high-powered handheld searchlight beam shot onto my face. I shut my eyes tight against the glare.

There was no shutting out the sound of a woman screaming.

Twelve

"Is he—?" she shrieked.

A cough began rumbling deep in my lungs. I doubled over, hugging my arms, unable to speak for the shakes, and the rumble.

"Do you know this man, Endora?" another woman called out from back in the cottage.

"Of course, of course," Endora's voice shouted.

"Then stop blinding the poor bastard and let him in out of the rain," the other woman said, her voice getting louder as she came closer.

I stepped inside, and someone, perhaps the other woman, slammed the door behind me.

The glaring light dropped away, and the world outside my eyelids darkened from bright orange to a soft red. I opened my eyes enough to see into the soft gloom of a room lit with stubs of candles stuck in ashtrays, furnished sparsely with straight-backed chairs, a braided rug, and a table made of pine planks. An ancient cast-iron stove stood in the corner, its door open, sending out heat and a little more light.

The woman standing beside Endora possessed her height, slimness, and beauty. The only real difference was her silver hair. That, and she was holding not a high-powered searchlight but rather a snub-nosed revolver, aimed at my chest.

"She knows me, Mrs. Wilson," I managed, through manly chattering teeth. My eyes were wide open now. Behind me, the storm raged against the door.

The gun dropped, pointing at my crotch. It was small improvement.

"You're sure he's all right, Endora?" her mother asked. The gun moved restlessly in her hand, as though anxious for explosion.

"Of course, of course," Endora said again, almost inaudibly. She wore faded jeans and a man's flannel shirt and stood stock-still, staring down at the big-lensed searchlight in her hand, unwilling to look at my face.

"Leo's not here?" I asked.

She raised her head slowly. "He's not dead?" she asked softly.

"Leo? Dead?" I said, confused, too.

She shook her head. "I thought that's what you came to say."

Theodea Wilson put the revolver into a leather holster clipped to her belt. "This man knows nothing, Endora. That's good news."

She motioned me to sit in a ladder-back chair directly in front of the wood-burning stove. "You may shed your wet pants if you'd like, whatever your name is."

"Dek Elstrom, Mother," Endora said, her voice a little more alive.

"That oddball friend of Leo's who lives in a castle?"

"A mere part of one," I said, taking off my two coats. Incredibly, the blue button-down shirt underneath was dry.

"A part of which?" Theodea asked. "Part oddball, or part castle?"

I remembered then that her neighbor back in Blenton told me Theodea Wilson was a teacher. Certainly she possessed her daughter's fast intellect, along with Attila the Hun's directness.

"Perhaps both," I stammered through my still-chattering teeth. I went to stand by the stove.

It was then that I noticed Ma Brumsky. She sat in almost total darkness in the far corner of the room. I couldn't see her eyes. Her head was down. She'd not said a word since I came in.

Noticing me noticing Ma Brumsky, Endora said, "She's been like that since we got here. She's frightened and isn't saying much." We sat, I in the chair by the stove, she across the table. "Tell me about Leo," she said.

"I thought I'd find him here with you."

Theodea handed me a water glass half full of whiskey. "This will work quicker than the stove."

"You're sure you've brought no bad news?" Endora asked.

"I've brought no news at all. They're building a new house on Leo's block; he's disappeared, and you and Ma are on the run. What's going on?"

"Were you followed?" Theodea cut in.

A new wave of chills grabbed me. I leaned closer to the stove. "There was a man, back at the ferry ticket shack in Mackinaw City." I took two long sips of the whiskey.

Theodea touched the handle of the gun at her belt. "You think he could have followed you here, to Eustace?"

"Not even Arnie Pine will venture out again in this storm."

"Later?"

"No doubt."

"How can you not know anything?" Endora asked, struggling to keep her voice steady. "You're Leo's best friend."

"Leo told you nothing?"

"He was frightened. He said to take his father's old Ford because no one knew that car. He didn't want to know where we were going. He said he couldn't say more because it would endanger us."

I looked over to the corner. Ma Brumsky sat passively. I couldn't tell if she was listening. I wondered if she was in shock.

I told them what little I knew, beginning with the phone call Leo received.

"You never thought to return Leo's call when you were in Iowa?" Endora's words came fast, clipped. Furious.

"It's like that with us—"

"Damn it, Dek. You could have returned his call."

I lifted my glass of whiskey to hide behind another sip.

"And now you've led someone to us?" she added, her voice shaking.

"Endora!" her mother said.

Ma Brumsky stood up, grabbed an umbrella from a brass urn, and went toward the back of the tiny cottage. A second later, a door slammed.

"I'm sorry I put you in jeopardy" was all I could think to say.

Theodea Wilson shook her head and offered a half-smile. "No. Outhouse. She brought lots of little bottles of alcohol. And big bags of prunes."

It cut the tension. Even Endora laughed, briefly. Then, "How do we help Leo?"

"I need to hear anything else you can remember."

The wind blew hard. Endora looked over at the front door, as though someone were about to charge in. "Leo said we had to be careful, to make sure no one was following us. He said we were in danger. He said to stay away, until he called. I'm not using the phone, to save the battery—"

The door began banging in rapid succession, as though someone huge were pounding on it. Mrs. Wilson took a yellow slicker from a hook by the door, slipped it on, and stepped outside. She was back in less than a minute. "The wind's blowing forty, fifty miles an hour. The lake is white. Not even Arnie Pine would attempt the crossing now."

"Leo said powerful people might try to get to us," Endora said, turning to me.

"Why?"

"I told you I don't know!"

"He said nothing about something he'd been given, a long time ago?"

She shook her head.

"How about a Snark Evans?"

"Who?"

"It was a name he mentioned, during that phone call I overheard."

"No; never."

The plywood shuddered against the window as Mrs. Wilson hung her slicker on a peg by the door. "This is a cheap movie," she said.

"*Key Largo*," Endora said.

Her mother forced a laugh. "*Key Largo*," she agreed. Her hand had strayed again to the handle of her revolver.

Ma Brumsky came in the back, a huge gust of wet wind slamming the door shut behind her. She eased out of her coat and took her place in her chair. She said nothing.

"You're sure: He told you nothing about where he'd be?" I asked Endora.

"Only that he'd be safe. He was angrier than I'd ever seen him. Angry, and frightened at the same time."

We went over it all again, but Endora could offer nothing more. Leo had kept everything to himself.

Theodea heated canned stew on a tiny propane stove. When it was done, she and Endora and I ate it with pieces from a thin wheel of Swedish cracker bread suspended on a string from the ceiling, safe from mice. It was rustic. Through it all, Ma sat silent in the corner, seemingly unaware of anything. Again I wondered if she were in shock.

By now, every shutter was beating on the tiny cottage. We tried to talk above the clatter but finally gave up. Our ears wanted only to listen for sounds beneath the storm, of a man who shouldn't have been able to get to Eustace. We sat silent, Endora and her mother drinking whiskey, me drinking coffee, afraid of what Arnie Pine might bring, if the money was right and he drank dinner the way he drank lunch.

Several times, Theodea got up to open the front door. There was nothing to see except rain.

Then, an hour later, when the candles were low and the whiskey was gone, something crashed on the rocks below.

Theodea jumped up and hurried to put on her slicker. "Probably flotsam hitting the rocks," she said, in an unnaturally high voice. She grabbed the big spotlight and opened the door.

Sounds of men yelling came in with the rain.

"What the hell?" she shouted down, above the drum of the storm.

I pulled on my sodden coats and followed her out. Down below, two high-powered flashlight beams were being aimed at the frothing water at the shore. Two men, one the elderly person who'd slammed the door on me, the other much younger, perhaps a seasonal worker, were standing on the rocks.

Arnie Pine's *Rabbit* lay at the edge of their pools of light, crashed up on the rocks. A huge hole had been torn in its hull.

"Get back inside," I shouted to Theodea. "Lock the door, keep your gun in your hand. If someone tries to get in, and it's not me, shoot through the wood."

She hurried back toward her cottage. She'd seen what was lying directly in the centers of the searchlight beams.

I worked my way down to the dock and stopped. I could see well enough, even from a distance.

Arnie Pine lay sprawled facedown on the rocks. His hat was gone; his light gray hair was matted back. The rain and the splash from the roiling lake hadn't completely washed away the spot of glistening red at the back of his head.

"Anyone in the boat?" I called to the two men.

The younger man shook his head.

"Got a radio?"

"An old ship-to-shore," the old man shouted back. "Sometimes it works, sometimes it doesn't."

"Pray it works. Call the cops."

He gave a contorted laugh, his face shiny with sleet. "You think they'll come out in this," he yelled, "especially for a damned drunk fool?"

He was right. It would be hours before anyone could come and see it was a bullet, and not bad boating, that had dropped Arnie Pine. Pine had taken on a passenger who'd waved enough big bills to get him to go back out in the storm, a man who'd become menacing enough for Pine to run his boat aground to try to get away. A man who'd shot him in the head, to keep him from raising an alarm.

That shooter was now on Eustace Island.

Thirteen

Lightning flashed as I got up to the row of cottages. I turned and looked around. Only the two men stood in the sleet, staring at Pine. The bulky man I was looking for had already made it to the shadows.

I ducked behind the first cottage in the row and waited for lightning. When it came, I edged out to watch the path. No one was coming up.

The sky went dark. I ran to Theodea's cottage and pounded on her door. "It's me," I said, trying to keep my voice low. She opened the door, and I ducked in.

Theodea had kept her slicker on, its vinyl still dripping rain. Her gun was in her hand. "Arnie Pine?"

"Anybody got a big boat on this island?" I asked.

"He's come?" Endora asked. "The man by the ticket shack?"

"It can only be him," I said.

"McNulty has a boat," Theodea said, her face drawn with fear. "He fishes," she added, like that mattered.

"We need to get away now."

No one demanded another word; they could read everything on my face.

"No bullshit," Theodea said. "Everyone follow me." She started toward the candles burning on the blank table.

"Leave them," I said. "He needs to think we're still inside."

"They might burn the place down."

"Worse things will happen if he sees the line of light below the door go dark and thinks to search for us outside."

"Of course," she said, moving to bundle Ma in the old wool coat she'd worn since Leo and I were in high school.

We followed Theodea out the back door and up the slope, away from the cottages and the men below. With luck, the man who'd come to Eustace Island had started searching for Leo or me at the old hotel, several hundred yards away.

The fierce sleet had iced the rocky path, and we had to move slowly. Even with Endora on one side of her and me on the other, Ma's steps were tentative, unsure on the slippery granite.

Worse, jagged bolts of lighting cut through the sky every few seconds, lighting us up to be seen with every slow step. I had no idea where the bulky man might be, but I was afraid he was inside the hotel, on the top floor. One look out the window, he'd see us trudging along the path.

After what seemed like an hour, we started down the backside of the island. Lightning struck five times in succession, lighting up a cottage not much bigger than a maintenance shed down below.

Theodea beat on the door. An enormous bearded man in jeans and a red flannel shirt opened it. We huddled in close, under the overhang.

"Theodea." His voice boomed, big like him. "Please, all of you come in." One lone candle burned behind him.

"No time. We need to get to Mackinaw City," she said.

"We'll go at dawn," he said without hesitation. "Storm will be done by then."

"We can't wait," Theodea said.

He looked at her for the briefest of seconds before he picked up the largest black oilcloth slicker I'd ever seen from the back of a chair. It looked like it weighed twenty pounds. "All right, then," he said.

"McNulty?" Theodea said.

"Yes?"

"You've got a gun?"

"Two, actually. One for the hand, one for the arm."

"Bring both."

He walked to a closet across the room. He put a revolver in his pocket, took out a rifle in a vinyl case, and came back. "We're off, then," he said.

We followed a gravel path to a solid-looking pier resting between thick metal posts. Tied to the pier was a stubby fishing boat, twice the size of Arnie Pine's *Rabbit*. A dozen plastic coolers were lashed to the open deck behind the wheelhouse. We climbed aboard.

There was barely room in the wheelhouse for Ma to stand next to McNulty. Theodea, Endora, and I hunched behind it, out in the rain.

His engine roared to life. "Best keep the lights off?" McNulty shouted back to Theodea.

"That would be appropriate," she called up.

"No problem. No one else will be out."

The water was rougher than when I'd crossed with Pine, but McNulty's boat, or maybe it was McNulty himself, handled the chop more smoothly. I kept my eyes on Ma. She stood upright, barely swaying at the boat's incessant shifting, rolling from side to side.

"I didn't know you were on the island, Theodea," McNulty shouted.

"I've had guests."

"Fine time of year for entertaining," he said.

"The balm of spring," she said. They both laughed.

Endora leaned to the side and whispered to me, "I think my mother shares a secret life with that man."

"I'll bet it's marvelous," I said.

She grinned.

McNulty didn't fight the waves; he used them, so expertly that in no time he slowed his engines, approaching the faint lights at the shore.

I stepped forward. "Someplace secluded, and as far away from the ferryboat dock as you can," I said. The man who'd killed Arnie Pine would still be back on Eustace Island, but there was no knowing if he'd left a sharp-eyed accomplice in Mackinaw City to watch the piers. Theodea looked at Ma, then at me. I shook my head. Better to have Ma wait in the rain for me to pick her up than to chance us all walking through town, even though it was past midnight.

McNulty nudged the side of his boat against a small pier two hundred yards from the ferryboat dock. Endora and I jumped out, and while McNulty revved his engine to keep the boat solid against the dock, we helped Ma up onto the deck. McNulty tried to give Theodea his handgun. She shook her head, gave him a kiss, and jumped onto the dock.

"I miss our chess games," he shouted.

"We'll play when I get back," she called back.

"And here all I thought you did on that rock was read poetry," Endora said to her mother.

"McNulty's that most enjoyable of the male species, a quiet one."

Only Ma Brumsky didn't try to laugh.

My genius for avoiding a tail, tarnished though it was by leading a killer to Eustace Island, offered up a new inspiration: Endora would drive the LTD out of Mackinaw City. I'd follow immediately behind. Gradually, I'd lag back, increasing the distance between us, until she was at least two miles ahead. That way, I could keep watch for anyone attempting to join us. If no one did, she could continue safely south, or east, when I turned west to go back to Chicago.

"What if your bulky friend does tuck between us?" Endora asked.

"I'll run him off the road," I said.

"In a short-wheelbase, lightweight Jeep?"

"The theory needs polishing."

"We'll shoot him, then," Theodea said to her daughter, patting the hip where her holster was. I had no doubt that she was serious.

Endora and I walked quickly through the deserted town, got the two cars, and drove back to pick up Theodea and Ma. They piled into the LTD, I stayed in the Jeep, and we rolled out of town a little before two in the morning. The temperature had risen enough to change the sleet over to rain and keep ice from building on the roads.

We maintained a steady sixty miles an hour, keeping track of the mile markers by cell phone. By the time we got ten miles south of Mackinaw City, I was passing their markers a full two minutes behind, which meant two miles separated us.

Thirty minutes after that, the rain stopped. I could see more clearly behind me now, but it didn't much matter. It must have been the bulky man who followed me down to Center Bridge, and he didn't mind running without lights. I dropped back another half mile. The road stayed free of cars.

"This is working well," I said into my cell phone.

"Unless we're being tailed by someone running without lights, like that car in Center Bridge you told us about?" Endora asked.

"I've been thinking about that, yes."

"Have you also been thinking about what you're going to do when you get back to Rivertown?"

"My head is already being bombarded with more inspirations."

"Meaning you don't have a clue about your next step?" she asked.

"It's a long drive back to Rivertown. Surely it will be productive."

When she got to Grayling, where 75 veered southeast, she made her last call, as agreed.

"You'll stay on 75 to points unknown to me?" I asked.

"My mother has thought of a place. Not even I know where we're going."

"You won't return to Illinois until I give the all clear?" I asked. I needed to be sure.

"Find Leo, Dek."

I told her that surely would be a piece of cake.

Fourteen

The adrenaline that had been propelling me since I'd first gotten to Mackinaw City vaporized like steam in a strong wind just west of Kalamazoo. I pulled into a McDonald's drive-through for coffee and a McMuffin, drove to the back of the parking lot to eat, and fell asleep before I could touch either.

When I awoke, it was after ten. I drank the cold coffee, ate the cold McMuffin, and called Jenny as I pulled onto the interstate.

"Nothing so far, Dek, except a record of his birth, in Champaign," she said. "I called three different sources, including one with the FBI. No Edwin G., no Snark. But don't forget, juvenile records get expunged. One thing I do know, and don't ask how: He hasn't filed an income tax return under that name, either. Maybe he changed his name."

"Or he really is dead, as I heard."

"No one's found that, but that's not surprising, especially when it's that far back and the deceased died in a small town. How does this fit with what you're not telling me about Leo?"

"I'll call you," I said.

"We must do this again," she said and clicked off.

I got to Rivertown's city hall at one and blew straight into Tebbins's office. He looked up, red faced and sweating, as though anticipating

a heart attack. Or me, coming to agitate him about things he hoped I
didn't understand, such as a killer who'd followed me up to Eustace
Island.

"I just got back from an amazing trip," I said. I couldn't tell if that
upset him, since his face was already so deeply flushed.

"What's that supposed to mean?"

"I was on a little island, off Mackinac. A guy crashed his boat and
died."

He sat up straighter in his chair, but it might not have been from
surprise. "I have no time for this, Elstrom."

I'd decided I'd come at him fresh and not tell him I'd learned
anything from his boss, Robinson. "Tell me about Snark Evans."

"Like I said the last time, I had all kinds of kids washing trucks."

"This one had a little burglary business on the side."

"Where the hell would you hear such a thing?"

"Good news gets around."

"I don't know anything about burglaries."

"You had to brace him about selling stuff out of the city garage."

"All kinds of punks worked for the city. Not all of them were memorable."

"Why cover for him after all these years?"

He took a couple of long breaths and said nothing.

I sat down in the guest chair, uninvited, and smiled. "So, what's
new?"

"OK," he said after a moment, "maybe I do remember one of them
selling junk in the garage. But it was only junk."

"I'm guessing it was more than that."

"Look, I remember Snark Evans enough to know I should have
canned him right away. I found out about his little extracurricular ac-
tivities, but I tried to cut him a break. I was hoping, with regular work,
he'd quit thieving. It didn't matter. He quit before the summer was
over."

"What else?"

"He died, later that summer."

I was tired. I was confused. "What the hell else, Tebbins?" I yelled.

A vein in his cheek started pulsing. "What do you care, anyway?" he asked. "And don't give me any crap about being here for Leo Brumsky."

"Ever wonder if Snark is really dead?" It was all I could think to shout.

"Adios, Elstrom," he said, after his face didn't change.

I had one more button to push. "About that house going up across town? What the hell is going on?"

That got a response. He pushed himself up out of his chair, drawing shallow breaths, his face a wet purple mask of fury. "Get the hell out of here, Elstrom."

His mouth hadn't said much, but the beads of sweat blooming larger on his forehead were saying a lot more.

I left.

I drove to Kutz's. I wasn't hungry for the greasy hot dogs Kutz floated in tepid water no one had ever seen him change. I needed a calm place to think, and maybe I needed a laugh, if only for a moment.

The wienie wagon beneath the viaduct was more Leo's place than mine, so much so that he prided himself on being among the very first to visit Kutz's each spring. That year, Kutz had roused himself early in the calendar and had opened the peeling wood trailer just a few weeks before. There'd been plenty of snow on the ground, and ice stuck to the bare branches of the trees. No matter. Leo breezed over to the turret that morning, grinning his wide grin. He always knew, always, when Kutz would open.

"Spring has arrived," he said, stomping snow off his red galoshes. "Kutz is cooking."

"It's February. There's more than a foot of snow on the ground." Kutz never opened for the season until the first of his most relentless visitors, the flies that called Kutz's trailer their summer home, were ready to take wing. That wouldn't happen for weeks.

"Which is why I'll suffer a ride in your Jeep. I'm assuming your ultralow four-wheel drive will work today?"

It was a cheap shot. My low-gear transmission worked more than half the time. That day, it worked particularly fine, blazing a new trail in the snow, for there were no other tire marks. Only Kutz's snowshoe tracks led down to the trailer beneath the viaduct.

Leo and I were first for the new season. Again.

"I could say I'm pleased to see you jerks, but I'm not, so I won't," Kutz had said, as Leo and I trudged across the snow.

As always, a scowl creased his grizzled, unshaved face. Young Kutz, as he was most formally known, was on the wrong side of eighty and looked every bit of it. That day, he was bundled up in thick coats and a sagging knit hat, as shiny with old grease as the hot dogs he served up.

Charitable people said his lack of social grace stemmed from his advanced years. Others, who'd known Kutz for many of those eighty years, said it was less complicated: Kutz had always been a mean son of a bitch.

"Happy to see you too, Mr. Kutz," Leo said, effervescing at the thought of the delights to come. He ordered his usual six dogs, cheese fries, and huge root beer.

"And you?" Kutz fixed his beady eyes on me.

"My usual as well. One hot dog, and a small Diet Coke to soften part of the grease."

Waiting for Kutz to snag the hot dogs from the muck of last year's water, we stomped our feet and studied the peeling paint on the menu board. The items were the same, but he'd lined out last year's prices and marked in new ones.

"Your prices have gone up twenty percent," I said.

"Ain't you heard? There's been a depression."

"Recession."

"Recession, depression, whatever. They all mean the same thing: hard times."

"Exactly. And that's why you raised your prices, because people are having a harder time getting by?"

"Some TV asshole says I got to embrace my financial destiny. That means I charge more. I keep the recession away from me, it spreads. Pretty soon the whole planet is doing better."

Clearly, Kutz hadn't been idling over the winter. He'd been watching Lester Lance Leamington, same as me.

Our lunch was slid out beneath the scarred Plexiglas window in less time than would be needed if he served things hot, and we stomped around to the picnic tables in back. We brushed the snow off a table and two benches and sat down.

Surrounded by drifted snow that was almost knee deep, Leo lined up his six hot dogs like torpedoes in a row. "Ah," he said, as he took his first bite of the season. With Leo, so much was ritual.

That had been less than a month ago.

"Where's the other jerk, the tiny one?" Kutz asked now, as I walked up alone.

"In the hospital, with tubes in every orifice, draining what he ate here the last time."

His face lit up with joy. He loved compliments.

I pretended to examine the unmarked snow around the trailer. "Business good?"

"Word's getting around. We got celebrities coming here now. We're going to be on the news, any day."

"Board of Health?"

"Laugh your ass. That broad from Channel 8, she came around."

"Jennifer Gale?"

"That's the one. Nice rack, though you can't see much when she's wearing a coat."

"She was here to eat?"

"She said she didn't have time, but she heard I was real popular with the construction trade, and was they coming around, now that they was building that new mansion? Millionaires is coming for sure, I told her. I'm going to be busting my butt real soon, with all the new houses going up."

I took my hot dog and diet around to the back. Most of the snow was gone off the same table Leo and I had used that first time this season. I sat there. With me, things could be ritual, too.

I took a sip of the Coke and tried to think. Stumbling around, I'd exposed Endora and Ma to a bulky killer. Stumbling around,

I'd turned one of Rivertown's building inspectors purple at the mention of the only new construction to come to town in years. Stumbling around, I was seeing Jennifer Gale everywhere.

I took out my cell phone and called her. She didn't answer. I left a message and took a bite of the hot dog. It was cold. I was cold.

I downed the last of the Coke, left the hot dog on the table for the pigeons, and got out of there.

Fifteen

The simultaneous ringing of my cell phone and the thunder of some-one pounding on my door jerked me out of the La-Z-Boy the next morning. I'd fallen asleep with my clothes on, sometime in the middle of the night, when my nerves had at last become exhausted.

I grabbed my phone and ran down the wrought-iron stairs to the front door.

"Dek?" Jenny Galecki was saying, simultaneously to her cell phone and to me as I pulled open the door.

"You're returning my call?"

She was out of breath, and her face was flushed. "What?"

"I called you yesterday."

"Five times." She pushed past me and pulled the door shut. "You know Tebbins at city hall?"

"A lizard," I said. "You want coffee?"

"Where were you this morning?"

"Sleeping."

"Alone?"

"I have intimacy issues. What's with Tebbins?"

"You were screaming at him yesterday."

"He wasn't being productive. Neither were you. As you said, I called five times."

"Leo Brumsky? Was he screaming at him, too?"

"Leo, with Tebbins? What are you talking about?"

"Snark Evans, for openers. Remember him? That guy I checked out for you? Who is he? Was he there with Tebbins, Leo, and you?"

"You're talking riddles. I need coffee." I feinted a turn to go up the stairs.

"Tebbins's secretary said she heard you yelling at him. Leo's name came up, along with your vanishing man, Snark."

"You're really not going to tell me what's going on?"

"I'll buy you breakfast, but only if you move quickly."

"Why's that?"

"So we won't be interrupted by the police arresting you. Someone, if not you or Leo or Snark Evans, just killed Tebbins."

One of the advantages of falling asleep in one's clothes is it takes no time to get ready to go out. I followed her to her Prius, fast.

"How do Snark Evans, Leo Brumsky, and you relate to Tebbins?" she asked, pulling away from the curb.

Things had just gotten elevated. I'd have to trust her if I wanted to get any new information.

"Back when Leo was in college, he and Snark worked for Tebbins at the city garage. Years passed, and then, a few days ago, Snark called Leo, looking for something he supposedly left with him, back in the day."

"What was it?"

"I have no idea."

"And now Leo has disappeared?"

I said nothing.

"And that's why you were questioning Tebbins? Don't be coy, Dek. I followed the cops to Leo's next-door neighbor this morning. They're looking for him like they're looking for you. The neighbor told them Leo and his mother went on vacation. She also told them Mrs. Brumsky never goes on vacation, and Leo never forgets to have his snow removed. And she said you acted quite surprised when she told you all of that."

"Perhaps he simply forgot to tell me."

"That nice neighbor lady said you broke into his garage, and then his house." She pulled to a stop in front of a small coffee shop.

The murmuring started as soon as we walked in. Unlike the barbecue joint we'd gone to, the coffee shop was well lit and had only one large room. The hostess recognized Jennifer Gale right off and walked us to a table in the middle of the restaurant. No doubt she'd take a cell phone photo: Celebrities ate there.

I pointed to a booth in the corner. "That one," I said.

Jenny appeared not to notice. I knew her well enough to know acting nonchalant was just that—acting. She didn't like being watched. The hostess frowned when Jenny sat facing the wall, and me the craning necks. A waitress fairly raced over with coffee. Jenny ordered whole wheat toast, dry. I ordered Cheerios and skim milk.

"Cheerios?" she asked, but she was only trying to calm herself down.

"Tebbins?" I countered.

"Found dead by the cleaning lady in his rec room. He was tortured with cigarettes, and shot, probably late last evening." She took a fast sip of coffee. "Where's Leo?"

I looked around the restaurant, at the faces trying not to look at us.

"I don't know," I said and told her only about Leo's phone call. "I think Snark Evans is key to Leo's disappearance."

"And Leo's vanished, Dek?"

"Tell me what's going on in Rivertown."

"It can't fit with Leo disappearing."

"Not long ago," I said, "you first came to Rivertown to cover our illustrious zoning commissioner, Elvis Derbil, being busted for changing stale-dated labels on bottles of salad dressing."

"Yep." It was old ground.

"The Feds dropped that case, along with the next thing you looked into, our lizards using citizen committees to extract phony expense reimbursements," I said.

"Old news, too."

"Something bigger than dead-ended stories about salad oil

schemes and expense report hustles brought you back. When I asked about it, you gave me pap about boredom and features, but I've done some Googling, now and again, since you left last fall."

"Keeping track of me?"

"You've been getting great press in San Francisco, Jennifer Gale. They love you. Yet you requested a leave, rather abruptly. You returned to Chicago, but not to Channel 8. Instead, you've been sniffing around the construction site in Leo's neighborhood, a hot dog stand where the construction workers might have lunch, and who knows where else. And now, wonder of wonders, you've become Johnny on the spot in the Tebbins killing."

"*Jenny* on the spot," she corrected with a forced smile.

"Tebbins was Rivertown's junior building inspector, the guy who monitors construction compliance with the city's building codes. You've been staking out the only new construction the town has seen in years. What gives?"

Our waitress came then, with our microbreakfasts.

"I still don't see how Leo can fit into any of it," she said, reaching for the toast.

"But . . . ?"

"But I think Rivertown's going wrong, big-time wrong. I got a tip that something was going on in your lovely little town, and that even more doors than usual were being kept closed at city hall."

"A tip out of the blue about closed doors was enough to kiss off San Francisco?"

"I hadn't seen my mother since last fall, and I thought I'd spend some time with her and maybe take a fast look around."

"What have you learned?"

"Things I don't understand. Your town fathers are nervous about that new house going up."

"Who's building it?"

"The owner is being anonymously represented by a lawyer downtown."

"Your source is Elvis Derbil. He's the one you know best in Rivertown."

"Robinson and Tebbins have issued work-stop orders, citing problems with permits and performance bonds and everything else they can think of. The architect is constantly revising the blueprints to meet the city's objections. It's a real battle."

"You think Tebbins is dead because of that construction?"

She looked at me with unblinking eyes. "You think Leo is missing because he lives right down the block?"

Sixteen

No cops were waiting at the turret.

"I don't understand," she said, looking down the street at city hall.

Jenny's lines into law enforcement throughout northern Illinois had never been the ordinary wires reporters worked at keeping taut. Hers were thick, like bundled high-speed information cables. It wasn't like her to have gotten wrong information.

"Look," she said, "your priority's your friendship with Leo. I understand that. But the Tebbins murder is going to get big. You're sure Leo couldn't have killed Tebbins?"

"Leo's no killer."

"I like Leo. I hope you're right."

She drove away, and I walked down to city hall. The police department was out of sight, around the back. In Rivertown, law enforcement wasn't so much a civic necessity as it was a payroll to feed lizard relatives. I walked past a municipal Dumpster adorned, like so many things, with the image of my turret, and up to the door.

It was locked.

I peered in the window. There was no desk sergeant inside, but that was normal. There were very few uniformed officers in Rivertown. The department had lieutenants, mostly, because the pay grade was higher. Almost always, they were to be found safeguarding the taverns along Thompson Avenue, no matter what the hour.

The locked door, though, was odd, even for Rivertown.

There was a doorbell, just like a house. I rang it twice.

Nothing happened.

I tapped it two more times. A little speaker scratched to life. "Huh?"

"Dek Elstrom," I said, like I was delivering pizza.

"Who?"

"Isn't this a police station?"

"Who is it?"

"Dek Elstrom," I shouted.

The electric lock clicked open, and I stepped inside.

A chair scraped in back, and feet landed hard on the linoleum. Footsteps started up the hall, grew louder, and stopped. Someone was pausing to make sure it was I before coming further.

"Hello?" I shouted. "Dek Elstrom here to see somebody."

The footsteps resumed, and finally Benny Fittle emerged from the gloom of the hall. He was about thirty, short and big-bellied. He wore his usual cold-weather outfit of a hoodie sweatshirt, sagging cargo shorts, and scuffed running shoes. It was the same as his hot-weather outfit, except then he swapped the hoodie for a T-shirt.

Everybody in town knew Benny. He patrolled the city's parking meters—one dollar for fifteen minutes—bagging the quarters and making sure the timers were running fast. Though he was naturally slow moving, the lizards prized Benny for his efficiency. He rarely paused to distinguish between meters that had already expired and those he was certain were likely to do so sometime soon.

He was no police officer, but Benny was pleased with his role in law enforcement. The last time he'd ticketed me, for being parked in front of a meter whirring in overdrive, its clock gone berserk, he'd given me a business card. BENNY FITTLE, it read. PARKING ENFORCEMENT PERSON. It, too, was adorned with the image of my turret.

Benny's was an outdoor job. Never had I heard of him being left in charge at the police station.

"Hey, Mr. Elstrom," he said, rubbing too hard at a sugary crumb stuck to the uppermost of his unshaven chins. Benny was never far from a doughnut.

"Tebbins," I said.

"He was kilt," he said, looking over my shoulder at the entrance door.

"I know. I heard I might be a person of interest."

"A what?" he asked, his eyes still on the door.

"Someone the police want to talk to about a crime."

He swallowed hard, and for once I didn't think it was from processing a doughnut.

"Benny, are you all right?"

"There's nobody here now."

"They're all at Tebbins's house?"

He shook his head. "Only two. The rest might be in a meeting."

"Here?"

"No way."

"Should I go there?"

"Where?"

"Where they're having the meeting."

"Someplace on Thompson Avenue is all I know."

Thompson Avenue was code. The first-shift officers were at a bar, drinking like on every other day. Even in Rivertown that made no sense. On such a day, the cops should have been out combing the town for leads in the killing of one of their own.

"Tebbins's house? I'm a person of interest."

"You could go there."

"Where is it?"

"Tebbins's house?"

"Yes." He was looking at the door again, and I realized it was fear that was worrying his eyes, like he was afraid someone bad was going to charge into the police station.

"I'll get the house's address," he said. He fairly ran to the back and returned with it written jerkily on one of his cards.

I was barely out the door before the electronic lock clicked on.

Seventeen

Tebbins had lived in one of the modestly upgraded bungalows in Rivertown. Its bricks were glazed and beige instead of the usual smudgy brown, and the roof was covered with green barrel tiles instead of curling asphalt shingles. In spite of what Benny had said, I'd still expected a swarm of cops, but Benny had been telling the truth. Only one Escalade was parked in front.

A lieutenant in a beige suit that almost matched the bricks opened the door a crack. I told him I was expected. He looked at me like I was nuts.

"My name's Elstrom," I said. "I live in the turret across from city—"

He slammed the door.

I waited so they could take a good look at me from a window. After they realized I wasn't going away, the door was opened again, this time by another cop. This one I knew.

"Are you having a mental episode?" he asked.

"A fit of good citizenry," I said. "I heard you think I might know something about the murder of Mr. Tebbins."

He stepped out onto the brick porch and looked up and down the street. "We already checked out your little shouting match. You're clear."

"The secretary overheard?"

"The secretary is hysterical. She said you and Tebbins got into it, screaming about a Leo Brumsky and someone named Shark."

"That would be Snark, not Shark. And we weren't screaming."

"Whatever. We already checked out Brumsky. He's off on vacation, and besides, a shouting match doesn't mean murder."

"Tebbins was upset," I said. "Red faced and sweating. Something agitated him before I got there."

"You can run along."

"What happened here?"

He looked up and down the street again. "A burglary gone bad. Tebbins caught a bullet, right to the head."

"A burglary, really?" Like murder, burglary was unheard of in Rivertown. Out-of-town thugs knew to stay clear of the locally connected cadre of car boosters, dope peddlers, hookers, and pimps who kicked back to the lizards like franchise operators.

When I didn't turn to leave, the cop said, "Look, Elstrom, we're figuring some itinerant, probably a druggie, was passing by on foot and broke in. Tebbins caught him; the burglar shot him."

"Isn't it unusual, an itinerant burgling a place, then hanging around to torture the homeowner?"

"We know where you live," he said, "like everybody knows where you live. If we need you, we'll find you." He took a last look up and down the street and stepped back inside.

It was a relief. And not. Not only did the cop not suspect me of the killing, he hadn't pressed me about anything Tebbins and I had been shouting about. One thing was certain: It wasn't some drifter the lieutenant's eyes had been nervously looking for, up and down the street. The cop had been looking over my shoulder for someone else.

Someone who he feared was coming back.

I drove to Leo's bungalow, thinking I'd give the place another once-over. I wasn't optimistic about finding something I'd missed earlier. I needed something to do.

Once again, Leo's back door yielded to my thin scraper. I walked in and immediately saw different.

The wide ribbon of pistachio shells that had been dragged from the front room toward the kitchen looked pretty much the same, but the trail from the kitchen and out the back door had been almost pulverized. What had been a trail of solid shells was now, in spots, little more than thick beige dust. Someone had broken in and walked over the shells since I'd last been in the house.

Leo's bedroom looked the same. His closet door remained wide open; his shirts and slacks still hung neatly inside. Ditto, Ma's bedroom. Her closet was in the same order, and the same two drawers remained tugged out as before. I quickly checked the dining room and the front room. They were unchanged as well. Whoever had broken in hadn't disturbed anything but the floor in the kitchen and the path to the back door.

I went down to the basement. No shells at all had been dragged down there. I thought that odd: Someone prowling a house would surely explore down there as well.

I went into Leo's office and sat behind his desk. Every piece of furniture was in its proper place. Bo Derek was as wet and beautiful as when I'd first laid eyes on her. Leo's childhood ideal of a bucolic farm scene, done up in lavenders, pinks, and greens, still brightened the wall, half obscured, above the light table.

Nothing had changed in the house, except everything. New footfalls had ground the shells lying between the back door and into the kitchen.

Bo Derek smiled back, wet and ripe and taunting.

"Well, damn it all," I said to her and to Leo, suddenly inspired. I hustled up the stairs to the kitchen to be sure. I opened the refrigerator door. I always remembered food.

There was new disarray. Certainly there was less milk.

I left, savoring the possibility of relief.

Eighteen

Still, I decided on caution.

I waited until eleven o'clock, that hour when even the most nocturnal of the working folks in Leo's neighborhood were sure to be asleep. I parked three blocks away and came up to the bungalow on the front sidewalk, slow and purposeful and out in the open, like someone with nothing to hide, just coming home late. I'd decided against the alleys because Leo and I had spent too many summer nights out on his front stoop, drinking his fine Czech Pilsner Urquell, talking about not much of anything at all, and laughing every time a marauding raccoon set off a backyard security light. Rivertown was too lousy with backyard security lights to come up the back way.

I'd just walked onto Leo's block when headlamps switched on, farther down. A car pulled from the curb, sweeping its lights across the stacks of cement forms piled in front of the excavation. It was only as I bent down, as though to tie my shoe, that I realized I couldn't hear the car's motor. I turned my head just enough to be sure. It was a Prius passing by. I couldn't see the driver, or be absolutely sure of the car's color in the dark, but I knew it was green, the color of Jenny Galecki's. I wondered what needed watching, that late at night.

I straightened up and ducked into the dark of the gangway next to Leo's house. The back door was locked, as I'd left it. I slipped the bolt with my thin scraper and stepped inside, as quietly as I could. My shoes ground into the shells on the floor. I stood still for a moment. The house was silent, a tomb.

I didn't need to be stealthy. I didn't even need to slink in the dark. I could turn on the lights, dance around, sing show tunes. I knew who would be coming.

It was his game that was being played, though, not mine. I left the lights off and tiptoed silently through the darkness to the front room.

I'd decided on the triangular space behind the big-screen television. When he'd first brought it home, Leo had pushed it flat against one wall. But once Ma discovered what could be found on her new television, and in such glistening clarity, she insisted that the new set be angled in the corner, so that all her lady friends could come and behold the miracle of naughty pay-per-view.

Leo and I had laughed at that, too, on more than one of those summer nights, when the girls were over and we were relegated to the lawn chairs in the backyard, safely away from any moans that might slip through the front-room screens. "Can you believe it?" he'd ask. "Septuagenarians and octogenarians, primly munching bridge mix and prunes, cranking up their hearing aids to catch the softest of the grunts?"

"Every old lady should have a son like you to destroy her morals," I'd said, more than once.

He'd shake his head at the absurdity of it all. Then we'd laugh again.

I slipped behind the television and settled on the floor. Soon I'd know what he was up to.

A car door slammed outside. Two voices sounded and then went away. Neighbors, coming home.

I relaxed against the wall, and my mind drifted to the last time I'd done late-night surveillance, and how Leo never let me forget it. It had been summer. I was perched in a vacant garage, watching a Dumpster behind a restaurant. I'd set up my long-lens camera carefully, at the ready to snap proof of a money drop. Then I'd fallen asleep. Leo loved that, and he rarely went a month without slipping some reference to my ace surveillance skills into a conversation.

This night, there would be no nodding off. Surely I'd be able to help, as soon as I understood what sent him into hiding.

The familiar tick of the banjo clock across the room, bingo booty Ma lugged home from church, brought back the times I'd spent in that house as a kid—the after-school hours, the dinners, the hundreds of unanticipated sleepovers when there'd been confusion, or perhaps it had just been indifference, about where I was supposed to be staying.

My mother, a high school sophomore, had taken off the day after my birth, never to be heard from again. My father, supposedly a Norwegian sailor named Elstrom, had moved on long before that. One of my aunts told me he hadn't been around long enough to learn he was going to be a father.

My mother's three sisters, all much older, agreed to raise me. Blood counted thick with them, though nurturing did not, at least not with two of them. A solution to keep me safe was reached . . . with exceptions. I spent a month with each of them on a rotating basis. By the time I got to kindergarten, I'd become an experienced traveler. I had a fiberboard suitcase and marching orders that required I move on at the first of every month.

Wires often got crossed. Vacations, doctor visits, and other things arose that sometimes resulted in locked doors. Often I slept outside, hugging my cardboard suitcase, rather than show up where I was not expected, or wanted.

That changed in seventh grade, when Leo Brumsky became my friend.

Ma Brumsky never said much to the boy Leo brought home, but she never said no. Many nights I spent in a spare sleeping bag on the floor of Leo's bedroom. Many mornings I lugged my battered fiberboard suitcase to school, made slightly heavier by two thick sandwiches wrapped in Saran for that day's lunch. There wasn't a day, from seventh grade clear through the end of high school, that I didn't wish I could spend the rest of my nights sleeping on a floor, any floor, in Ma Brumsky's bungalow.

The click of a lock echoed loudly through the still house. The back door creaked slowly open. I moved lower behind the big wide TV, smug with relief. I'd been brilliant, and I was going to be brilliant some more. Whatever was going on, whatever the reason he felt he had to hide, I would fix it.

His footsteps crunched on the pistachio shells as he went into the kitchen. He needed to eat.

Glass rattled, but no light came on. I'd already noticed that he'd unscrewed the refrigerator bulb. He always thought of everything.

Cabinets opened; cabinets closed; minutes passed. There was no scrape of a chair; he was eating standing up. Then his footsteps sounded, and again the back door creaked. The lock clicked. He was gone.

It was as I'd expected, and now I'd hurry to learn where he was hiding. I pushed myself up.

Footfalls pounded up the basement stairs. I slipped back behind the television, struggling to think. No one else was supposed to be in the house. I'd come in; I'd hidden.

I'd never imagined someone else was already inside, hiding in the basement. Someone who hadn't heard me come in.

The footsteps got to the back of the house. The door creaked open, fast. He crossed the back porch. Then he was outside, in the gangway, crunching the snow below my head.

It was wrong. There was only supposed to have been Leo, sneaking back to his house every night for food, playing a strange game I didn't understand at all.

Instead, there'd been two—and I wasn't sure which was which.

I ran to the back door.

Nineteen

My teeth had begun chattering when I hit the outside air, but it wasn't from the cold. It was jitters. I was trailing a man trailing a man, and one of them was sure to be packing a gun.

I ran up the gangway. I'd shoveled well enough, but there was still too much ice and snow for silence. Each of my footfalls ground down hard, echoing loudly off the bricks in the narrow passageway and announcing that I was there, a third man in the night.

I stopped at the front and edged out just enough to see. Light came from the streetlight down the block, at the corner past the excavation. At first I saw nothing, but then one of the shadows in front of a house four doors down changed shape. A man was moving there, hunched down, tight against the houses. His feet crunched noisily on the crusted snow. He wasn't worried about that. The houses were dark. No one would be out.

Except this night. Another man followed fifty yards behind, tight to the same dark buildings. He, too, moved low, but he was going slower, stepping more deliberately, careful to not alarm the hunched figure in front.

A loud crack filled the night. The trailing man had snapped a branch.

The hunched figure in front spun around and rose. In that instant, he was backlit by the pale milky light at the corner, a man wrapped so thickly against the cold he appeared more square than tall. He stood frozen, straining to hear.

The trailing man melted into the darkness of the bungalows.

I eased back a little into Leo's gangway, still watching.

The bundled-up man dropped back into his hunch and hurried toward the end of the block.

The trailing man stepped out from the shadows and followed.

I moved behind them. I didn't know who was leading, or following, or what I could do. It was a fool's mission I was on, and I'd come unarmed.

The bundled-up man stopped just before the excavation, at the house slated for demolition. Again he turned to look back. Satisfied that he was alone, he ran up the stairs of the vacant house.

The trailing man reemerged from the shadows and began running across the frozen lawns. No longer was he worried about being heard; his quarry had gone inside. He turned and ran up the stairs of the empty bungalow. A door banged loudly against an interior wall.

I was still two houses back when flashes, bright and blue, lit the front windows, one, two, three. Gunshots, muffled by thick old plaster and old glass.

I ran up the steps. The old door, stripped of its knob and latch, was ajar. I slammed through it and stopped.

A man stood in the center of the room, indistinct in the haze of gunpowder lit faintly from the streetlamp outside the window. His body was rounded by the coats he wore, probably two. A long-barreled revolver dangled heavy in his right hand.

He turned slowly to look at me, seemingly unsurprised by the new intrusion.

Behind him a man lay with his back against the wall facing the dining room, where a small sofa or a piano topped with graduation pictures might have once stood. Three spots made black by the gauzy gray light showed on the blank wall, higher up. Bullet holes, surrounded by splatters made large by the heavy gun.

Relief touched at my chest. I took a breath, then another.

I said his name. "Leo."

"You're here for your friend?" he asked, in a slow, soft monotone I'd never heard. He was in shock.

"What?"

"You're here for your friend?" he repeated, in that same chilling, slow voice.

"Leo!"

"Leo?" He did not know the name.

"Damn it, I'm Dek. Dek Elstrom."

He might have made a smile. By then, I wasn't watching his face. He'd raised the heavy, long-barreled revolver. His knuckles got larger as he began to squeeze the trigger.

I dropped and charged; the gun fired. I hit him low at the knees, not knowing whether I'd been shot. There'd never been weight to him, and he crumpled like rags. Something thudded a few feet away. The gun, coming loose from his hand.

I flipped him over, waiting for pain, but he'd missed me. I got him in an easy chokehold. He didn't fight; he didn't yell. None of his senses were working fast enough for those.

I got up to my knees and leveraged us both up to stand. He was dead weight and barely breathing.

"What the hell have you been doing here?" I managed, loosening my arm a little around his neck.

He shook his head, heavy with shock.

"Walk with me," I said.

He offered no resistance. I removed my elbow from his neck, and we walked slowly toward the back of the house. The layout was identical to Ma's, built in the same fast binge in the late 1920s when America, and Rivertown, were solid in their hope for the future.

We walked through the kitchen. The cabinets, counters, and doors had been ripped away.

As I thought, his clothes were piled in the back bedroom, the bedroom that was his in another bungalow, just a few houses down. He was a man of habit. I'd have to come back for them.

I put an arm across his shoulders and turned back toward the front room. His revolver glinted dully on the floor. I picked it up and jammed it in my peacoat.

We walked outside, my arm ready to grab him if he tried to bolt. But he went passively down the steps and down the blocks to the Jeep, and got in as solemnly as a scolded child.

He sat erect, unseeing, as we drove away. His eyes didn't flicker as we passed the neon carnival that was Thompson Avenue, nor did anything within them flash in recognition when I got to the turret. This Leo had never been there before. We climbed the wrought-iron stairs to the second floor.

I sat him in the La-Z-Boy. His head fell to his shoulders. He was asleep.

He wore two coats. I inspected the thick wool outer one for signs of blood splatter. There seemed to be none. A thin insulated windbreaker was underneath. There appeared to be no blood evidence there, either, but that didn't mean a crime lab examiner wouldn't find some. I unbuttoned his topcoat but left it on. Later, I'd get him to change clothes and ditch what he was wearing.

I had rope that I used to secure my ladder when I climbed more than two stories. As he softly snored, I tied him loosely to the La-Z-Boy, around the chest, around the legs. He didn't stir even when I duct-taped his wrists together.

I knew that if I paused to think, I'd realize I was acting like a crazy man. Leo needed medical help. I had to go out again, though, and I couldn't risk leaving him loose, perhaps to wander over to Thompson Avenue and announce he'd just killed somebody.

I tugged at the rope. It was taut.

Now I had to clean things up.

Twenty

The sky was dark, and clouds obscured the moon. Nothing moved in Leo's neighborhood, yet I was sure I felt a hundred pairs of knowing eyes watching as I parked around the block from the empty bungalow where the dead man lay.

I dropped the shovel I'd brought next to the excavation and hurried up the steps of the vacant bungalow. Now hidden in the shadows of the front porch, I chanced a look at the dig next door. The wall forms still lay piled outside the hole, but the cement footings had been poured, and gravel had been roughly spread between them. All that remained was to pour the basement walls, and then the basement floor. With luck, it would all be done within a week.

All I had to do was make sure the dead man was a part of all that.

I went inside. The air still stank of the gunpowder from Leo's revolver.

The dead man facing the wall was huge. He wore a leather jacket, dark jeans, and black sneakers.

I bent down. His was the face I'd seen by the ticket shack in Mackinaw City, the last face Arnie Pine had seen before he crashed his boat onto the rocks on Eustace Island.

I patted his pockets and found a penlight clipped on a key ring containing an electronic remote and a single car key. He carried no cell phone and no wallet. That was no surprise. The man was a professional killer.

I patted him down again, to be sure. He had no gun. I swept the beam of his penlight low across the floor, thinking it must have fallen out of his hand when Leo shot him. I saw nothing. There was no gun.

There was no more time, either. I jammed the key ring into my pocket, grabbed the man under his arms so I wouldn't smear blood from his chest or his back on the floor, and began dragging him toward the front door. He was every bit as heavy as he looked, two hundred and fifty pounds at least.

I tugged him over the threshold and paused to look up and down the block. No lights were on, but here and there a glint came off a car parked along the street. The sky had lightened. A sliver of bright moon was peeking out from the clouds.

I went backward, pulling him behind me, and dropped him.

I was exposed now, out in the faint moonlight, and had to get him out of there fast. I grabbed his ankles, turned him around, and tugged. Air banged out of him as his back and head hit each step, gasps from a dead man.

At the bottom, someone started humming the heavy bass line of an old Bob Seger tune, *Night Moves*. I wanted to giggle. It was me.

I dragged him to the edge of the excavation, switched ends, and pushed at his shoulders until he tipped over the edge. He hit bottom with a horrible grunt. I grabbed the shovel, rolled onto my belly, and dropped into the hole.

Something moved on the gravel. I froze, unable to breathe until I realized it was my shadow. A bigger piece of the moon had slipped out of the clouds and was lighting the whole excavation with milky blue light. The good darkness was gone.

I bumped him over the low concrete footings to the center of the excavation and ran back for the shovel. After scooping away the surface gravel, I began digging like a crazy man. I had to go down four or five feet.

At two feet I hit hard clay, rock solid and frozen. Furious, panicked, I stabbed the shovel harder at the frozen ground. It was no use. Only tiny bits broke free.

The gravel around my shadow was getting whiter. The moon was now half free.

I dropped to my knees. Raising the shovel high over my head, I brought it down with all the force I could muster. Over and over, I attacked the frozen ground. Again and again, the shovel fell from my bloody hands, unable to cut in at all.

"Hey?" someone yelled. A house door slammed across the street.

I found a foothold in the dirt and pushed up just enough to see. A man was walking toward the street, a dark shadow in the moonlight. He was looking at the excavation. I held my breath. If he came over, he'd see the corpse lying uncovered in the moonlight.

"Hey?" he called again.

He'd stopped by a car. A minute passed, and then, satisfied he was alone in the night, he opened the car door and set a rectangular lunch-box inside.

He was so close I was sure he could hear me breathe.

He looked over at the excavation a last, long moment and then got in and pulled the door closed. A second later, he drove away.

My arms were shaking too badly from nerves and pain to strike at the earth anymore. I pulled the big hulking man into the shallow grave, spaded him over with frozen clay, and covered it all with gravel.

The moon was now as bright as an examining lamp. There was a slight mound where the dead man lay, but it cast no shadow. I could only hope the cement men wouldn't think to work at leveling the gravel further.

I threw the shovel out of the hole, scrambled out after it, and shuffled across the snow to the abandoned bungalow. I'd never be able to get rid of the holes in the wall, or the splatter, but obliterating the drag marks might buy enough time to get the body cemented over without anyone thinking to inspect the inside of the bungalow.

I scooped up Leo's clothes from the back bedroom, snatched up the shovel, and ran around the block to the Jeep. Five minutes later, I was back at the turret.

Leo still slept, in spite of the uncomfortable way I'd bound him. I cut away the tape and undid the rope. I left him in his coats. I was too tired to do anything else.

I left myself in my own coats as well and lay down in front of the stairs. He'd wake me if he tried to leave the turret.

In the brief seconds before I crashed into sleep, I supposed I'd been as cunning as I could be, in trying to hide a corpse in frozen ground.

Twenty-one

His slight cough woke me.

Leo's hands were clasped primly in front of him, as attentive as a small child in a museum, as he stood facing the curved wall. First-time daytime visitors to the turret are always dazzled by the way the sun streaming in through the slit windows changes the hues and the shadows on the limestone blocks every few minutes. It's quite a show.

Leo had seen it before, hundreds of times.

I got up off the floor. "Coffee?" I asked.

He turned at the sound of my voice, his face as blank as it had been the night before. Leo, the Leo I knew, was still checked out from the trauma of his gun work.

"Follow me," I said.

He understood. We crossed the hall to my almost-finished kitchen. I pulled out a chair, told him to sit at the plywood table.

I had Cheerios, and I had bowls. I mated one into the other in front of him. The fact that I had no milk didn't concern him. I gave him a spoon. He just stared at everything.

It chilled me worse than anything the night before. I tugged at my peacoat, to pull it tighter. I saw dirt and grime—and blood.

"Damn it," I said. I had the thing off in an instant.

Leo watched me like he'd watched the limestone—silently, with mild interest, nothing more.

I laid the coat on the counter, sloshed Tide on the dark wool, and scrubbed it with my fingers. After a minute, I put it in the sink, ran water on it, and rubbed at it some more. It wasn't just the blood I was trying to wash away; it was the memory.

I set the coat on the back of a chair to dry and looked again at Leo. He was eating the Cheerios, uninterested in my sudden laundering.

Amnesia was supposed to give the brain time to heal from trauma, but amnesia meant Leo couldn't tell me anything to make him safe. I was certain the man he'd killed hadn't been the only cranky monkey in the circus. That bruiser had worked for someone who would simply hire another cranky monkey, but for what, I could not imagine.

I set a cup of coffee in front of Leo. Invariably, he refused to drink my coffee, claiming I brewed the worst stuff on the planet. It was true enough, since I rarely indulged in absolutely new grounds. Now he was drinking it slowly, passively, without expression.

I called the Bohemian.

I'd known Anton Chernek since the day my marriage to Amanda Phelps was dissolved. He was a CPA and certified financial manager and worked out of a fancy factory rehab full of licenses, degrees, and awards, but the wall shingling told only a small part of Chernek's story. Mostly, he was a quietly influential adviser to many of the wealthiest people in Chicago and their offspring, of which my ex-wife was one.

He'd come to the settlement conference with her three-man team of lawyers. I came alone. The conference lasted barely ten minutes, and that long only because her lawyers brought a huge sheaf of papers for me to sign. I read none of them. I wanted none of her money.

Chernek liked that. He also liked that I was half Bohemian and had been tagged with the thoroughly ethnic and quite unwieldy name of Vlodek. He enjoyed rolling it on his tongue: *Vuh-lo-dek*. We reached an accommodation: I let him call me something I wouldn't name a dog; he offered his quite considerable resources when I got in a jam.

"Vuh-lo-dek," he said now, relishing the three syllables when we both knew there were merely two. "What sort of mess are you in, these days?"

"I need a very private, very discreet medical clinic, for a friend."

His tone changed from kidding to serious. "To treat what?"

"Amnesia, I think, and shock. Lots of other head stuff, potentially."

"How discreet?"

"Discreet enough to admit him under an assumed name and to never tell anyone he's a patient. Do you know of such a place?"

"I must put you on hold."

He was back in five minutes. "As a matter of fact, I do know such a place. It's very pricey."

"I have about forty-five hundred dollars."

"Amazingly, Vlodek, that is precisely what I estimate it will cost for an indefinite stay." He chuckled. He'd find a way to take care of the balance, through favors he was owed, or merely his own considerable funds. Friendship with me isn't always cheap.

"Is there a capital crime associated with the amnesia?" he asked.

"Yes. I think his life is in danger, too, but the immediate problem is his amnesia."

He did not hesitate. He'd heard worse, from the people who ran most of Chicago. "Does your friend require transportation?"

"I don't know how to do that. He is with me at the turret. It's probably being watched."

"What does your friend look like?"

"Five-six, one-forty, pale skin, bald as an egg."

"Do you own a hat, Vlodek?"

I was probably the only one he'd ever had to ask such a question.

"Chicago Cubs," I said. "It's one of two I own, the other being a knit."

"In about an hour, put your Cubs hat on your friend, along with your peacoat—"

"You remember I have a peacoat?" I interrupted.

"Every time I've seen you in cold weather, you've worn navy surplus. I assumed it's your only outer garment."

"Please continue."

"Thusly attired, put your friend in your Jeep and drive to this address on Archer Avenue." He gave me the street number. "It's a spring coil manufacturer. They have a ground-level loading dock. They will be waiting for you. When they open the receiving door, drive in. Your friend will be immediately transported in a windowless service van to a clinic. You, however, will wait thirty minutes before driving out of the factory. You will be accompanied by one of their employees, who will be wearing your surplus coat and Cubs hat, sitting slouched down in your, ah, vehicle. That person will instruct you what to do. It's the best I can offer on such short notice."

"Don't tell me where you're taking my friend."

"I wouldn't dream of it. He'll be admitted as John Smith. All communication will be done through me."

He hung up before I could thank him.

I called Endora. "I have good news and some temporarily not so good news. I have him with me, but he's suffered a mild concussion. It's resulted in a bit of amnesia."

"We'll leave now."

"Absolutely not. Leo wanted you out of town because he got into something bad. I don't know what that is yet. He'll be at a clinic, safe, getting his health back. You stay out of Chicago until I know what's going on."

"Which clinic?"

"Someone I trust made the arrangements. I told him I don't want to know where Leo is."

She paused, then, "It's like up at Eustace?"

"Have you heard anything about how Arnie Pine died?"

"I forbade my mother to call her friend."

I'd told her I'd call her later.

I held out my peacoat, still damp, and Cubs cap. Leo put them on without asking why and followed me docilely out to the Jeep. I walked with my sport jacket open, his revolver tucked inside the waistband of my khakis. I didn't like packing the gun, a murder weapon with his and my fingerprints on it, but I liked the idea of being defenseless against some friend of the dead man's even less.

The spring coil company was in an old factory building that took up most of a city block. The street-level dock door opened as soon as I drove up. I pulled in next to a beat-up panel van with the company's logo on it. A man in a quilted down jacket with a reassuring bulge under his left armpit stood by the driver's door. A woman who might have been a nurse got out of the van as soon as the dock door closed. She came over and led Leo to the sliding door at the side of the van. She came back with my peacoat, the Cubs hat, and what I took for a reassuring smile. She and the driver got in the van and backed out of the adjacent bay.

I sat in the Jeep for fifteen minutes, watching shipping department people move large wood pallets of thick wire, until a small Latina, no more than twenty-five, came up to the passenger's side. She put on the peacoat over her hot pink ski jacket, tucked her long hair up inside the Cubs hat, and gave me the whitest smile I'd ever seen. The transformation was good enough. She slouched down in the passenger seat like she was asleep, the dock door opened, and we drove away.

She directed me through the old factory district. At the westbound entrance to the expressway, she told me to park between two cars in front of a crowded strip of stores. She tugged off the peacoat, dropped the Cubs hat, and slipped out. Even in hot pink, she disappeared into one of the stores in an instant.

The Bohemian, that knower of all things, had done me well. Leo was in sharp, professional hands. Protected, for now.

Only for now.

Twenty-two

I parked in the Rivertown city hall lot and went inside. Robinson was alone in his office. He wore a white shirt, a dark suit and tie, and a nervous face.

"Tebbins's funeral?" I asked.

He leaned back in his desk chair and tugged at his tie like it was a noose. "Awful; just awful."

"Heard anything about the police investigation?"

"Drifter is all anyone's saying."

"You believe that?"

"Sure. What else . . . ?" His face changed. "No, no way in hell his murder was about Snark, or Leo, right?"

"I don't know."

"Shit. Why else would you be here?" He motioned me to the chair next to his desk. "Coffee? I just made the coffee. I make very decent coffee." He was babbling, now even more nervous.

"Coffee would be good."

He got up and went to a small table against the wall. "Our secretary said you and Tebbins had strong words. I told the police I was here, and you had no such things." His hands shook as he set down my coffee on his desk. He dropped into his chair.

I sipped the coffee. He was right. It was very decent coffee. Then again, my standards were compromised; I was used to reruns.

"Look, you got to be straight with me," he said. "You think Tebbins's death had something to do with Snarky?"

"Tebbins tried lying about not remembering him."

"Of course he did. He tried hard with that boy. He knew darned well Snark was fencing stolen stuff."

"How?"

"Look, we wanted no drugs in that garage so, like I told you, we had a master key to all the lockers. Every time Tebbins found something small-time stolen in Snarky's, he hauled him around to the back, where nobody could hear, and tried to yell some sense into the punk's head . . ." His face lost focus as his voice trailed away. Then he said, "Son of a bitch," but it was more to himself than to me.

"What are you saying?"

"Tebbins had a side business installing home security systems. They were half-assed little things, mostly hardware-store motion sensors and the like, but part of the setup was boxes with tiny flashing lights visible from outside the windows, and security system signs stuck in the flower beds. In those unsophisticated, predigital times, Tebbins's little installations worked as well as any to frighten would-be burglars away, or so he told customers." He cleared his throat. "From time to time, Tebbins would need extra help, and he'd hire guys from the garage to work after hours and on weekends."

He was watching my face, to see if I'd caught his drift.

"Extra guys like Snark Evans?" I asked.

"And a couple of mechanics from the garage. And your friend, Leo Brumsky."

"Snark stole from Tebbins's customers?"

"Until now, I never considered that. Tebbins never mentioned a connection between his after-hours jobs and Snark's little inventories, but now that it's come up, it's something to think about. Maybe that's why he was watching Snark so close. And right after Snark quit so sudden and left town, Tebbins never again worked on another security system."

"Cops ever come around?"

"You mean cops from other towns, following up on reports of stolen goods?" He frowned. "Not that I know, but people came around sometimes. Customers of his, I think. I never paid it any mind."

"Snark died at the end of that summer?"

"Tebbins was real broke up about it, when he heard." Robinson's face froze for an instant, and then he popped out of his chair like it was on fire. "You're not saying Snark was killed for his thieving, are you? That somehow, Tebbins got shot for it after all these years?"

"Anybody ever think Snark's death notice was a put-up job, a faked notice in his local newspaper to shake the law off his tail?"

"Nobody wanted to talk about Snark, period. He was bad news, and everybody was glad he quit." He sat back down. "Listen, you got to tell me why young Master Leo is taking an interest in this, after all these years. Has he found out something?"

"Not such a young master anymore," I said, evading his question.

"Leo absolutely hated us calling him a young master," he said, relaxing into a laugh, "but we couldn't help it. His mother packed him such precise lunches."

"Precise lunches?"

"Two sandwiches every day: rare roast beef and yellow cheese on white bread. Cut on a diagonal and wrapped precisely in waxed paper folded, I swear, with hospital corners." He started laughing again. "Get this: She always sent along exactly sixteen potato chips in a little Baggie."

"How could you know there were sixteen?"

"Leo quickly became the object of much interest, as you might imagine. A college boy with such a doting mama wasn't ordinarily found in our grimy garage. Somebody snatched his chips one day, held them up. Leo told him he'd give him eight. The guy said he wanted half. Leo said that was half, that his mother always sent sixteen chips." Robinson was laughing so hard tears had begun to glisten in the corners of his eyes. "Know why?"

I could only shake my head. I'd never heard anything about Leo lunching on a precise number of potato chips, but I knew Ma Brum-sky, and Robinson's story sounded right.

"Leo said his mother figured he'd take four bites per half of sand-wich, and that this way, he'd have one chip per bite."

That did it for Robinson. He started hugging his ribs because he was laughing so hard.

I laughed hard, too. "A young master indeed?"

"Absolutely, and that's why I'll always think of him as a nice young kid with two sandwiches and sixteen potato chips." His face turned serious. "Why won't you tell me why the not-so-young master is all of a sudden so interested in Snark Evans?"

I lied by shrugging.

"And how, after all these years, Snarky's thieving could tie in to Tebbins's death?"

"I'm not sure of anything."

"I'll call Leo myself. I can get the number, you know, even if it's unlisted."

"He's away," I said.

"Where?"

"Vacation."

He licked his lips. His nervousness had returned. "Remember the last time, I told you Leo got sick that summer?"

I nodded.

"It was just a few days before Snarky left," he said.

"What are you saying, Mr. Robinson?"

"Bruno; call me Bruno."

"You think that Leo faked being sick so he could quit your garage?"

"Now you got me wondering about everything." He wiped sweat from his forehead. "Not one damned thing could have happened that summer that would be worth killing over. Not one damned thing."

"Tell me you're positive that Tebbins was killed by a homeless man."

The outer door opened. "Robinson?" a woman's voice shouted. "You in here?"

I recognized the woman's voice.

Robinson jumped up and hurried out of his office to meet her.

"You've got to stay on top of those bastards . . ." The woman's voice dropped away. Robinson must have told her someone was in his office.

A minute later, the outer door opened and closed again, and Robinson came back, carrying a topcoat. "I need to leave."

"J. J. Derbil?" I asked, getting up.

"Smart as hell, or at least thinks she is. She's ten times more dangerous than her fool brother."

I stopped us at the hall door to throw down a wild card. "I hear there are problems with that new McMansion."

His face went pale. "We're not used to new construction, is all." He led me through the empty office to open the outer door. "I think you can forget Snark Evans. Besides . . ."

"Besides?" I asked, stepping into the hall.

"Now that Tebbins is gone, I don't know who's left besides me who would even know about him," he said, "except . . ."

"Leo," I said, walking toward the stairs.

Twenty-three

Robinson beat it down the hall ahead of me. I went into the zoning office, smiling.

An attractive blond woman, a bit younger than me, turned from some papers on the visitors' side of the counter.

Her hands were trembling. "May I help you?" she asked.

I recognized the voice. Again.

"J. J. Derbil?" I asked. "Elvis's sister?"

"I tell people we've got different genes, Elvis and me," she said squeezing one of the papers in front of her. Apparently I'd not completely masked my surprise.

"You must have gone to private schools, away from Rivertown."

"Finishing up at Harvard, undergrad and MBA. What do you want?"

"I want to talk about a building."

She took a deep breath. The trembling had stopped. "Dek Elstrom?"

"Yes."

"Make an appointment," she said, moving around the counter to her office.

"I'm curious about that big house that's going—"

That was as far as I got. She went in her office and slammed the door.

Bingo, bango, bongo; I'd mentioned the new house to Tebbins, Robinson, and now J. J. Derbil. Each time, I'd set a head to bobbling.

I went up the stairs and out into a world that felt even more tense, tired, and unsure. The temperature was around freezing, not quite above, not quite below. The sky was gray and vague and dribbling big flakes of snow mixed with tight drops of rain. Three men were dead— Tebbins, Arnie Pine, and the guy Leo shot—people were jittering about a house, and nobody seemed sure of anything.

I drove to Leo's block, hoping for good news of the flowing concrete variety. For an instant, I saw it. The wood forms had been lowered into the hole and set up on top of the footings, ready to make the basement walls. A floor could come then, to cover the man I'd buried under too little gravel.

Except there was a crowd. A hundred people milled about in the snow and the dirt and the muck that wasn't quite either. Some of them belonged there, construction men in thick jeans and canvas coats and high rubber boots who should have been down in the hole, readying the foundation for a pour, instead of standing around, spitting and smoking and stomping their feet to keep warm.

It was the others that dried my throat. Women in sensible long dark wool, housewives from the neighborhood, had been drawn from their houses and now stood talking in tight clusters, shifting uneasily.

They were all looking at the same thing. Two Rivertown lieutenants in tan trench coats, their gin-joint complexions reddened even further by the cold, were stretching yellow police tape across the front steps of the vacant bungalow.

I drove down to Leo's, parked, and reached behind the passenger's seat for my peacoat. Pulling it out, I saw faint smears of blood and mud on the dark wool that I hadn't gotten out earlier. I stuffed it back behind the seat, pulled up the collar of my blazer, and walked back to the crowd. I told myself I looked normal, mildly curious, and not at all like someone who'd buried a body less than fifty feet from the cops pulling the yellow tape.

Jenny was on the sidewalk, talking to a woman. Robinson was

there as well, twenty feet behind her, talking to a man in a dress coat and a hard hat.

Jenny noticed me coming up. She shot a quizzical look at my blazer. I shrugged like it was a balmy day in May. She said something to the woman and came over.

"Where's your peacoat? You'll catch your death."

"I've built up a defense, living in the turret. What's going on?"

"I just got here. Any word on Leo?" she asked, by way of not answering.

"I just talked to him. I was alarmed over nothing."

"Where was he?"

"What's the ruckus here?" I asked in as even a tone as I could manage.

"See those steps?"

"Police tape is always hard to miss."

"Look harder."

I did. "I see concrete steps."

"See those little stains on the edges of them, halfway down? Rusty red?"

I saw. Now it was like they were outlined in neon, bright and red even in the gray of the day. I shook my head like I was confused.

"I see nothing."

"Bloodstains, maybe," she said, watching my eyes.

"I suppose, or paint."

"That woman I was just talking to? About three o'clock this morning, her husband came out to go to work. He thought he heard something coming from the new construction. He dismissed it as being the wind; no one's out in this neighborhood that time of morning. He drove to work, thought nothing more of it until he got home. Then he looked across the street, and in the daylight, he could see those little rusty red stains. He crossed over for a better look. Then he called the police to tell them he'd just spotted what might be blood."

"Rivertown cops confirmed that?"

"They don't have the expertise, as you well know. The sheriff's crime scene team is inside the bungalow now, looking for other evidence."

"Unusual, for Rivertown cops to call in the sheriff," I said. "They like to control everything here."

"As I told you, everyone's nervous since Tebbins got shot."

"As well as before," I said. "They're thinking those stains on the steps relate to Tebbins?"

"I don't know what they're thinking."

"One thing after another seems to shut down that construction."

"Unexplained blood is good reason to shut everything down. Where was Leo?"

"Ill."

"Want to know what I learned about Edwin G. Evans, of Center Bridge, Illinois?"

"Sure."

"Where was Leo?"

"Just ill. What did you learn about Snark Evans?"

"Not a thing," she said. "Now tell me about Leo. Head trauma?"

"What?" I said it too sharply; she'd hit too close to home.

She turned to look at the cops guarding the bloodstained steps, a small smile on her face. She'd sensed the beginnings of victory.

"How ill?" she asked, after a minute.

"They're at a relative's."

"That's why his mother is gone, too?"

"He's her life's work."

She sighed. "I'm going to check out those steps."

She walked toward the house, and I followed her, hanging back. Suddenly I was desperate for a glance into the hole next door, to be sure there was no trace of the dead man's belly poking out of the gravel.

However smooth the snow had been last night, whatever the drag marks and blood smears I'd left, all of it was now obliterated. The bungalow's front yard had been stomped over by dozens of babushkas. For the first time in my years in Rivertown, I was grateful for the incompetence of its police.

I shot a quick look into the excavation. Nobody's belly showed through the gravel between the foundation forms. In fact, the stones reflected no disturbance at all, almost as though they'd been freshly raked that morning. I'd gotten lucky. Everything was ready to pour the walls and, after that, the top of the dead man's grave.

A crime scene technician came out of the bungalow holding two clear plastic bags. Inside one was a gun. Inside the other were small chunks of plaster, stained bloodred.

"Where was the gun?" Jenny shouted out.

The crime scene technician didn't even glance at her as he came down the stairs.

She nudged closer to one of the Rivertown lieutenants. He smiled. Most people did when they recognized Jennifer Gale. Males smiled the most widely.

She began questioning him. He nodded, still smiling. She pointed up the stairs. He shook his head. She touched his sleeve. He smiled more broadly.

Smoke came then, thick, black, and noxious, accompanied by the loud clatter of pistons slapping too loosely at cylinder walls. Like everyone else, I turned at the racket, but I'd already recognized the sound of Benny Fittle's ancient orange Ford Maverick. He was making his morning rounds, looking to meet his ticket quota, and had gotten blocked by the people standing in the street. Never one to be constrained by social grace, he'd begun revving his engine to frighten the people away. It worked. People hurried to the curb, convinced they were fleeing an impending hailstorm of ball bearings. Benny grinned, displaying a mouth chock full of Boston crème, and began to drive on.

He stopped suddenly, this time of his own accord. Leaving his engine running, he got out with his pad of tickets and walked up to the crime scene technician, who was closing his trunk lid on the evidence he'd collected. Benny assumed his official stand-up writing position, squinting at the crime scene technician's rear license plate. A conversation between them began, or rather half of one did. The technician was doing all the talking. Benny simply shook his head, kept chewing, and kept writing. The technician got angrier. He pointed to the county sheriff's seal on the door of his car.

Benny was well known for maintaining his focus. He kept shaking his head, chewing, and writing.

One of the Rivertown lieutenants guarding the police tape had noticed and came over to put his arm on Benny's shoulder. Benny shook his head and wrote on.

The lieutenant smiled at the furious crime scene technician. No matter, he seemed to be signaling.

Benny left the lieutenant and went to place the ticket under the windshield wiper of the county car. The crime scene tech's fists were clenched, but his feet were not. He started toward Benny. The lieutenant stepped in front to block him until Benny had gotten back in his Maverick, sent up a loud cloud, and driven away. The lieutenant took the ticket from the windshield, put it in his pocket, and walked the evidence technician back to the vacant bungalow. Once again, things would be fixed in Rivertown.

Fear began prickling along my scalp. I hadn't considered that Benny would be writing tickets on the side streets.

Jenny came back. "Those two evidence bags? Nine-millimeter automatic. Serial numbers ground off. And three bullets, with blood spatter, embedded in plaster."

The slugs would be found to match Leo's gun, if I didn't get rid of it. Certainly they'd be tied to the dead man's blood DNA, if it were on file.

Benny turned at the corner past Leo's house. "And no corpse," I said.

"Why would you say that?"

I'd said it because I'd been stupid, talking to myself out loud. My mind was elsewhere, riding in a smoking orange Maverick.

"I just assumed the blood on the stairs means the wounded man left the house," I said.

She laughed. "I suppose that's a fine assumption, but I do believe there's something else on your mind. Want to know what else is on mine?"

"Sure."

"Let's suppose someone was driving down the street, a good three hours before the man from the house across the street came out to go to work. Let's also suppose that the person driving down the street was a reporter, someone who prided herself on having an acute sense of observation."

I turned to watch the lieutenants guarding the front steps, because it seemed the safest place to park my eyes.

"Let's also suppose that this reporter saw someone on the sidewalk suddenly bend down to tie his shoe," she went on.

"Sounds newsworthy, someone tightening loose laces."

"Ultimately, I'll find out, you know."

I told her I had to get back to the turret. She said that was fine.

As I walked down the block to the Jeep, trying to not break into a run, I was sure she was reading my mind through the back of my head.

Twenty-four

Benny was sure to ticket the dead man's car.

Rivertown had funny parking restrictions. There was no side-street parking, anywhere, between the hours of 9:00 A.M. and 4:00 P.M., unless exempted by a special residents-only, hundred-dollar parking permit. The lizards passed off the fee grab by saying it would prevent nonlocal commuters from leaving their cars on the side streets, in order to dodge the exorbitant parking-lot fee at the train station. Residents knew better. It was a way of sucking more money into city hall. Still, so it went. Every year, residents had to shell out a hundred dollars just to leave their cars parked in front of their houses during the day.

It was bare windshields Benny Fittle was looking to ticket that morning, cars that displayed no street parking permits. That would include the dead man's automobile, since he must have parked nearby. Which was a problem, because later, maybe not for a day or two or even a week, someone from the sheriff's department would think to instruct the Rivertown coppers to keep their eyes open for an abandoned vehicle, especially if the blood DNA they'd recovered from the bungalow hadn't turned up the dead man's identity. The Rivertown cops would search through their unpaid parking tickets for any car sitting abandoned on a local street, and from that trace the name of its owner, who would be found to have disappeared. Alarms would go off.

I had to find the car and make it disappear, but I couldn't risk anything in broad daylight. Benny Fittle was loose on the streets. He knew me, and he'd remember me lurking around a car he didn't recognize.

I had hours to kill until dark. I started cleaning, beginning with myself. All morning, I'd been fighting the irrational thought that the dead man's blood was embedded in more than my peacoat. I felt like it was inside my skin.

My bathing system is rudimentary. It consists of a garden hose rigged from a tiny two-foot-high water heater to a fiberglass shower enclosure. A second hose, much larger, runs from the shower to a drain. The system is not elegant, but so long as one is speedy, it's functional.

That day, speed didn't matter. I scrubbed long after the water ran cold. Only after I'd gone through a whole bar of soap, making sure I scrubbed each of the eight million goose bumps I sprouted, did I dry off. Then, dressed and chattering, I threw my laundry, along with Leo's coat and jacket, into a cardboard box, which is way more elegant than the black garbage bag I usually use, and drove to a Laundromat. I dumped my washables in, added soap and quarters, and hit play.

There was a two-hour dry cleaner three blocks down. They took my blazer, my peacoat, and Leo's coat and jacket and said I could come back in two hours.

I went back to the Laundromat. It was wonderfully warm inside, though damp right down to the magazines littering the dirty yellow plastic chairs. No matter. I settled back to catch up on the lives of Hollywood celebrities I'd never heard of.

Apparently, their lives were wonderfully damp, too. They spent lots of time on various beaches and on yachts, and lots of time, if the court papers were to be believed, sweating it up with people who were not their spouses. I had the thought that celebrities could get just as damp and be better off financially if they simply took to hanging out in Laundromats with people like me.

One story in particular was fascinating. A married movie star had an affair with the family nanny. Apparently, the nanny had film aspirations of her own. She'd secretly made a documentary of the affair, certain the film would become a financial success. Unfortunately, she was indicted for blackmail before she could realize any profit, though the film did attain some popularity with the aggrieved wife's divorce lawyers and everyone on the Internet.

"Dek?" It was Endora on the phone, shouting over a vacuum cleaner and the sounds of an irregular loud pinging. I knew that pinging.

"You must not be in Rivertown, Endora," I shouted, hoping I'd guessed wrong at the vacuum cleaner sounds.

"Listen, there's a reporter—"

"It's not safe," I yelled.

"I told Ma Leo was all right. Next thing I knew, I caught her trying to start the LTD. She hasn't driven in years."

"So you drove her home?"

"She was hyperventilating. I was worried she'd pass out."

"The reporter; it's a woman?"

"The one that used to be on Channel 8. Very nice, not at all pushy, but I'm making her wait outside. I told Ma to vacuum everything again while I called, so the reporter can't hear through the door."

"Did your mother ever call McNulty on Eustace Island?"

"Yes. The police think some drunk shooting out into the water from Mackinaw City accidentally shot Arnie Pine."

"Did McNulty tell you about any missing boats?"

"No—"

"Arnie Pine had a passenger. After he found out we were gone, he left Eustace in a boat that's going to be found missing."

"He's still after Leo?"

"Not him, maybe, but one of his friends might come. You and Ma have to get out of there now. Tell the reporter you've talked to me and I said she should go. She'll leave without any trouble."

"You'll call me tomorrow and explain this better than you have." It was a demand, not a request.

"I'll try."

"Do better than that," she said and hung up.

My clothes were dry. I tossed them in the Jeep, picked up the coats down the street, and started back to the turret.

I called Jenny. "What the hell are you doing?"

"Angering you, apparently. I left. Who's the brunette?"

"Leo's girlfriend. She knows nothing."

"I saw her and an old woman inside. I went up the stairs and knocked. By the way, what were you doing hunched over on a sidewalk in that neighborhood last night?"

"We must have dinner sometime."

"You keeping your laces tied, Dek?"

Without waiting for a response, she laughed and hung up. At another time, it might have been musical.

Twenty-five

By six o'clock, it was dark enough to drive to Leo's neighborhood. The construction site was deserted. The empty bungalow next door was no longer guarded, its yellow tape already beginning to sag.

Only a single lamp shone behind the thick lace in Leo's front-room windows. No other lights were on. I hoped it meant merely that Ma Brumsky had set a timer before Endora dragged her away.

I continued on slowly and began thumbing the dead man's key remote. The junior-grade daytime delinquents that hung out at the health center, Rivertown's community college for budding thieves, prized such devices for their efficiency: Someone new to the health center leaves his keys in his locker. As soon as he goes upstairs, the supposedly dozing attendant cuts his lock, rifles the pockets, keeps the cash, and beats it outside to sell the keys to the slit-eyed juniors loafing about. He gets extra for remotes; all that's needed is to wave them around to see what chirps. The victim's car is long gone before the victim makes it to the showers.

Three blocks over and two blocks up, I lit the taillights of an older bronze Malibu with a ticket under its windshield. No surprise, it was the car that I thought I'd lost at the shopping center, before heading up to Michigan. I parked two blocks farther on, slipped on gloves, and hoofed my way back.

The dome bulb didn't light, and the interior smelled of years of spilled coffee, fast hamburgers, and cigarettes. It was a surveillance car. I drove it to the Rivertown Health Center.

The parking lot was dark, as usual. The daytime crowd of junior-grade thumpers was content to lounge about in the open, but the night was reserved for the older criminals, the professional car strippers meeting to exchange cash for keys, and retailers of serious drugs. Once, after a particularly nasty midnight fight between rival drug retailers, the parking lot had been fitted with bright lights and security cameras. The nighttimers regarded the new brightness as counterproductive to the conduct of their businesses and smashed the new lamps and lenses. The folks that ran the health center, a derelict lot that rented rooms to other derelicts, understood. The parking lot was allowed to slip back into its former darkness.

I pulled in, immediately switched off my headlights in keeping with the after-hours protocol, and crept the car around the craters to the darkest of the dark corners.

I used the dead man's penlight to search the car. The glove box contained a stash of poorly refolded maps of Wisconsin, Indiana, Iowa, and Illinois, a garage door opener, and a jumbo-sized Swiss Army knife. There was nothing jammed under the seats or in the door pockets.

I left the maps and the knife, pocketed the opener, and got out. I unlocked the trunk. The man had been careful there as well; the bulb was gone. The trunk appeared empty, but to be sure I undid the spare tire cover—and discovered treasure. A wallet was wedged beside the spare tire, along with another ring of keys. More ominous were the three automatic handguns. I put everything in my coat pockets and slammed the trunk lid.

I stuck the key back into the ignition and powered down the driver's window, to ease the work of the cherubs flitting unseen in the darkness, and took off.

It took twenty minutes to walk across town to Leo's neighborhood. I'd turned up his street, to make sure his bungalow looked well and empty of Endora and Ma Brumsky, when I saw something move in the shadows of his front porch.

An old, boxy station wagon was idling at the curb. Several heads moved inside.

I paused behind a tree, trying to decide which was dumber: charging up the stairs to accost the person by the door, or sneaking up to see who lurked in the idling car.

Neither felt particularly brilliant, but the three guns I had in my coat pockets offered a fortifying weight.

Pulling out the heaviest of the automatics, I ran across the street, jerked open the front passenger's door, and thrust the gun barrel inside.

"*Teef, teef!*" the babushka in the front passenger's seat screamed.

"*Teef, morder?*" the two octogenarians chorused from the back.

"*Teef?*" an old woman's voice shouted from the darkness of Leo's porch. Something metal—a four-footed metal cane—began clanking down the cement stairs.

They screamed other words then, but all of it was foreign. The ancient idling station wagon had become a Polish henhouse, erupted into chaos. I jammed the gun back in my coat and retreated to safety in the middle of the street

The woman with the clanking cane had rounded the front of the station wagon and now leaned against its front fender to catch her breath. "*Creeminal,*" she yelled, raising the metal cane two-handed like a battering ram at me, the would-be criminal.

I held up my empty hands. By now, all the windows in the station wagon had been powered down. "*Creeminal, creeminal,*" everyone but me screamed.

"No criminal," I shouted back. "No thief; no murder."

The aged woman at the front of the idling car lowered her cane and, leaning on it, pushed herself off the front fender and started hobbling toward me. I recognized her then. She was the friend of Ma's who ordered the special movies that came in unmarked envelopes.

"Mrs. Roshiska," I shouted. "I'm Dek Elstrom, Leo's friend."

The good black wool wrapped around her face fluttered. "Leo? You frenn?"

"Friend, yes. Dek Elstrom."

"Dake?" Behind her, I heard more Dakes, cackled, coming from the car.

"Elstrom."

At last, she recognized me. She lowered her cane. "Where Mrs. Baroomsky?"

"Away, on vacation."

The old woman shook her head. "No goot; mus' be home. Call today for us come over." Then she gave me a sly look and added, "Moofies."

"Moofies," the girls in the car chortled.

It all came clear, then. Ma Brumsky had wasted no time after she returned. With Leo all right, things could get back to normal. She called her friends. Movies would resume. Endora must surely have had to drag her away.

"Vacation," I repeated and walked away. I could add no words that would salve their disappointment.

I drove the long way back to the turret, so I could pass the health center. The old Malibu was gone, safely on its way to becoming parts of other old Malibus.

Two blocks later, I put fifty dollars in the parking ticket envelope and dropped it in a city box. Now, no Rivertown official would ever have cause to think of the Malibu.

I parked at the turret, but before going in, I walked down to the river. Broken sheets of ice moved white in the faint moonlight, drifting lazily downstream. They would shatter against each other when they hit the debris trapped by the dam.

Blue lights were pulsing rhythmically down there, along with two very bright yellow search beams aimed at the far bank. Cops and a city crew had been called out. Something had gotten stuck, impeding the flow of the water. I didn't envy them, having to work so late.

The gaps between the ice sheets in front of me were wide enough to take guns that would never fall into the hands of kids. I threw the three automatics into them, one by one, and went inside.

I treated myself to a cup of cold coffee, sat at the makeshift plywood table, and opened the dead man's wallet. The bright gold of a badge flashed at me. It had the seal of the State of Illinois set in the center of it, a wide-winged eagle at the top, and said PRIVATE DETECTIVE in letters circling the seal. It was the kind of thing that anyone could buy to impress morons.

There were two laminated detective licenses, however, that were the real deal. Robert Wozanga, a man who until yesterday had been alive, was licensed by the states of Missouri and Illinois to sniff around. He had an address in a suburb near O'Hare International. The wallet also contained a driver's license, a Visa card, and a picture of a white Shelby Ford Mustang from the sixties.

There was a little money, just a few singles, two fives, and one ten. Mixed in with them, apparently forgotten, was the ticket stub for a ferry ride from Mackinaw City out to Mackinac Island.

I thought back to the three guns I'd just thrown into the Willahock. No doubt their serial numbers had been ground off, like the weapon the cops had recovered from the empty bungalow. For all of Wozanga's legitimate licenses, he was ultimately just a thug who killed people.

The question was, for whom.

I went out and drove north, toward O'Hare.

Twenty-six

Robert Wozanga had lived behind a screen of tall bushes next to a 7-Eleven. The other houses on the block were just like his, modest two-bedroom homes painted in conservative whites, beiges, and pale blues that were sure to draw no attention. Wozanga's was one of the blue ones, perhaps as blue as Wozanga himself was now, lying in the frozen ground beneath what was destined to become a rich person's rec room.

I parked behind the 7-Eleven, went in to get coffee like that was the objective, and took it to the bare tendrils of the privet hedge that bordered Wozanga's property. Without leaves to block the light, his backyard was as bright as the parking lot. I set my coffee down at the edge of the asphalt and pushed through the branches. I was still fifty feet away when I saw I wouldn't need to take out his keys. The back door was ajar, its window smashed. I slipped inside the kitchen and stopped.

No sounds came from the rest of the house. I hoped that meant whoever had broken in had left.

The wattage from the convenience store seemed to light the whole of the house as brightly as the backyard. Wozanga looked to have lived neatly, and apparently alone. There was one dirty bowl and one milk-smeared glass in the sink. Nothing cluttered the counters except for one yellow box of Cheerios, and that gave me pause. The little life-extending O's might have been Wozanga's last meal. He'd been disciplined, eating for better health. Yet the low-fat cholesterol-scrubbing O's had ultimately done nothing to prolong his life. Somehow, that seemed like a cruel irony, even on a killer.

The living room was as tidy as the kitchen. A three-seat sofa was set against a long wall. A worn upholstered chair was placed next to it, alongside a scarred low table that held a dozen car magazines stacked neatly. A big flat-screen television was hung so it could be seen from both the sofa and the chair.

There were two bedrooms. The largest had a queen-sized bed, a lamp table, and a dresser. The bed was made, but the drawers and accordion closet doors had been pulled open in a hurry. The room had been searched.

He'd used the smaller second bedroom as an office. It was trashed. The desk drawers had been pulled out and upended. File folders lay on the floor in front of a black four-drawer cabinet. A computer keyboard rested on the desk, but there was no computer. Whoever had ransacked his office had carted it away, perhaps along with some of the paper files.

A shelf hung from brackets on the wall. It held two tiny cacti in little clay pots, a larger framed version of the picture of the Shelby Mustang, and a three-ring binder imprinted with the name of an office furniture store, set upright next to the picture of the car.

The binder was meant to hold catalogs. It was a good binder and would be useful to a frugal man for holding more than catalogs. Wozanga had been such a frugal man. Inside were copies of the invoices he sent clients. It was what I needed.

I went out to the garage. I didn't need the door opener I found in his Malibu. The side service door had been kicked in, like the door to the kitchen. Inside was the Mustang, pristine in white with two wide blue strips running trunk to hood. I guessed the car was worth more than his house.

Behind the car, a lawn mower sat next to a snow blower, two shovels, and some quarts of weed killer. Like the Shelby, he'd never need them again. I crossed the brightness of the lawn and pushed through the branches to the parking lot.

The coffee was still warm. I took a sip as I stepped back to study the hedge. I'd left marks where I'd pushed through. So had someone else, a few yards down. The man who'd ransacked Wozanga's had left not long before. Since Wozanga was less than twenty-four hours dead, the other person was likely either a mystic or someone who'd found out fast that Wozanga was dead.

That meant either he'd been tailing Wozanga or he was his client, come to remove any link between the killer detective and himself.

I wondered, then, if that also meant that the intruder knew about Leo killing Wozanga. And about me, thumping the man's corpse down front stairs and into the frozen ground of an excavation.

Twenty-seven

I was fresh with new inspirations early the next morning. I drove to Leo's, smashed his back-door glass, called the cops, and settled back smug in the Jeep.

Delightfully, I had a cement truck to watch while I waited. It had beaten me to Leo's block and was churning in front of the excavation as two workers set up chutes to pour the foundation walls. After that, it would only be two or three more days before they did the basement floor. Then I could breathe deeply, free from the worry that Robert Wozanga might get jostled out of the gravel and point a frozen finger at Leo and me for having put him there.

A burgundy Escalade roared up to the excavation and skidded to a stop. Robinson jumped out and started waving his arms at the cement truck, the chutes, and the excavation. Worse, he was shaking his head.

It was over in a minute. Robinson stormed back to his Escalade and drove off, one of the workers made a slashing motion to the truck driver, and the cement truck rumbled away. The workers took apart the chutes, and they left, too. There'd be no pour. Wozanga, the unknowing Leo, and I would have to wait for another day.

Two of Rivertown's rarest—cops in uniform—arrived thirty minutes later. "I'm the one that called," I said, getting out of the Jeep.

The two officers stayed in the car. They smelled of whiskey.

"You go in?" the driver asked, looking up through the open window.

"No."

He nodded but made no move to get out.

"Aren't you going to investigate?"

He shut off the engine, and they got out. Both of them had mud on their shoes.

"Sloppy morning?" I asked.

"Up all night. Floater, by the dam. Took forever to snag him out."

The buzz in my brain came from remembering the blue lights I'd seen the night before, as I'd stood by the Willahock, throwing in guns. The tingle in my neck came from remembering Jenny saying that bad things were beginning in Rivertown.

"Drowning?" I asked.

"Guy had a bad smash to the head that could have come from banging against the dam."

"Who was it?"

"Medical examiner's working on that." The driver turned to scrutinize the front of Leo's bungalow. "Everything looks OK," he ventured, his eyes shifting nervously between the front porch and the gangway.

It was a wrong response. They should have been moving toward the house.

"The break-in occurred around back," I said.

"You go in?"

"Not on your life. I saw the broken glass and said to myself, this is evidence of a crime. The perpetrator might still be inside, armed and dangerous. Being unarmed and not dangerous, I called you."

The driver looked at his partner uneasily.

"Surely you can't think this relates to Tebbins," I said. It was a wild shot, but something more than the possibility of confronting a burglar had to be making them so nervous.

"No one knows shit around here anymore," the partner said.

I recognized him. A few years back, he'd been a thumper, one of the junior-grade punks hanging out at the health center. He'd had a spiky haircut that made him resemble a porcupine, aroused. Certainly it was nothing that would fit under a normal cap. Yet here he was, in uniform, wearing a glossy-brimmed police cap. I shifted to see if there were any spikes pushing up at the fabric.

He looked at me, alarmed by such an odd, obvious inspection.

"Let's go around back." I started toward the gangway.

They had no choice but to follow, both of them looking up as though someone dangerous might be in the windows, watching. I led them to the flimsy wood door that went to the wood porch and stopped.

"This is as far as I go, gents," I said.

"You'd best come in with us," the former porcupine snapped. "You're the one who called. Besides, we might need you to identify stuff."

I put on a look of horror. "You mean like corpses?"

"He means like damage," the driver said.

I winced appropriately and shook my head, a coward through and through. "I'm staying outside, back by the garage."

"Just exactly what is your relationship to the people who live here?" the porcupine asked. It was a legitimate cop question, but I wondered if he'd asked it simply to delay having to go up into the house.

"Leo Brumsky lives here with his mother. He is a friend of mine. They're gone on a trip, and I've been keeping an eye on the place. I came over this morning, saw the shattered back-door glass, and called you brave young men."

The neighbor's door banged open. "What the hell's going on?"

We stepped back into the yard. The ever-vigilant babushka from next door had come out, done up in her black down coat and a red watch cap.

"Nothing, ma'am," the former porcupine said.

"Well, what about down the block? Bad enough there's an empty house just sitting there, waiting to attract prostitutes, thieves, and drug dealers, without you using yellow tape to advertise this block as being unsafe. And just this morning, a cement truck drove up and took off, too afraid to stay long enough to deliver its load. I watch TV. I know when a whole block's gone bad."

"Precautions, ma'am," the driver cop said. "We were only inspecting unusual stains in that empty bungalow."

"I heard blood," the woman said.

"Probably nothing to it," the former porcupine said.

"What about those bullets dug out of the front-room wall, and that gun they found?" she asked, no one's fool.

"Sounds like a crime wave to me," I said, smiling at her.

"Damn it." The former porcupine's eyes flashed as he bit his lip, looking at me

"Don't forget Tebbins," I went on. "And now a floater's been found murdered in the Willahock."

"I left my front door unlocked," the babushka said, hotfooting it back inside. I'd ruined her day. It was wonderful.

"Thanks a bunch, Elstrom," the driver cop said, half tugging his partner through the flimsy door and up into Leo's porch.

I went across the yard to the garage, but wasn't alone for more than a minute when my cell phone rang. "Mr. Elstrom?" It was my new insurance client, the fellow that was about to set me on the same road as Lester Lance Leamington. "We'd like you to go to Lincoln, Nebraska, as soon as possible. We've got an insured that's reporting unusual inventory losses. They think it's internal—"

I cut him off. "Employee theft?"

"That's the supposition, but we'll wait for your report."

"I'm tied up."

He cleared his throat. "Pardon me?"

"I'm tied up," I said again.

"We discussed putting you on retainer," he said.

"I'd like that, very much."

"But?"

"But I'm tied up—"

Now it was his turn to cut me off. "Retainer means you drop everything for us."

"Ordinarily—"

He gave me a long, loud sigh. "We'll get back to you, Elstrom," he said and hung up.

Maybe he would, when pigs flew. Right now, the only things flying were my prospects for further income from that client, right out the window.

The cops came out in less than five minutes.

"When's the last time you were here?" the former porcupine asked.

"You mean, do I know how long the door glass might have been broken?"

He nodded.

"Not long; a day at most."

"We can't tell if anything is missing," he said. "Best you look around, and best you get that window glass replaced."

They left like rockets.

Other than my financial future vaporizing, the morning had transpired magnificently. Leo had had no keys when I hauled him out of the abandoned bungalow. Yet he'd used a key when he snuck home for food. If he'd left his keys or anything else in the empty house, the cops had it by now. A phantom burglar was ideal for explaining away anything of Leo's they might find there.

I'd also had another objective for my faked burglary: bait.

I drove to the hardware store for a new lock and glass for the back door. Next up was the signage shop in a suburb south of Rivertown. The rush order I'd phoned in, for two outdoor-quality signs, was ready. Back at Leo's, I drove both into his small front yard. I'd gotten the idea from Robinson, recalling Tebbins's little side business.

The signs were big, the same size Realtors used. The first was ordinary, and read ELSTROM SECURITY SYSTEMS. AFFORDABLE PROTECTION. I'd been more creative with the second: BURGLED ONCE? SHAME ON THE THIEF! BURGLED TWICE? SHAME ON THE HOMEOWNER . . . FOR NOT USING AN ELSTROM SECURITY SYSTEM!

I went inside and installed the new lock and door glass.

My tool bag contained small spools of different-colored wire, black electrical tape, and the doorbell I planned to hook up one day at the turret. I hoped they looked like the components of a security system. I left it on the kitchen table and went home, to think about my vaporized financial future and wait for someone to call.

Twenty-eight

Someone called less than an hour after I got home.

"I'm inquiring about your security systems." He spoke smoothly, but there was an element of rough behind it. He was a Chicago guy, probably South Side.

"Yes?" I asked, a businessman anxious for clients.

"I'd like to look at a current job." Definitely, he was smooth.

"I've just begun installing systems. I've got a friend, see, who was recently burgled—"

"Oh, no," he said, with almost no inflection. "Was anything taken?"

"I don't think so."

"You're not sure?"

"My friend's gone, off on a trip with his mother. I found the door glass broken. Lucky for him I've been reading up about security systems, what with the economy and all, and me needing work of any sort. I offered to rig his place right away, so long as I could use it as a showplace. He wasn't crazy about the showplace part, but he needs a system fast. I'm already hard at work and only came home to make a sandwich for lunch later."

I paused for breath.

"You think nothing was taken?" he asked. An ordinary buyer wouldn't have asked such a thing.

"He was big-time lucky," I said. "Now I'm rushing to get the system installed."

"I suppose the police will keep an eye on his place until you're finished?" It was another question asked too smoothly.

I made a fake laugh and threw in a freebie. "Not a chance. He lives in Rivertown." The information wasn't necessary. My caller knew where Leo lived; he'd been on his block, probably watching as I put up the signs.

With Wozanga gone, unaccounted for, likely enough the caller was his employer.

"Yes, everybody knows about Rivertown," he said, rushing now. "I'd like to see the installation."

"I'll be back there in fifteen minutes."

He had the presence of mind to ask for the address, as though he weren't already parked nearby.

I had the presence of mind to not laugh at the charade as I gave it to him.

He got out of a black S-Class Mercedes, smoked windows, top of the line, before I'd even slid out of the Jeep. He knew whom to expect, from watching the house.

He was silver haired, wore a dark wool topcoat, and had a ten-thousand-dollar gold Rolex around his wrist. Or maybe it cost more. It had been light-years since I'd priced new Rolexes. I'd worn a used one once, but that was back in the day. I'd sold it after I'd become a news item.

Before I could extend my hand, he put his in his coat pockets like mine might be dirty. He gave me a nod, but not a name. It was just as well. The name would have been false. I'd already memorized his license plate, but that wouldn't matter either. Guys with his kind of dough leased their Mercedeses, so they could switch them out when the floor mats got crudded up.

I took him around back. "It's a modest job, you'll see, but it's a start."

"Burglary, you mentioned," he said, when I unlocked the kitchen door.

"Through the back door here."

"But nothing was taken?" Again he asked the question that shouldn't have mattered to him.

"Maybe I just don't know."

He'd brushed past me to step into Leo's bedroom. Right off, he knew to duck beneath the last of the psychedelic squadron dangling from the ceiling. He'd already gotten a description of the room, from his man Wozanga.

"My friend told me some of the things he's worried might have been stolen."

It was like tossing chum off a fishing boat. He spun around. "Jewelry?" he asked, but something in his monotone made him sound like he thought it was what I wanted to hear.

The thought of someone lifting Ma Brumsky's rosaries was a laugh. "Sure. And the flat screens, the camera, stereo . . ."

He wasn't interested. He walked to Leo's closet, looking down at what might have been behind the clothes. "Nothing else?"

"Like what?" I asked, a doofus.

"I don't know; other things," he said, fingering one of Leo's more outlandish tropical shirts, a medley of colors that should never have been joined. "Flamboyant fellow, your friend."

"One of the neighbors saw a suspicious-looking guy hanging around." It was more chum.

His fingers froze on the sleeve of Leo's shirt. "What did he look like?" he asked, without turning around.

I gave him a vague description of Wozanga, lying just a few hundred yards down the block, awaiting a ton of concrete.

He could have been an excellent poker player, or there was the chance he hadn't known the dead detective. "That's it?" he asked, turning to look around the room, at the desk, the dresser, even the long curtains Ma had made from a hard-to-find pattern of dancing ducks. "Just a vague description of a big man?"

"Any questions about what I plan to do in the other rooms?" I asked, chumming for the third time.

He beat me to the door. "Good idea. Let's look around."

No doubt, the man was looking for something. Passing through the kitchen, he gestured at my tool bag. "When will you be done?"

"Very soon."

He stopped in the dining room. It offered a view of Ma's bedroom.

"Mind if we talk about what you're planning to do in here?" He pointed at the wide window that faced the bricks of the bungalow next door. That's what windows in brick bungalows in Rivertown mostly did; they looked out on more bricks.

"Sensors," I said, hoping he wouldn't ask questions. I had no idea what kind of sensors a home security system would require.

"Of course," he said, but he was no longer looking at the window. He was looking past my shoulder, through the door of Ma's bedroom.

We went up to the front room. He stopped in the center and looked everywhere but at the lace-covered windows stretching across the front of the house.

"Charming room," he said. Then, "Same thing in here?" He'd stepped through the arch into the little room set behind the front porch. Most bungalows in Rivertown had them, though for reasons nobody seemed to understand.

"More sensors," I said. It was a preposterous game. He was definitely looking for something.

"How about the basement?" he asked.

"Same thing, except smaller windows, higher up."

He turned and started toward the back of the house. Instead of walking straight through, he ducked into Ma's bedroom. Like the dining room, it had windows that faced the bricks of the bungalow on the other side. To live in Rivertown required joy at the sight of bricks.

"Sensors," I said.

He smiled a little as he scoped out the room. When she'd come back with Endora, Ma had straightened Christ on the cross and closed her closet door. His eyes lingered on that closet door. No doubt, he wanted a peek inside.

"I guess that about does it," I said. He hadn't seen enough, but I had. He was looking for something that was big enough to be left in plain view and easy to spot.

He hurried through the kitchen and down the basement stairs.

"As I said, more windows, higher up," I said, at the bottom of the stairs.

"And more sensors, I suppose?" he asked, eyeing the massive pile in the center of the room. He must have been imagining how long it would take to go through it all.

"Shall we go up?" I asked.

He started toward Leo's office. I hurried to step in front of him. "We'd better avoid going into Mr. Brumsky's private office."

He stopped. "Where do you put the control panel?" he asked.

I smiled. "Can't tell you that."

"Good man."

I followed him up the stairs but paused as he went out the back door. We'd made plywood key racks in seventh-grade wood shop, Leo and I. They were cut in the shape of a key and were about eight inches long. I'd dropped mine in a Dumpster, the day we were supposed to bring them home to delighted parents. Ma Brumsky had hung Leo's, the only one in the whole class striped yellow and black, like a wasp, by the back door. It had hung there ever since.

Leo's key ring wasn't there, of course, but a spare set for the Porsche dangled from the middle hook. I had an inspiration and snagged them before easing the back door shut to follow my inquiring guest down the back steps.

"Give me a call if you have more questions," I said.

My visitor nodded as he disappeared into the gangway.

I'd left the service door to the garage open. I ran in, pressed the electric opener to raise the big door, slipped into Leo's Porsche, and gunned it out of the alley.

My visitor drove sedately, perhaps pleased by his tour of Leo's bungalow. I hung back, keeping cars between us. He was smart enough to be checking his rearview, but he'd be looking for a red Jeep, not a purple Porsche with a brown rub on its fender.

We headed west, past the ruined ground of Crystal Waters and the other, healthier gated communities west along the highway. He pulled into Falling Star, one of the oldest of the secured communities, and stopped to give the guard in the gatehouse a good look at him. The thin white gate rose, and the nameless man in the S-Class Mercedes motored on in.

I hadn't gotten much, but it might have been enough.

Twenty-nine

I figured he wouldn't make a move until well after nightfall.

After switching cars, I went back to the turret and called an acquaintance who worked for the State of Illinois. Like so many Illinois bureaucrats, he was willing to break the law, by providing me with information from the state's confidential database. What made him rare was that he didn't charge for doing it. That ran contrary to the public service culture in a state where two of our former governors were simultaneously doing time in federal prisons.

"Leased vehicle, Dek," my acquaintance said, after looking up the auto license number I gave him.

"From a dealership in Westmont, according to the license plate frame."

"You know more than I," he said and clicked me away.

I didn't expect much from the license plate, but I had better luck going through Robert Wozanga's tidy notebook of invoice copies. He'd done work for a Mr. R. Cassone, of 15 Falling Star Lane. Two weeks before, Wozanga billed thirty-eight hours for unspecified services. I would have bet Wozanga had done more work since then, including taking a bumpy boat ride to and from Eustace Island.

The name Cassone nagged. I'd heard it but couldn't remember where.

I started with the county's property tax Web site. It told me that Cassone owned the home at 15 Falling Star Lane and that it was worth a little over four million, even in current depressed dollars. He had no mortgage.

Switching over to Google lit my computer screen with the promise of ten thousand sites and lit my memory at last. Rudy Cassone was one of the quieter hoodlums that worked the Chicago area. He'd been in the news for years, linked to charges of illegal gambling, prostitution, and construction-bid rigging in the suburbs around Chicago. Always, though, he'd been a rumored participant, never a primary suspect. I found no incidences where he'd been arrested.

He was a careful, successful man. He drove a hundred-thousand-dollar Benz and lived in a four-million-dollar house, set inside a well-guarded community.

I had an inspiration. I went back to the county assessor's property tax Web site. Cassone had lived at Falling Star for decades. He'd been able to afford very nice things for a long time.

I hustled over to city hall. Robinson was at his desk, studying a blueprint for a huge house. The drawing must have been for the house under construction on Leo's block, and I would have bet Robinson was looking for flaws.

"I saw you," I said.

He looked up, startled. "Where?" His hands shook as he reached for his coffee.

"That new construction. You shut down the concrete work. Who's building that place?"

"A lawyer, fronting for another lawyer."

"That wasn't why I stopped by. I was wondering if you'd heard."

"Heard?"

"They fished a floater out of the Willahock last night."

He set his cup down without taking a sip. "I heard. No one knows about that, too."

"Ever hear of Rudy Cassone?"

"The gangster?"

"The very same."

"I suppose Master Leo wants to know about him, too?"

"No. Personal curiosity."

"I've been trying to call Leo," he said, ignoring my lie. "Nobody's answering his home number. I even looked up his address and stopped by. The neighbor lady said he's still on vacation."

"That's about it," I said.

"He's calling you from wherever he is, asking all these questions?"

"Look—"

"Never mind," he said, glancing down at the blueprint. "I got bigger things to worry about. All I know about Rudy Cassone is he lived, or maybe still lives, in a big fancy house in one of those protected communities west of here."

"Did Tebbins sell him a security system?"

"I think it was the last one he did, as a matter of fact."

"Anybody else help?"

"Sure. Snark—" Robinson jerked upright in his chair as he realized what I was inferring. "This is about stolen goods?"

"I'm not sure."

"Yes you are, Elstrom. This is all about something that got stolen years ago? Leo's thinking Snark stole something from Cassone? No chance. Tebbins sure as hell knew Cassone was a . . ."

"A big time badass?"

"Snark Evans might have been a stupid punk, but he'd never mess with a guy like Cassone."

"How can you be so certain?"

"I . . . it's inconceivable."

"Maybe he was acting under orders."

A sweat had broken out on Robinson's forehead. "You mean Tebbins? You're thinking Tebbins had Snark steal from Cassone, and because of that, Cassone killed Tebbins all these years later?" He wiped at his forehead and cradled his head in his hands. "Oh, sweet Jesus."

"What do you hear about Tebbins's death?"

He looked up. "Nothing new. A transient. Nothing to do with Rudy Cassone."

"Bad things happened to people who worked at his house that summer."

"You mean Snarky?" His face got defiant. "Snarky died somewhere else that summer. Tebbins got killed by a transient."

I met his stare, said nothing.

"Look," he said, "I got to get back to work. Why don't you ask your friend Leo Brumsky about all this?" he asked. "Or is . . ." His face lost its defiance. "Is that what this is all about? Leo's worried he's in trouble, too? Because of Snarky? Because of Tebbins?" His hands shook as he squeezed the arms of his chair. "That can't be. I think Leo was out of here long before Tebbins and Snarky did the job at Cassone's."

I left him to his nerves and his caffeine.

Walking back to the turret, I called the Bohemian. "Vuh-lo-dek," he said. "I was just about to call you."

"What is it, Anton?"

"Your Mr. Smith has become quite frantic."

Thirty

The clinic was at the Illinois-Wisconsin line, set unmarked and se-cluded well back from the road. If the Bohemian's instructions hadn't been precise, I never would have found the driveway through the trees.

The reception area was designed to receive no one comfortably. It consisted of two hard plastic chairs and a stern-faced woman tucked behind a high counter. I was made to wait for only a moment before a woman in a cardigan sweater came through doors that opened with a faint electric snick. She smiled in spite of the surroundings.

"I'm Dr. Feldott," she said, extending her hand. She was about forty, prematurely gray, and wore bright red glasses that would surely please Leo if he were feeling well. "Mr. Smith is doing quite well, con-sidering," she went on as she led me back, through the electronically locked doors.

"Considering?"

"He's begun acting in a most determined manner. We believe he's trying to tell us something."

"He's not speaking?"

"Occasionally, but he's not communicating with words. You'll see."

We walked down a hall that looked more residential than

institutional. Paintings hung on the walls, glass vases filled with fresh flowers sat on narrow tables. The only tip off that we were in a health-care facility was the doors. They were wider than residential doors. They had keypad locks, and they were all closed.

"His blood is good; everything physically seems to be fine," she said as we turned a corner. "His issue stems from a shock. You know about his shock?"

I nodded.

"It would help if we could discuss the details of that."

"I cannot."

"He's been eating and sleeping well, and smiling almost all the time, until this morning, when he went into a sort of frenzy. He grabbed a pen from one of our nurses and began motioning for paper. I was called. We took it for an encouraging sign, this new desire to share. But almost immediately, he threw the pen down. He wanted another writing instrument. It was only after some time that we realized he wanted crayons—" She stopped abruptly, seeing the smile on my face. "Something is funny about this?"

"He likes colors. Like no one you've ever met. Did you get him the sixty-four-piece set?"

"Not at first," she said. "We brought him one of the small packs we keep here for children. He got furious, shook his head back and forth. I went out to Walgreens, brought back the largest set, though we removed the little sharpener. He's been drawing on typing paper ever since, not happy, not unhappy, just . . . purposeful; driven. He hasn't eaten at all today, so fixated has he been on drawing. As you'll see, he draws only one picture, over and over, and presses one upon everyone he sees. At first, we thought he was offering his artwork as gifts, but as he kept drawing the same thing over and over, we realized he's trying to tell us something with the pictures. We're hoping they'll mean something to you." She stopped at a door, entered a code on the keypad, and pushed it open. She motioned for me to go in first.

Leo sat at a small table, stabbing a white sheet of typing paper with the stub of a red crayon. He wore khakis and a light blue knit shirt. The Leo I knew would never have sported such a boring ensemble. The tip of his tongue was sticking out of the corner of his mouth as it sometimes did when he concentrated. He looked up as I came closer.

His face was even more pale than usual, and haggard. Too haggard.

"About time," he said.

It was the beginning of relief. "You know me?"

"Of course."

"Who is he?" Dr. Feldott asked, coming up to stand beside me.

"The gun man." Not gunman; gun man. Two syllables.

Dr. Feldott inhaled sharply.

Leo was beginning to remember, linking me with the gun he'd used on Wozanga, the gun he'd been about to use on me.

"Relax," I told the doctor. "I haven't killed for a month, maybe more."

She smiled, sort of, but took a couple of steps back anyway.

I looked down at the picture Leo was drawing. It wasn't much, just a hundred red dots in several clusters.

"What are you drawing?" I asked.

He began attacking the paper in front of him with more red dots.

I looked over at Dr. Feldott and shook my head. I had no idea what he was trying to draw.

"Are you going to give this nice man your drawing?" Dr. Feldott asked him. She hadn't asked my name because she expected I'd give her something phony.

"Not nice man; gun man," he said.

Apparently satisfied with the hundreds of dots he'd put on the paper, he put the stub of the red crayon back into the flip-up box and studied the other colors. Like the red crayon, many of the others had been worn down to stubs. His fingers dug deep into the box, pulling out a lavender crayon even shorter than the red one.

"That's one of your favorites, isn't it?" Dr. Feldott asked.

"No time." He drew a rectangle on the sheet of paper and began filling it with broad strokes of lavender.

I knew then, as surely as I'd ever known anything.

"You're going to give your friend this drawing?" I heard Dr. Feldott ask again.

"The gun man," Leo corrected, running the lavender crayon back and forth.

I turned to the doctor. "You said there are other pictures?"

"All the same," she said. "Can the gun *man* see some of the others?" she asked Leo.

His coloring hand stopped in the middle of a stroke. "Excellent!" he shouted. He opened the table drawer and pulled out a sheaf of papers. Thrusting them at me, he yelled, "Gun man."

"Gun man?" Dr. Feldott persisted, but it was so unnecessary.

He'd handed me the sheaf upside down. I turned them over. As Dr. Feldott had said, the picture on top was the same as the one he was now drawing. It had hundreds of the same red dots, meant to show leaves. The lavender was there, too; broad swipes of plenty of it, all over a barn; along with pink, green-spotted cows against a background of orange rolling hills. The only thing missing was the "Leo B." in the lower right corner, and that was only because he couldn't yet recall his own name.

"I understand," I said quickly, though I didn't, at least not all of it.

Dr. Feldott looked alarmed. Leo looked up from his coloring and smiled.

I jabbed the sheaf of pictures back at the doctor and ran out of the room and down the hall. Dr. Feldott came running after me. She knew the electronic locks on the door would stop me.

She demanded to know nothing as she punched in the code to make the doors swing free.

"You'll call me?" she shouted, as I sprinted into the reception area.

"I'm the gun man," I yelled back, running for the Jeep.

Thirty-one

I'd started the day establishing a burglary explanation for anything of Leo's the cops might find in the empty bungalow. Then I'd stuck signs in Leo's yard, hoping to lure one of Wozanga's compatriots, or maybe even his boss, into revealing himself.

I'd won. I could explain anything of Leo's that popped up any-place inconvenient, and I'd flushed out Rudy Cassone.

I'd lost, too, because the picture that had caused Leo to get lost, and Snark Evans to get dead, was likely to get stolen away before I could use it to figure what was going on.

Traffic was a gnarled nightmare southbound on 294, a twisted jumble of obstinate idiots hell-bent on keeping me from Rivertown. I bobbed, weaved, and swore, and none of it did any good at all. It took over an hour just to get to O'Hare, and another thirty minutes to thread east through the last of the day's rush on the Eisenhower Expressway. By the time I charged onto Leo's block, it was dark, and it had started to snow.

A corner of my eye took in the unchanged excavation. Every day that passed without progress meant another day that Wozanga's corpse might be discovered. It was a worry for later. My fear now was I was getting to Leo's too late to act on the only signal he could send me.

I cut my lights and coasted to a stop across the street. The lamp on Ma's timer was on, casting a soft, semitransparent glow in the front room behind the lace curtains. I could make out the shape of part of the big-screen television, just to the right, and the high back of the sofa that Ma had kept pristine with so many generations of white-piped clear plastic slipcovers. I wanted to hope that the light from the front-room lamp, or the threat of my make-believe security system, or even the potential of drive-bys by the Rivertown cops would keep Cassone away.

I'd kept him out of Leo's office. Surely he'd not yet seen the supposed child's fanciful drawing of a lavender barn, pink and green cows, and red-leafed trees.

Still, my gut said to stay in the Jeep for a time, be cautious, and watch. Cassone, after all, was likely a killer, just like his man Wozanga. So I stayed behind the steering wheel and squinted at the light behind the lace. I watched for five minutes, and for ten more.

Then the faintest of shadows moved quickly by the big-screen television, right where I'd hidden the night my friend killed Wozanga.

The shadow retreated from the light behind the lace.

I'd been a fool. I should have brought Leo's gun. Not to fire, but simply to use to threaten.

I remembered the aluminum baseball bat I'd picked out of the snow the morning after Ma and her friends had gone berserk trying to open pistachio nuts. I reached behind the passenger's seat, felt its cold opportunity.

I grabbed it and eased out of the Jeep.

Every room in the babushka's house next door was lit up brightly, an old woman's defense against the night. I moved low through the gangway, trying for invisibility. I turned the corner at the porch and moved to the shadows next to Leo's outer door to wait. There were no basement windows back there, so I could not see the movement of a flashlight, but surely he'd go down there, and into Leo's office at the front. He'd look behind the cabinets and under the desk and behind the huge overstuffed chair. He'd look at the walls, at Bo Derek. At some point, he'd notice the painting above the file cabinets, with its oddly colored cows and barn and leaves. He'd know it not by the colors it was now but simply by its size. I didn't understand why, but I knew: The intruder would smile.

A half hour passed, in minutes each longer and colder than the one before. I huddled against the back of the building, ten feet from the door to the porch, too afraid to stomp my feet to keep warm. The snow was falling harder, big flakes, wet flakes.

The kitchen door creaked, cracking the hushing cover of the falling snow. Footsteps thudded across the porch floor. He paused at the steps, and then he came down, softly because the babushka next door might be in her backyard, having sensed a disturbance in the night.

The flimsy wood door at the bottom groaned as he slowly pushed it open. He came out, carrying the rectangle.

I swung as he turned toward the gangway, slamming the tip of the bat square between his shoulder blades, at the base of his neck. He dropped onto the cushion of snow with a soft thump and was still.

I dropped the bat. I tugged to roll him over, to be sure of the face. He wheezed, unconscious, a sack of live bone and meat that was Rudy Cassone.

I grabbed the rectangle. He'd wrapped it in layers of cloth, a sheet torn from one of the beds.

He moaned and shifted a little on the snow.

I ran through the spill of light in the gangway, across the parkway. Grabbing at the Jeep's door handle, I jumped in. My trembling fingers searched my pocket, found the keys, and dropped them like they'd been greased. Fumbling, frantic, I ran my hands around the floor. Surely the babushka had heard me pounding through the gangway and raced to a front window.

I found the keys, poked the rubber-headed one into the ignition, and was off. It was only when I reached the corner that I thought to switch on the headlights.

I saw the black Mercedes as I made the turn. Cassone had parked on the side street. He'd known to be cautious.

I unwrapped the rectangle on the card table, on the second floor. As I expected, several pink, green-spotted cows were standing in front of a lavender barn, looking right back at me.

They didn't look like they knew anything at all.

Thirty-two

A nightmare jerked my hand off the side of Leo's revolver the next morning.

I dreamed my feet were encased in hardened concrete, as tons of thick cement cascaded down from the chutes of a dozen monstrous churning trucks, into the excavation. Rudy Cassone was up above, running from truck to truck, working the levers, and laughing as I swung my bat futilely at the block of concrete trapping my feet. The block wouldn't chip. It was too hard. And the concrete kept coming, a dozen thick rivers filling the hole like a tub, up to my ankles, up to my calves, up to my arms until I could swing no more.

I pushed myself out of bed and into cold clothes and went to the window still groggy enough to fear seeing cement trucks lined up, churning. Mercifully, there was only new snow, six inches of fresh fluff lying on top of the Jeep.

It had been a nightmare like all nightmares, built of a jumble of a few very real blocks. The cement, Cassone, the bat . . .

The bat.

I pounded down the stairs and out to the Jeep. I pawed through the Burger King wrappers, beneath the gym bag, and under the towel I keep to wipe the inside of the windshield when it's raining

and the defroster has gotten too bored to work. I searched everywhere. The bat wasn't there.

I'd clubbed Cassone; I'd dropped it; and then I'd forgotten it,
anxious only to get away, to protect the painting.

I hustled back into the turret, shivering from cold but more from
fear, thinking that Cassone had likely regained consciousness in
something of a foul mood and interested to know who clubbed him.
He'd have grabbed the bat, and although Rivertown was small-town
cheesy crooked, Chicago wasn't. Outfit guys knew cops, and cops
could check fingerprints. Mine had been on file since the court case
that had ruined me.

Still, he might have hobbled away, without noticing the bat. There
was the snow, too. Enough might have fallen to cover it up after I'd
knocked him unconscious.

I sped over to Leo's thinking I'd surely appear innocent, coming
only to shovel the walk. No attacker, any right-thinking person would
reason, would have the nerve to show up after beating a man sense-
less at that very place just a few hours before. With luck, I'd fish the
bat out of the fresh snow and toss it away somewhere.

The babushka was on her front porch, dressed in dark clothes for
another dark day. She moved her head back and forth, making a
pointed comparison between her own neatly shoveled walk and Leo's,
covered thickly with new snow.

"Wonderful day, is it not?" I asked, pasting on what I was sure was
a fine wide grin.

She frowned. "Last night was disturbing."

I lessened my smile, fearing I might resemble a crazed jack-o'-
lantern. "All the new snow?" I asked, hoping it was only the snow.
"Not to worry; I came to shovel."

"Odd soft noises, coming from the Brumsky place." She pointed
at Leo's bungalow as though I didn't know where it was.

"Noises from the snow?" I asked, an idiot, but an innocent.

"Not from the snow, you fool. There was a shout, like people were
fighting in the backyard. By the time I could get to my back room to
look out, someone was escaping up the gangway. I got to the front

just as a car started. The snow was falling thick, and the sneak was crafty. He pulled away without turning on his headlamps. I couldn't see dink squat." Pausing for air, she stared at me, then, "Only one person's been interested in coming around much, lately."

"I've been working here, rigging up a burglar alarm, checking the furnace and the hot water."

"That's another thing about last night," she said. "I didn't hear any alarm."

"I'm not done," I said. "See anything else?"

"You'd best get shoveling, then," she said.

"Oh, you bet." She'd seen nothing, called no one.

I high-stepped to the back and saw that the snowfall had obliterated any signs of my clubbing Cassone. I got the shovel from the garage, came back, and began stabbing at the new blanket of snow, hoping to hear the clink of aluminum.

"What on earth are you doing?" the neighbor shouted across the chain-link fence. She'd made no sound coming out her back door, a true stealth-babushka.

"Chipping ice off the shovel."

"Shoveling the walk will get rid of it quicker." She went back inside.

I shoveled my way to the front, did the walk and the steps, and returned to the back to take more stabs at the snow. Nothing clanked; the bat was gone. He'd taken it with him.

I went up the back porch stairs. There was no broken glass, but the door was open. Cassone had jimmied the new high-security lock I'd installed. I went inside.

He'd not trashed the house. He'd known the dimensions of what he was looking for. The clothes in Ma's and Leo's bedroom closets had been pushed to the sides, so he could peer behind them, but he'd been unhurried and orderly, a professional.

I went down to the basement. The clutter had been spread farther out and gone through carefully. Nothing appeared to be broken.

He'd found what he wanted in Leo's office, of course, on the wall above the file cabinets. I went upstairs.

"I suppose I should call the police," the babushka said from her back step.

I stomped across the snow to her fence, one last probe for the bat. "About that ruckus last night?"

"They could search the property, like maybe you've just been doing."

"I came to shovel and thought I might as well check the furnace and the hot water heater," I said.

"Why are you standing in deep snow?"

"To hear you clearly," I said, giving her my best smile.

She snorted and turned her back.

Thirty-three

By most accounts, my grandfather was a courtly, small-time brewmeister, a guy looking to make good beer and, of course, a castle. Part of his being in the bootlegging business during Prohibition must have required a place to stash money and perhaps long guns, because I'd come across his hiding place, a large cavity tucked into the floor, quite accidentally only months before.

I lifted the fitted planks and brought Leo's painting down to the lighted Luxo magnifier on my card table desk.

At first glance, it was nothing more than a kid's painting, eighteen by twenty-four inches, done by a child fated for a career in anything but art. The lavender barn was lopsided. The pink, green-spotted cows had misshapen legs, each of which was a different length, and the tree trunks were tendrils, too spindly to support so many red leaves. He'd signed it "Leo B." in the lower right corner.

I turned the painting over. Always a stickler for detail, he'd written "To Ma, from Leo," in a big, looping child's hand.

Something irregular caught my eye. I moved the magnifier and saw that a tiny seam had opened up along the inside edge of the wood frame. An artist's canvas was always stretched around a wood frame and tacked in back. A seam inside the frame made no sense.

I used my fingernail to pull gently at the seam. A tiny speck of glue fell away, revealing what looked like an older piece of canvas underneath.

It was obvious what Leo had done. He'd painted a ridiculously colored farm scene right over another picture. He'd thought to disguise the back of the old painting as well, by gluing on a piece of new canvas.

It was enough to build a scenario: Snark Evans, installing a security system at Cassone's house for Tebbins, had stolen a picture. Likely enough, Snark didn't know what he had, other than a raging case of second thoughts. He dumped the picture on an unsuspecting Leo, thinking maybe he'd come back for it when things cooled. Snark hightailed it out of Rivertown, going so far as to fake a report of his own death so Cassone wouldn't come hunting for him. Leo, a kid finishing his first year of college, probably thought nothing of adding a picture to the pile of other artifacts mounded in the middle of his basement.

For years, Snark's ploy worked. Snark drifted on to new things under a different name. Cassone settled into believing his picture was gone for all time. Leo forgot about the painting in his basement.

Then, just a week or a month before, something triggered each of them into action. Snark called Leo, wanting his picture back. Cassone hired Wozanga, who ultimately traced the painting to Leo. Leo dug out the picture and saw something he hadn't seen before, something that needed camouflaging with a child's version of a lavender barn and pink, green-spotted cows.

My scenario was sure to have big holes, but I knew one thing: Leo was the most honorable of men. He would have researched the painting and likely found out it belonged to Cassone. He would have returned it to him, whether or not the man was a hood. That he hadn't meant he'd learned something that prevented that.

I called Jenny. "I need a favor."

"How's Leo?" Jenny asked.

"Improving."

"Are you going to take me to someplace memorable if I do this favor for you?"

"I took you to the beach once."

"You took me to a trailer park *near* the Indiana dunes. We found a corpse covered with flies."

"Wasn't that memorable?"

"What do you want, Elstrom?"

"I want you to call your police friends and find out whether Rudy Cassone ever reported a theft from his house in Falling Star."

"Rudy Cassone, the big-time gangster?"

"Yes."

"This has to do with Leo?"

"Yes."

She hung up without waiting for me to dodge a next question. I told myself it was gamesmanship.

I looked across the room to admire the black char in the fireplace, the residue of the only fire that had ever been lit there. Jenny and I had inaugurated that fireplace, not two hours after we discovered the corpse in Indiana. Shivering, although it was July, we'd spoken of our ghosts, her dead husband and my ex-wife. Sometime into the night, the adrenaline gave out, and she fell asleep in the electric blue La-Z-Boy as I sat beside her, alert, lecherous of thought but virtuous of action, until I became too aware of myself watching her breathe, and I covered her with a blanket and went upstairs to the bed across from another fireplace, one that I'd inaugurated with Amanda, my ex-wife.

Amanda knew art. She used to write big glossy art histories before her estranged father found the right way to lure her into his electric utility and back into his life. Amanda didn't write art histories anymore. She no longer taught at the Art Institute. I hadn't spoken to her since late in the previous year.

Still, she knew art.

I did not stop to wonder about motives and needs and what used to be. I dialed her number.

"Dek?" Vicki, her assistant asked, surprised. It had indeed been months.

"Alas, the very same."

"She called you already?"

"What?" I asked, confused.

"You're on her call list. I was supposed to remind her to call you later this afternoon."

It didn't make sense. "Is she free now?"

"Hold, please."

"Dek?" Amanda asked, after a longer wait than ever before.

"I have an art question," I said quickly and preemptively.

"I know," she said, stunning me.

Thirty-four

She had people . . . I said I'd be hanging . . . She said she'd call.

It was like that with us. We'd not been married long, really only weeks, before we developed senses of each other that were ordinarily reserved for people who'd been together for decades. She knew the endings of my sentences, as I knew hers. Answers to the big questions, though, we never had the time to figure out, and we crashed when I was wrongly accused of falsifying evidence in a suburban mayor's insurance scheme. I'd looked around for anyone other than myself to blame and saw Amanda, a rich man's daughter who'd brought me notoriety because of her father's prominence. Or so I reasoned, through the ninety-proof haze I'd taken to using to blur my shame. It killed my self-respect, her tolerance, and our marriage.

Our abilities to finish each other's sentences were taking longer to die. Even the last time we'd spoken, months before, we laughed awkwardly at that last stubborn vestige of our marriage.

Her knowing that I was calling about an art question, though, went way beyond that.

The afternoon faded into dusk, and the dusk into darkness. An hour after that someone knocked on the door.

Cassone wouldn't knock. Still, I grabbed Leo's revolver before running down the stairs. I turned on the outside light, raised the gun, and jerked the door open.

Her beautiful brown eyes, made even darker by the hood on her black parka, went wide at the sight of the gun. She was carrying one of those small plastic-wrapped bundles of firewood that gas stations sold. A little white bag was perched on top. I tugged her inside.

"What the hell, Dek?" she asked, staring at the gun.

"What a wonderful surprise, Amanda," I said, slamming and bolting the door with the hand that wasn't holding an armament.

"Don't give me that."

"Damned out of season trick-or-treaters?"

"Nor that."

I jammed the gun, barrel down, in the waistband of my jeans, hoping it would not shoot off anything vital, and took the firewood and the little white bag that most certainly looked like it came from a bakery.

"Are you in danger?" she asked, in a small voice.

"Nah."

"We'll talk." She put a smile on her face, trying to summon up some of the old playful sternness she used to level at me, but her eyes weren't going along. They were wary, maybe from the gun I'd added to my wardrobe, or maybe from the fact that so many months had passed since we'd last talked. I followed her up to the second-floor fireplace. Certainly there would be no banter about bringing the firewood up to the one on the third floor, opposite the bed. I set the wood down next to the hearth and turned to her.

She was looking past me, into the huge fireplace. The last time she'd come to the turret, it had been unmarked. For a moment, neither of us said anything.

"Coffee?" I finally thought to ask.

"Great," she said, relieved.

We walked across the hall. "My," she said, looking at the cabinets, trim, counters, and absolute lack of new appliances. "You've done nothing with the kitchen since I was last here."

"I found work, for a time."

"Insurance?"

"Profitable, too."

"It's coming back, finally?" The document scandal had left a long-lasting residue of doubt in the minds of my former clients.

"Slowly," I said.

"Are you going to build a special cabinet in here so visitors won't have to look at your revolver?"

"Ah." I took it out of my waistband and set it on the farthest counter.

We talked of safe things while I made coffee. The little white bag contained croissants from a Chicago bakery I'd never heard of. We brought them and the coffee back across the hall, and I started a fire with scraps of trim wood I'd conveniently left all over the floor. When those caught, I added three of the split short logs she'd brought. She sat in the electric blue La-Z-Boy, I sat on the tilted red desk chair, and we ate the croissants as the fire found strength.

"I only brought enough wood for a quick fire," she said, warming.

"Always thinking."

"What's with the damned gun?"

"Extra precaution for a little project I'm working on."

"Leo?"

I paused midbite, a rare enough occurrence. "When I called, you said you were expecting to hear from me. Because of Leo?"

"Actually, I was expecting to hear from him, not you. He called me a few days ago—"

"How many days ago?" I cut in.

"I don't remember, exactly. It was the day we got a lot of snow, before the last day we got a lot of snow."

It was the day he'd sent Ma and Endora away and disappeared himself. "Sorry. Go on."

"He'd called about the provenance of an obscure set of paintings that had been in the news recently. He wanted to know if I had any sources."

"Isn't that the sort of thing you'd be asking him about, and not the other way around?"

"Absolutely; origins are his specialty, not mine. I figured he was being extra careful, covering all his bases, because of the publicity." She smiled softly. "When I told you I wasn't surprised to hear from you, it was because I'd wondered if Leo's calling me had been a way of staying in touch. I don't think he's ever given up on us."

I looked away, toward the fire. "He's a romantic."

"And the most loyal of friends."

"You mentioned publicity? A series of paintings has been in the news?" I asked.

"A big Hollywood divorce. Two wealthy people are fighting for control of a set of paintings."

"Wait here," I said. I went up to the fifth floor, brought down the picture, and set it on the card table. I switched on the Luxo.

"My, my," she said, coming over. "Primitive. Not Grandma Moses primitive, just plain awful primitive."

I pointed to the signature in the lower corner.

She started to grin. "Leo B.," she read. Then the smile disappeared. She bent down and sniffed.

"I would have said grammar school artistry," she murmured, "but the paint's too fresh. He painted this eclectic monstrosity in acrylic, and very recently." She turned the painting over.

"See the open seam?" I asked.

She was already picking at it as I had, gently with a fingernail.

"That doesn't belong, does it?" I asked. "It's been pasted on, as though to cover up the back of the original canvas?"

She said nothing as she reached for the plastic ruler I keep in a coffee mug, along with pencils. She measured the painting.

"Amanda?"

"Leo, Leo," she whispered, setting the ruler back in the mug with exaggerated slowness.

"Amanda!"

"I thought he was talking about one of the three," she muttered. "One of the divorce attorneys . . ."

She straightened up, blinking her eyes as though she'd just emerged from a cave.

"What are you talking about?" I asked, wanting to yell.

"The fourth flower."

Thirty-five

She said she needed something stronger than coffee. All I had was the ancient gallon of Gallo that I'd kept, mostly untouched, since the aftermath of our divorce. Sometimes the old jug mocked me; sometimes it beckoned me. Always it challenged me.

I got the jug and poured wine into our coffee cups.

Only after she took a long, slow sip did she begin. "You know of the Nazis seizing famous art before and during World War II?"

"I've read snippets about looting."

"It was more than simple looting, and it was huge. Adolf Hitler had the idea to build a grand *Führermuseum,* a gigantic cultural museum that would dwarf anything in Paris, London, Vienna, or Florence. To stock it, he had his Nazi sickos plunder, loot, confiscate, and, as a last resort, buy all the great art they could find in Occupied Europe. They grabbed so much, they had to store it in multiple locations in Munich, Czechoslovakia, Austria, and other places. Toward the end of the war, as things began going badly, they moved most of it into salt mines near Salzburg. And there it all sat, until the U.S. Army discovered it." She took another sip of wine. "That brought on new problems."

"Not all the art got returned to its rightful owners?"

"Even now, there's litigation over the identities of the rightful owners. Remember I said that Hitler's minions actually paid for some of the pieces?"

"Yes."

"A sale doesn't make for a proper legal transaction, a rightful transfer of ownership, if it's the result of a threat, or worse, a drawn gun."

"Sell or else?"

"Exactly, and those happened all the time. Then there are different sorts of issues, ones concerning entitlement. In those cases, a Nazi did indeed pay fair market value for a work of art. The army found the work after the war, yet did not return the work to the Nazi or his family, because the Nazi had been convicted as a war criminal, and his assets had been seized as retribution."

"Where would the art go then?"

"Victims' groups."

She raised her eyebrows to make sure I was following. I nodded.

"To muddle things even more, there are other cases where ownership records have been lost over the passage of more than half a century."

"Making it impossible to determine who truly is the rightful owner?"

"Yes."

"So many complications," I said.

"Now let me tell you about the Brueghels. They were a distinguished Flemish family of artists. One in particular, Jan the Elder, was known for his floral still lifes. He was nicknamed 'Velvet' for the velveteen sheen of his colors, or perhaps for his fondness for wearing velvet. In the late 1500s, Velvet Brueghel did a series of four paintings, one each of a daffodil, a daisy, a chrysanthemum, and a rose. They changed hands, legally, many times over the years."

"The four together?"

"Only at first. The set of four was broken up in the 1700s. Over the next two hundred years, each flower was separately sold—"

"Or confiscated, or sold under dubious circumstances, in the years leading up to World War II?"

"Exactly. Three of the flowers were part of the Nazi trove discovered by the army."

"Three of the four? That's a high percentage to have gotten into Nazi hands."

"They had an objective, but don't get ahead of me. The Daffodil, the Chrysanthemum, and the Rose were the ones recovered, and they were subsequently sold in the late 1940s, each to a different buyer. The proceeds were given to several authorized victims' groups."

"And the Daisy?"

"It was never recovered by the army."

"It's valuable?"

"In and of itself? Of course, as much as any of the other three, simply because it's a Brueghel. But let me add one more piece to the puzzle. The descendents of a Nazi captain successfully sued in Germany for the return of a collection of paintings he purchased."

"But he was a Nazi. Wouldn't his paintings have been subjected to claims from victims, just like all the others?"

"He'd been rumored to have helped outfit the death camps, but so far, that's never been proven. What's known for sure is he was only a captain, and he didn't acquire the paintings for the Reich. He bought them for himself, always paying with his own personal funds, always making sure he got a receipt. That's why his heirs won their lawsuit."

"You think he used his Nazi credentials to scare owners into selling cheap?"

"I have no doubt, but that can't be proven."

I was getting confused. "Included in his collection were the Four Flowers?"

"No. Remember I told you three had been recovered by the army, sold after the war, and their proceeds distributed to victims' groups?"

I nodded.

"Our Nazi bought only the long-missing Daisy, from a reputable dealer who had it on consignment from a man without heirs, who perished at Dachau. The dealer himself is long dead, and his records are lost."

I turned to look for a moment at the painting on the card table behind us. "Who has the Daisy now?"

"Where's Leo?" she asked.

Thirty-six

I hesitated too long before I lied.

"On vacation," I said. The less she knew about what was going on, the safer she'd be.

"It must be one hell of a vacation; he's not even answering his cell phone," she said softly. She'd recognized the lie.

"Recently there's been a new twist in the saga of the Four Flowers," she went on. "There is a particularly nasty divorce playing out in Los Angeles. A movie producer and his wife are battling over who gets to keep Brueghel's painting of the Rose, among other things."

"One of the Four Flowers?"

"Yes, but more interesting, the movie producer and his wife jointly hold purchase options on two more: the Daffodil and the Chrysanthemum."

"Bringing them effective control of three of the Four Flowers?"

"Yes."

"Just like the Nazis?"

"Precisely, but remember: The objective back then was to unite all four in the *Führermuseum*."

"Our own nasty little Nazi knew about the Reich's objective?"

She nodded. "That's my supposition. He hustled in, bought up the fourth flower for himself, and looked to make a killing if he could find a way of selling it anonymously to his own people, once the war was over."

"If the fourth flower, the Daisy, can be located, it would dramatically increase the value of the other three?"

"Tenfold, if all four flowers can be reunited and sold as a complete set. That's why the divorce story hit the *National Enquirer* and *People* magazine a couple of months ago. Both ran a picture of the long-missing Daisy, since enormous money would be at stake if the fourth flower was ever found. So far, that notion has just been a fantasy; excellent magazine fodder, nothing more."

It hadn't been happenstance that had brought Snark Evans back from the dead. He'd come across a *People,* or a *National Enquirer,* he'd seen the picture of the Daisy, and he recognized the painting he swiped from Rudy Cassone and passed off to Leo on his way out of Rivertown. Millions would be his if he could get it back from Leo.

Those same news flashes out of Hollywood had roused Rudy Cassone to take another run at Tebbins. I'd found the triggering event.

"How was Leo when he called you? Did he mention the Daisy specifically?"

"He was trying to sound casual, but there was tension in his voice."

"You really think it's the Daisy under that?" I asked, pointing at the picture on the table.

"Leo would certainly know how to camouflage it."

"Paint over a masterpiece?"

"It used to be done all the time, back when masters reused canvases. Of course, they didn't know they were going to become masters. Otherwise, they would have splurged on new canvas. Besides, Leo's painting was done in acrylic. It's water soluble. It can be removed."

"How do we find out?"

"I assume you want to investigate this very quietly?"

I nodded.

"It's not like Leo to not have called himself." Her eyes were unblinking on mine. She wanted an explanation.

"I'm handling this for him."

She leaned across the table. "Where's Leo, Dek?"

I couldn't lie, nor could I tell her a truth that would put her in danger.

"Safe," I said.

We both looked at the fireplace. The fire had died.

She stood up. "I know someone who can X-ray what's beneath Leo's pink cows," she said, standing up, "but Leo already knows what's under there."

"I'll pass that along." I got up, too, and we walked downstairs.

"Tell him everything is in the envelope."

"You sent him an envelope?" I grabbed my coat and started walking her outside. I needed to see her safely to her car and headed for home.

"I dropped it off on my way here."

My throat dried in an instant. "Drive straight back to your building. Don't let anyone into your condo."

"What's wrong with you?"

"Tell your building's security people you need a special watch on your place for the next few days."

"Damn it, Dek. What are you doing?"

I opened her car door. "Straight home, no stops."

I followed her out to Thompson Avenue. Only when she turned east toward Chicago did I cut through the side streets to Leo's house.

The envelope Amanda had left for him was still there. I jammed it in my pocket.

My call to Amanda's cell phone got sent to voice message. She set it that way, when she was driving.

"False alarm," I said. "Sorry for my irrational behavior tonight."

It felt odd, as it had for some time, to hang up without telling her I loved her.

Thirty-seven

Once before, I'd expected someone to come for me in the night.

It had been cold then, like now, and the ground had been covered with snow then, like now. Back then, my genius had told me to string sensor lights around the first and second floors. Someone might break through the timbered door, but that would trigger the big lights, and that would send him away. If it didn't, my genius added, I'd deal with him with impunity. Snugged up on the top floor, with the trapdoor bolted and the ladder pulled up behind me, all I had to do was watch the snow below. When light shot bright out of the slit windows, I'd know to call the cops, then wait, safe at the impregnable top of the turret.

I figured wrong, several ways. First, I forgot to bring up the phone. Then, when my visitor did arrive, he brought a helper. Neither of them was afraid of strong light, and they proceeded up through the second, third, and fourth floors like they were being welcomed at an overlit party. Finally, when they ran out of stairs and saw there was no ladder to get up to the top floor—because I'd so cleverly pulled it up behind me—they found a way to make me come to them. It was a mess. Only through blind luck did my genius, such as it was, survive to think again.

This time, I didn't have to risk an occasionally misfiring brain.

I had Leo's gun. There'd be no need to scuttle up to the top floor and hunker down with a cell phone. My timbered door was thick, perhaps the strongest in town except for the mayor's. At the first sound of someone trying to break in, I'd simply call the cops and wait, prone on the second floor, with the long barrel of Leo's gun aimed downward, straight at the doorway. Even if the cops took their usual leisurely time to amble over, and my intruder did get through the door, I had the gun. It was like a cheesy camera, Leo once told me. There was no safety to unclick, nothing to cock: Just point and pull the trigger, was all there was to it.

So I waited, stretched out on the floor above the door, gun at the ready.

Caffeine and adrenaline and the sounds of the night along Thompson Avenue kept me jittered and alert until well past four in the morning. When the tonks began to close and the last revelers shuffled away, bent double by bad booze or unrequited lust, the wind took up its cue and started to howl along the Willahock, sweeping up bits of bramble and branches to slam against the turret's slit windows. The noise of the night kept me ready, waiting for a killer.

He never came.

Then it was eight o'clock and it would be safe to sleep, at least for a time. He wouldn't try to break in with cars passing right by the turret on their way to city hall. I climbed up to the third floor and was asleep in an instant.

Someone at the door woke me too few hours later. Sunshine streamed in through the slit windows, making long, narrow ribbons of bright light on the wide-planked wood floor. It was late morning.

I hustled down the stairs and kept the gun in my hand out of sight, up against the inside wall as I opened the door.

A short, gray-haired man in a dark green trench coat stood outside. He flashed a Chicago cop's badge. "My name's Jarobi. Mind if I come in?"

He wasn't holding a gun, but he looked as though he could, in a hurry. I nodded.

"Mind putting that away, son?" he asked, giving the gun in my hand a slight nod as he gently pushed past me.

He headed toward the table saw, the centerpiece of my conversational furniture grouping. Sitting on one of the white plastic chairs, he made a show of eyeballing the saw, and the nothing that was in the rest of the room. "Lived here long?" He was sizing me up for a flake suit.

I took the other chair. "I'm fixing it up to sell."

"A table saw does a lot to liven up a room."

"What have I done to interest the Chicago police?"

"Nothing, officially. Wendell Phelps is a friend of my chief's. Mr. Phelps asked for an informal review of those people closest to his family, prior to a federal audit he's about to undergo. I imagine it has to do with Mr. Phelps's foreign interests."

"I fit in because I used to be married to his daughter?"

"I'm hoping you'll answer a few questions." He took out a little notebook, flipped it open, and asked me questions he could have gotten answered off the Internet. Mostly, he kept his eyes on my face.

"You don't look stupid, Captain," I said, when he closed his little notebook.

His face didn't change. "Why, thank you."

"Why are you here?"

"I told you, Mr. Wendell—"

I stood up. To his credit, he stood up, too. I walked him to the door.

I wondered if he was even a cop. Perfect badge copies could be bought in Chicago, in the wrong neighborhoods for the right price. I looked at the revolver I'd left lying on the table saw.

He'd followed my eyes and pulled out a business card. "Call my district, describe me. Hell, you can ask them to e-mail my picture."

He opened the door but paused before going out. "I did have someone fill me in. You've got an interesting history."

"Interesting enough to warrant a look-see, in person?"

"I've written my cell phone number on the back," he said, handing me the card. "Call me anytime."

"About what?" I asked.

"About anything."

"You have no jurisdiction." The words came out too stupid, and too fast.

"Over what?"

"Over anything in Rivertown," I said.

He shook his head with affected sadness. "Men like your ex-father-in-law have jurisdiction everywhere. Best you realize that."

Thirty-eight

I watched Jarobi drive away, but not so a man in a black Chevy Impala. He was parked across the spit of land on Thompson Avenue. He might have been a guy taking a break in his car, or an innocent, of sorts, readying to murmur desire to one of Rivertown's noontime belles. He might have been Wozanga's successor, sent by Cassone to find the right time to storm into the turret, or he might even have been Cassone himself. The car windows were tinted just enough to obscure the driver.

I wondered if there was another possibility. The man could have been a Chicago cop, left behind by Jarobi to keep an eye on me. The captain's story about a security audit was a fairy tale. I'd been out of Wendell's life too long, and the cop had asked too few good questions. What I couldn't imagine was why I'd matter to a cop.

I called Amanda's office. Her direct line sent me to voice mail. I tried her assistant, Vicki, and got voice mail there, too. Finally, I called Amanda's cell phone. I clicked off when her recorded voice asked me to leave a message. Amanda's life had gotten busy since she'd gone to work for her father.

I switched on my computer. I'd received three new e-mails. The first was from a pharmaceutical organization, offering me enhancement pills that would make me a bigger man than I'd ever been known to be. The second was from a Nigerian prince, offering the opportunity to become a wealthier man than I'd ever been known to be. The third was from Jenny, saying Rudy Cassone had never filed a police report for burglary.

I went to Google. The Hollywood couple battling for control of the three extant flower paintings was named Bennett. The producer was Henny; she was Mindy. She was a foot taller, but he was the titan. He'd produced a couple of thrillers I'd watched on late-night television, after I'd gotten tired of infomercials about effortless miracle polishes, sticky things that attracted lint, and Lester Lance Leamington, before he'd gone big-time. I remembered Henny Bennett's films as being cheesy, though I supposed it was unfair to judge the quality of anything viewed on a four-inch screen, where film artistry rarely registers without magnification.

Both Bennetts were very tan and had extremely white teeth. Her lips were plumper than most, as though she'd been exercising them by sucking on eels. Her chest was plumper than most, too, but I didn't think that had anything to do with eels.

They looked happy in their online photos. That could have been because, allegedly, they'd each been getting damp with others. The bottom line, though, was the bottom line: She wanted half of what he had. He wanted to give her two hundred thousand a month, flat. She said she couldn't live on that. He said she'd have to learn. Lawyers and accountants were called in. All agreed, billably, that there was much to discuss.

Two of the online sites mentioned that the couple's Velvet Brueghel Rose, when combined with the purchase options they jointly controlled on the other two Flowers known to exist, constituted a princely asset. The lawyers and the accountants disagreed, also billably, about which Bennett should retain control of the painting and the options.

Only one account mentioned, and then only in passing, that the combined value of the three Flowers would multiply exponentially if ever the long-lost Daisy was combined with the others into one collection. Nothing in the account pointed to such a likelihood.

I called Robinson at city hall. "That floater they pulled out of the Willahock?"

"Bad business," he said. His voice was shaky. "He'd been in the water for some time."

"There's been no mention of it on the radio or in the papers. Any ID?"

"His teeth were hammered out. Why are you asking?" His own teeth had started chattering.

"Curiosity. Are you all right, Mr. Robinson?"

"The floater's a . . . he's a John Doe."

"Are you all right, Mr. Robinson?"

"No, damn it," he said, his voice rising. "Someone is following me."

"Why?"

"I have no idea. I'm just a building inspector. All I can think is it might have something to do with Tebbins. He got into something here, then he got murdered, or . . ."

"Or what?"

"Or it has something to do with you and your questions, supposedly on behalf of Leo Brumsky."

My cell phone beeped. A call was waiting. I pulled the phone from my ear to check the screen, hoping it was Amanda, but it was an unfamiliar number.

"You're sure you're being followed?"

"Too much is happening in Rivertown." He clicked me away.

I thumbed on the new call. "Elstrom?" the new voice whispered, perhaps through a cloth.

"I've been expecting you." Indeed I had, the whole of the previous night.

"We'll meet. Public place."

It was a surprise; he was being too refined. I told him six thirty, before things in Rivertown got too rowdy, and named a bar.

Thirty-nine

The bar I'd named was on Thompson Avenue.

It had small tables jammed in the front window, a rarity in a town where people didn't much like to be seen, and had a good view of the turret. From one of those tables I'd see my sensor lights go on if someone smashed down my front door while Cassone had me otherwise engaged.

It made me feel clever until I realized I was not about to go speeding home to confront an intruder, even with Leo's revolver tucked in my peacoat.

Rudy Cassone came into the bar dressed immaculately, in a dark gray topcoat, navy business suit, white shirt, and muted blue tie. He sat across the table, three feet from my nose. A waitress came over, a big blowsy blond in her early sixties. I'd heard she used to work Chicago's Viagra Triangle off Rush Street when she was young. When she got older, she came west, to the curbs along Thompson Avenue. When the glare of the headlights became too unflattering, she moved to the alley behind the bowling alley. Now she served beer in small glasses. A lot of careers in Rivertown followed that trajectory. We ordered beer.

"Cop company?" Cassone asked, cocking his head toward the

street. One of his elbows was moving. He was feeling under the table for a microphone.

"I hadn't noticed."

"A man in a car seems to be very interested in you sitting here."

"Black car, Impala?" I hadn't noticed it, coming in.

He shook his head. "Crown Victoria. Chicken shit, if you're attracting cops and you lead them into this. Chicken shit, like a baseball bat." His eyes were steady on mine but, strangely, not angry. There was too much money at stake to give in to rage, at least for the time being.

I looked out the window. "I've got nobody watching us."

The waitress came with our beer. He held up his glass to the little light that came from the bar. A smear of lipstick was on the glass. He set it down, apparently concerned about where that lipstick had been previously.

"You took something of mine," he said. "I want it back."

"You were stealing it from somebody's house."

He turned his beer glass so that the lipstick stain faced me. It was only the lower lip, but it looked angry.

"I got robbed, years ago. Brumsky knows it; you know it."

"You never filed a police report."

"Why are you talking so stupid?"

"How about your insurance company? Did you file a claim?"

He raised his wrist and slid back a French cuff to check the gold Rolex. "We're wasting time."

He stood up, turning suddenly to look at the people standing clustered at the bar. A man in shadow, at the far end, abruptly turned away.

"Ten o'clock tomorrow morning, you will come to 15 Falling Star, where I live. I will tell the guard that you're expected, as I do when any friend comes to visit. You will bring a picture, a gift from you to me."

He went out the door, leaving me alone with the two untouched glasses of beer.

I got up, too, and put a ten between the two untouched glasses.

"Something wrong with the beer, honey?" The blowsy blond had come up, anxious to clear the table.

I felt a chill on the back of my neck. Someone else had gone out.

"Everything's fine, for you and for me," I said, and it was. Cassone hadn't tried to kill me, and the blond would be able to re-serve the beer.

Outside, I looked up and down the street. Every parking place was taken, even in the loading zones where the short-skirted women liked to lean into stopped cars. I didn't see a black Impala or a Crown Victoria. No one else seemed interested in me.

I called Jarobi. He picked up before the second ring. "Have you got people following me?" I asked.

"You mean at the request of your father-in-law?"

"Ex-father-in-law."

"Why do you ask?"

"Black Impala or a Crown Victoria?"

He made a laugh, but he didn't sound amused. "Such obvious cop cars? We're more cunning than that."

"Would you tell me if you did?"

"No."

"Why is Wendell Phelps interested in me?"

"I told you—"

"I know what you told me. I pose no threat to Wendell. I pose no threat to his daughter, as she'll tell you. So what's the interest?"

"Maybe it's time for you to tell me about your jitters, Elstrom. Why so nervous? You're in a bar, and all of a sudden you're seeing spooks, shadows in the night? Maybe it's your own shadow you're seeing . . . and that's becoming interesting."

"Jarobi?"

"Yes?"

"How do you know I was in a bar?"

He said nothing.

"Call them off anyway."

"What do you mean 'them'?"

"At least one outside, and the one at the bar."

"I told you: I had no—" I clicked him off. It was early enough, and I had things I needed to do.

I drove north, to a strip mall. I'd bought my box of Cheerios there, back when Amanda and I were still married. Tonight, it wasn't the supermarket I was headed for. I went into the giant craft store next door. I'd never before thought to enter such a place, because I'd never had the urge to get crafty with glitter and glue, or clay, or tubes of colors and brushes. That night, though, they had what I needed, and all for less than a hundred dollars. I had them partially disassemble the largest piece, so its shape would not be apparent when I strolled artily out, in case one of Jarobi's men had followed me. I ducked into the supermarket next, to make it look like a normal shopping trip, bought a small jar of olives and a large box of cupcakes, and drove back to the turret.

I had three of the olives and three of the cupcakes for dinner and went across the hall. I propped Leo's painting up at the back of the card table and put together the wood stretchers I'd had the craft store people disassemble. I now had a canvas the same size as Leo's.

I glued another piece of canvas to the back, careful to leave a slightly opened seam like Leo's original. I laid out all the tubes of acrylic colors and unscrewed their little caps.

Beyond primitive, Amanda had called Leo's repainting of the supposed Velvet Brueghel. I wished he were there at that moment, so I could laugh at him, but things had gone to hell. He was in an institution, fumbling to unscramble his brain.

I painted a new lavender barn and pink, green-spotted cows. I dabbed red leaves all over spindly black trunks and limbs, and I made orange rolling hills. I tried to work fast, but I had to work carefully, measuring everything on Leo's original before doing my own. There was no way of knowing how closely Cassone had looked at Leo's painting.

The person at the craft store said the acrylics would dry quickly. To make sure, I aimed a box fan at the painting before I went up to bed.

Though I was dead tired, sleep wouldn't come. I kept imagining a black Impala and a colorless Crown Victoria parked along Thompson Avenue. If they hadn't belonged to Cassone or Jarobi, one or both might have been a rental, picked up at Midway or O'Hare by someone fresh off a plane from L.A.

Forty

I sat for a time the next morning looking at the painting I'd faked the night before. What had seemed like a smart idea, copying Leo's farm scene, now seemed destined only to bring more trouble. Even if Cassone didn't recognize the poor copy right off, he would as soon as he sponged away the water-soluble acrylics and saw there was nothing underneath. Yet any decision to turn over something worth tens of millions wasn't mine; it was Leo's, and he wasn't communicating except with crayons.

At nine thirty, I threw the fake in the back of the Jeep and drove west to Falling Star, feeling not at all optimistic about anything.

A man in a private security uniform, looking as worried as me, stepped out of the guard shack when I pulled up to the gate.

"Dek Elstrom to see Mr. Cassone," I said.

His face got even more pinched. He stepped back and tugged the door tightly shut, as though I had anthrax on my nose and was about to sneeze. He picked up a phone and spoke for only a second or two. Then, most oddly of all, instead of opening the door to tell me how to proceed, he mimed the number fifteen with his right hand behind the glass—one finger, then five fingers—and pushed a button to raise the gate.

I've long enjoyed the belief that possessing big money offers the option of indulging behavioral aberrations that ordinary incomes keep in check. Furthermore, I fear such nuttiness can easily spread to the paid help. The guard's behavior seemed to go well beyond that. Finger miming was not something any class of grown-ups did. I let the thought recede as I motored in.

Tall arborvitae concealed a set-back eight-foot chain-link fence topped with barbed wire. Inside, big-buck brick houses with shake or slate roofs and perfectly manicured evergreens were laid out along gently curving streets. Driveways were filled with Cadillacs and Lexi, Beemers and Benzes, and absolutely no trace of the people who lived behind all the bricks.

Number fifteen was a splendid, rambling multilevel with small windows and a big, four-car attached garage. Framing the front doorway, though, were two huge cement pots filled with cheap plastic daisies. It might have been a whimsical touch: Daisies, like the one he'd lost in a theft. That morning, the whimsy was spoiled by the two sheriff's cruisers parked on the street.

A deputy waited by the curb. He used the barrel of his automatic to motion me to pull over. It was more compelling than using his hand.

He was alongside the driver's side window in an instant. "Hands on the steering wheel," he shouted, then, "Now, slide out real slow."

I slid out real slow.

He told me to put my hands behind me and snapped handcuffs around my wrists.

"Got time for a quick question?" I asked.

"You're a person of interest," he said.

"I've always thought so, but in what regard this time?"

"In whatever my superiors are interested in, smart-ass. My job is to encourage you to not run off."

"Your superiors will be pleased. I feel encouraged. I need to make a call."

"In due time."

"Where's Cassone?"

"Unavailable."

"Inside?"

"Unavailable."

"I'll sit in the car. It's cold."

"You'll stand outside, freezing your ass off, same as me."

So it went for more minutes than were necessary, until a captain came out of the house and walked up to the officer watching me.

"Aren't you cold?" he asked the cop.

"No, sir."

"I am," I offered.

The captain didn't even look at me.

"I need to make a call," I said. The Bohemian was the only one who could quickly get a lawyer in between the cops and me.

"In due time," the captain said.

So it went. I spent another hour stomping my feet to keep warm, yelling my fool head off about making a call.

"No chance," the freezing cop kept saying.

"I'm entitled to a phone call."

"After you're questioned."

"What's happened to Cassone?"

"Later."

"At least let me get back inside my car and run the heater."

"It's a Jeep," he said finally.

I must have looked confused.

"Not a car," he added.

"It's certainly not a truck," I said, ripening for any warming confrontation.

"It's not a truck," he said.

By then, I'd deciphered the rhythm of his logic. "Because it's a Jeep?"

He nodded.

"You're crazy. You know that?"

He shrugged, accepting. I gave him credit for not succumbing to self-doubt.

Twenty minutes later, incredibly, Jarobi showed up.

He barely acknowledged me as he went in the house. Fifteen

minutes later, he came out with the captain, who ordered the deputy to remove my handcuffs.

Jarobi motioned for me to get in the Jeep. "If you don't stay right behind me, I'll have squad cars surround you in less than five minutes."

"What's going on?"

"We'll stop, have coffee."

"What's going on?"

"Coffee," he said.

Forty-one

Jarobi led me to a Denny's just north of Rivertown. After he parked, he came up to peer between the strips of silver tape keeping my back window together.

"I noticed this painting, back at Cassone's," he said.

"What's going on, Jarobi?"

"Is it Leo Brumsky's painting?"

I looked at him, a cop in a green coat, short and gray and too wise to what was going on in my life. "Why is Cassone's house crawling with sheriff's deputies?"

"How about I lock it up while we eat?" He fingered a loose curl of tape. One soft tug and he'd have the painting in his hands anyway.

I nodded; anything to speed him up. I got it out, he aimed a remote to pop his trunk and locked it up, and we went into the restaurant.

The hostess asked where we wanted to sit. I said any damned place. She gave me a harsh look and led us to a booth by the window.

"What's going on, Jarobi?" I asked again.

"Amanda," he said.

The waitress came over with a Thermos pitcher.

"Leave the coffee," I said to her, keeping my eyes on Jarobi.

She banged down the Thermos.

"We'll eat," Jarobi said.

"Cheerios, then, small bowl, skim milk," I said.

Jarobi took too long to tell her that no, we'd have pancakes, scrambled eggs, bacon and sausage, and thick Greek toast.

"You must keep your strength," he said, after she huffed away.

The blades were out now, fencing inside my gut. "What about Amanda?"

"And calm," he added. "You must be calm."

He looked around. Midway between the breakfast and lunch rushes, the restaurant was practically deserted.

"She's been kidnapped," he said.

I pushed up out of the booth fast, going nowhere but needing to tower over him.

"Sit down, or you'll hear nothing." He lifted his coffee cup like he had hours to kill before catching a bus.

I dropped back down. "Everything. Now."

"Near as we can figure, she was grabbed just a few minutes after she left your place. Someone bumped her car, left a scrape. Most likely, he got out, waving what she must have thought was insurance information. It's an old carjacking trick."

I wanted to smash his face. "You came to me yesterday morning, just hours after she was abducted, and said nothing?"

"Mr. Phelps is running the show. You're broke; you live in a turret. He thinks you're involved. I came to check you out."

"She's my wife—" I stopped myself. "My ex-wife, but we're on good terms. She's safe? The kidnapper's called? Why the hell are we just sitting here?"

"I just got the painting, Elstrom. Now we're going to think."

I must have slumped back in the booth. For sure, I remember going blank for a moment, unable to think. He was talking gibberish.

"The painting?" I asked, finally. "Amanda wasn't grabbed for her father's money?"

"Money? Sure, two million, but the bastard's endgame is a painting." He cocked a thumb toward the parking lot. "He didn't specify, but it's that painting? That purple barn? Those pink cows? Really?"

"Camouflage. Why are we here if the cops are at Cassone's? He's your man."

"Because we're going to think. Go slow. Don't talk in riddles."

"Cassone's your man."

"It's a voice on the phone that wants two million in cash and that Brumsky painting. For now, we consider everything."

"You're sure Amanda's not at Cassone's?"

He nodded. "We don't know where she is, which is why we're going to think. Tell me about the picture, from the beginning."

The waitress came with our plates. She set Jarobi's down carefully. Mine, she dropped from an inch up. Jarobi dug right in.

When she left, I said, "A punk named Snark Evans stole the painting from Cassone years ago. Evans gave it to Leo Brumsky. Not knowing it was stolen, Leo kept it down in his basement ever since. Leo's away. I've been watching his house. I stuck signs in the lawn, advertising residential security systems, to see who got nervous. Cassone came around, sniffing. I played along, gave him a tour, telling him about a system I was supposedly installing. He left, but not for long. Middle of the night, day before yesterday, I drove past Leo's house and saw someone prowling inside. I waited by the back door. A burglar came out carrying something. I clubbed him and took what he had. It was that painting."

"It was Cassone you clubbed?"

"Yes."

"With what?"

"What does it matter?"

"With what?"

"A baseball bat."

"Go on."

"We're wasting time, Jarobi."

"Just go on."

"I called Amanda because she knows art."

"And because you knew she'd come to your place without question."

"Yeah, and then I followed her to abduct her on the street, instead of just holding her at my place. Man, if I had that kind of genius I could be a cop."

"Continue."

"Later on, that evening, Amanda came over to my place. She'd already been working with Leo, researching the painting. She studied it, told me it was valuable, and left around ten. And none of this makes any sense."

"Why?" He'd paused with a forkful of sausage halfway to his mouth.

"Because your people saw Cassone and me last night, talking calmly, having a beer. Cassone wanted his painting back and told me to deliver it this morning. No muscle, and no gun, and sure as hell no mention he was holding Amanda hostage."

"Maybe you made it so easy he didn't need any of that. Why cave so quickly? You clubbed Cassone to take the painting away, then overnight became willing to give it up? All before you knew Ms. Phelps was kidnapped?"

He'd cleaned his plate. He pushed it away. "Boy, if I had that kind of genius, I could live in a stone . . . whatever it is."

"I had second thoughts. I realized I was in over my head with a guy like Cassone. I wanted to be rid of the painting and rid of him." It was a lame lie, the best I could think up without telling him about Leo or that I wasn't yet ready to trust an arrogant peacock like Wendell Phelps to engineer the safe return of his daughter. For now, Jarobi could think the painting in his trunk was the real thing.

"You're lying, Elstrom, about a lot of things."

"Go back to Falling Star, help the sheriff sweat Cassone, and keep your eyes open for somebody else. You know Cassone doesn't need two million. He only wants the painting." I made to get up. "Let's go back to Falling Star."

"Cassone's dead."

I searched his face for any hint that he was toying with me. "That can't be," I finally managed.

"He was found early this morning lying behind a used car lot halfway between Rivertown and Falling Star. He was shot four times and then beaten so brutally his face was hamburger, super rare. Both his shoulders were smashed and his kneecaps pulverized."

"He was beaten postmortem?"

"I surely hope so. The sheriff's deputies are scratching for a motive. That's why they're going through his house. They don't know about Amanda or the fancy painting. Or, for that matter, the baseball bat you used on Cassone to get the painting back. If they did, they'd be real interested in you, Elstrom, because someone needed real rage to beat Cassone so badly after he was already dead."

"You know damned well I didn't kill Cassone."

"I know because I had two men watching you last night."

"Black Impala?"

"You asked that when you called from outside the bar. The answer's still no. I had one man in a white Crown Victoria, the other in a yellow Ford Explorer. The Crown Victoria followed you shopping after you left the tavern. The Explorer slipped your lock and had a look around inside your stone tube. Neither was in the bar with you and Cassone. Help Amanda, Elstrom. What don't I know?"

"Cassone noticed someone watching us."

"You told me that last night, and I just told you the Crown Victoria was mine."

"Someone else, inside the bar."

"Wasn't one of mine. Did you see his face?"

"No. I just felt a draft on the back of my neck as he left."

"Who else wants the painting?"

"Snark Evans, because he was the one who stole it in the first place. A divorcing couple out in Hollywood. Underneath the cows is a picture of a flower, one in a set of four. The couple owns or has options on the other three. The value of their pictures and options would go up immensely if they recovered the long-lost fourth in the series."

"We're done for now," he said, sliding out of the booth. "Mr. Phelps has got the two million ready, and now I have the painting. All we can do is wait, and be careful how we make the exchange."

"Wendell's the wrong man to be running this. He's too cocksure, convinced of his own wisdom."

"It's out of my hands."

"You can treat this as a kidnapping, have your people question anyone who might have been in the bar or on the sidewalk last night. Maybe someone saw somebody following Cassone."

"Like you pointed out when I came to your castle, I have no jurisdiction."

"Let me in on this, Jarobi."

He shook his head.

"I'll report her missing in Rivertown."

"On what grounds? That she left your place and hasn't been seen since?"

"Sure."

"They'll call Mr. Phelps. He'll say everything is fine. He wants this hushed, so he can control it himself."

Outside, I went to the trunk of his car, but it was for show.

"Not a chance," he said.

Forty-two

I drove back to the turret because I had nowhere else to drive.

Robinson was across the frozen lawn, standing with another man in the city hall parking lot. I walked over, because going inside the turret at that moment would make me feel caged, like an animal.

Robinson was trying to ease a jimmy bar down the passenger's door of a silver Escalade. His hands were shaking too badly to work the bar. He handed it to the other man.

"You wouldn't believe how many people used to drop their cars off at the garage and leave the keys locked inside," Robinson said.

"Maybe your hands are too cold," I said.

The other man jiggled the bar, drew it up along the glass, and popped the lock.

Robinson motioned for me to walk with him down to the Willahock. "You've got to help me," he said.

"You're sure you're being followed?" I had no room for his problem, but I asked anyway.

"He switches between a light-colored sedan and a small SUV, blue I think."

"Is it the same man?"

"He's always too far away to tell. He's not always there, but it's when I'm headed to work, or driving to lunch or driving home."

"A light-colored sedan or a small blue SUV? How about a black car, an Impala, maybe?"

"No. Just the light-colored car or the blue SUV."

"Do you have any idea why someone would be following you?"

He stopped and spun to face me. "No, but like I said before, I think you brought him to me. You came around saying Leo Brumsky wanted to know about Snark Evans. I told you Snarky was small time, a punk who lifted trinkets, and that he was dead. Next thing, Tebbins is dead, shot in his house, and you're back, asking about the floater that got stuck downriver. Now I just heard Rudy Cassone was beaten to death. I looked Leo up in the phone book, and still nobody's answering. Maybe he's dead, too. Three deaths, maybe four, all of them linked to that damned fool Snarky—and I'm linked to him, too, because I was there with the rest of them. You still think all this has to do with something Snarky stole off Cassone?"

"I don't know," I said, meaning I didn't know how much I should tell him.

"Listen, you got to find some way to stop this." He shook his head, hard. "No way; no way I knew about Snarky stealing off Cassone."

"You haven't heard who the floater is, Mr. Robinson?"

"You mean is it Snarky, if he didn't really die that summer? Hell, maybe it's Leo, since everybody that's dying around here goes back to that garage, that summer."

"It's not Leo."

A faint sweat had built on Robinson's forehead, despite the cold. "Look, Tebbins and Snarky I can understand getting killed, if they stole something expensive from Cassone, but that makes Cassone the killer, doesn't it? Yet now he's dead, too. There's nobody else, Elstrom, not now."

He was right. There was no reason to tail him. An exchange was already in progress: Amanda for the painting and a couple of million bucks.

Unless there was someone else after the painting, someone who didn't know a ransom demand had been made. Someone, nonetheless, who might be connected to the person who'd made the ransom demand.

Someone who might be the actual kidnapper.

"When's the last time you were tailed?" I asked.

"This morning, driving to work."

"What time do you quit?"

"Four thirty, but I've got to do a damned forms inspection before that. I'll be leaving around three."

I took the river walk back to the turret. Inside, I rummaged through an old address book and found Wendell Phelps's phone number. I called his office.

His secretary said he was out.

"Out, like in temporarily out?"

"I'll have him call you," she said and hung up. She hadn't asked for a message, or my number.

I called Jarobi. "I'm having nasty thoughts."

"Such as?"

"I think there are two parties after that painting, and they might know each other."

"You mean like that man and woman divorcing, out in California?"

I told him about Robinson.

"How can Robinson being tailed relate to Ms. Phelps?" he asked.

"I don't know."

"Look, Elstrom, the divorcing Bennetts are a possibility, I'll give you that. Both might know Ms. Phelps has been kidnapped, even if only one's got her. We'll make sure Mr. Phelps deals with the one that's got Amanda."

"How will he know? What if somehow he's negotiating with the wrong one?"

"Call Mr. Phelps."

"I tried. He's out, and his secretary is not taking messages."

"I'm out, too, Elstrom. I'm not in the loop much."

I sat then, and drank coffee, and made sense of nothing. At two forty-five, I drove to Thompson Avenue and parked where I could see across the spit of land.

Right at three, Robinson's burgundy Escalade left city hall and drove up to Thompson Avenue. I tucked a few cars behind it and followed it to Leo's neighborhood.

Robinson had gotten out in front of the new excavation by the time I drove by. I parked a few cars up.

Robinson handed a man wearing a hard hat a white business-sized envelope. The man shook his head, angry. Robinson shrugged and began walking around the hole, taking his time to look down at the forms that had been set up for the foundation walls.

I called Wendell again. The same secretary answered. I said we probably got cut off a half hour before. She said we hadn't. I asked if she'd asked Wendell to call me. She hung up on me again.

I called back. "Tell him to make sure the person has the goods."

She hung up.

Robinson got back in his Escalade and drove away. It was rush hour by now, and Thompson Avenue was thick with traffic. I followed him east into Chicago. He went food shopping and headed home to a bungalow three blocks from Leo's. I watched his house until ten thirty, when the lights went out. No one had tailed him.

I called Jarobi. "Anything?"

"Wendell's beside himself. Nothing."

"You told him about Robinson seeing a shadow?"

"Yes, though that can't have anything to do with Mrs. Phelps. I also told him about the people in California. He got your message, by the way. He knows to be careful."

I drove to Leo's house. Only one lamp was on, and that was in the front room. I hoped that meant Ma and Endora were staying away.

Down the block, the excavation looked as it had, and maybe as it always would. The envelope Robinson had handed the contractor might delay things for forever. I thought about calling Jenny, but whatever she knew about that house didn't matter much to Amanda's kidnapping.

I pulled my peacoat tighter and pushed away the thought that Amanda was lying somewhere, cold like Wozanga.

Forty-three

I was down the block from Robinson's bungalow by five the next morning. His lights went on at six, and he left for city hall at seven. The streets were mostly empty, and I tailed him from far back. No one else did.

I turned around and went back to the turret. I called Jarobi before I went inside. "I don't like this one damned bit. The kidnapper should have called by now."

"I want to think he's just being careful."

"No one's tailing Robinson, or they backed off, if they saw me."

"Mr. Phelps will concentrate on the one who calls."

"Give me something to do."

"Back away. Mr. Phelps wants you clear away from all this. For now, we wait for a call from our man."

"Or our woman?"

"California's a long shot, Elstrom. Don't get your hopes up." He promised me he'd call with news and hung up.

I called the Bohemian. "What do you hear about my friend Mr. Smith?"

"He's not so agitated. He quit drawing pictures as soon as you left. Now he's eating and leafing through magazines."

"Still in no shape to leave?"

"Not even close, they tell me."

I called Endora next. "Leo's improving," I said.

"Then we're coming home."

"There've been two more murders, plus a corpse found bobbing in the Willahock. Amanda was helping me, trying to puzzle through what Leo might have gotten caught up in. She's been kidnapped."

"My God, Dek!"

"I've got to go away later," I said. "I can't worry about you returning to Rivertown while I'm gone."

"Leo's safe; you're sure?"

"Hidden away from the world."

"Call me soon?"

"As soon as I know something," I said, which didn't sound like anytime soon at all.

The burgundy Escalade passed beneath my windows an hour later. I grabbed my coats and ran to the Jeep.

Robinson drove to the same Denny's Jarobi and I had gone to, just the day before. He and another man went in. They sat at a booth by the window, as Jarobi and I had. I watched them eat what looked like omelets. When they came out, I followed them back to city hall. Cars and trucks got between us, but again I spotted no one following Robinson.

My landline rang as soon as I got back inside.

"Did you get hungry, watching us?" Robinson asked. He sounded calmer.

"How was breakfast?"

"Excellent, like every morning. I spotted you following me home last night as well. I appreciate the thought, but if I noticed you, chances are my secret friend did, too. He's probably backed off for a while."

"Maybe you should ask the police for help."

"Rivertown police? You're kidding, right?"

"I've got to go out of town for a little while. I think you'll be all right." I made sure he had my cell phone number and told him to call me if his tail reappeared.

• • •

Jarobi called as I was walking from the indoor garage.

"Anything?" I asked.

I lost his words in the chatter of a group of people walking behind me, happy folks on their way to happy times.

"Tell me, Jarobi: anything?"

"I said—" His words vaporized as the nattering group passed by.

"Any word?"

"What the hell are you doing at the airport, Elstrom?" he shouted.

"Chasing the only idea I've got," I said, riding the escalator up to the ticketing area.

"There's a man less than fifty feet behind you. See him waving?"

I turned. Down at the base of the elevator, a man waved.

"You're wasting manpower tailing me."

"It's the only idea I've got," he said, mimicking my words. "He wants to stick a gun in your ribs before you can buy a ticket. What shall I tell him?"

"Tell him security people will frown at his gun, but if he's got a cop ID, he can come along."

"Those divorcing people?"

"I can't just sit."

"Your L.A. lovebirds won't tell you anything. They've got the money to hire professionals."

"I'll agitate. I'll fuss, I'll fidget, I'll look like I know more than I do. Tell me what else I can do. Tell me why the kidnapper hasn't called. Tell me how Amanda's feeling, right now."

"Wait here, be bait. Maybe our kidnapper thinks you still have the picture."

"He knows better if he's already contacted Wendell. You can put a man on my turret, though, to see if anyone comes. Or you can pick my lock like the last time and wait inside."

"As I remember, it's too cold inside your place."

"I'm hoping I'll heat things up in L.A."

Forty-four

Right after I landed, I used a nicely anonymous prepaid cell phone to call each of the two divorce lawyers named in the *National Enquirer*. I gave each receptionist the same message: "This evening only, I'm in town to see if you're interested in a daisy."

Each receptionist asked me to hold. Neither lawyer surprised me by then picking up the phone himself. Each agreed to meet immediately, accompanied by his principal.

Neither had pretended even a moment's confusion, and I took that behavior as ambiguous news. Both knew the painting was about to become available; likely each had already been in contact with someone looking to sell a flower. It meant, too, that neither had sent one of his own to kidnap Amanda. Whoever had been hired to grab her was local to Chicago.

I called Jarobi to update him with the latest news. He didn't answer. I let myself dare to hope that perhaps the kidnapper was calling at that very moment, and that was why he couldn't answer his phone.

I also let myself dare to hope that the kidnapper knew Wendell Phelps had the resources to unleash every hound in hell if even one of the hairs on his daughter's head was harmed.

I rented the cheapest thing Hertz had, a tiny Korean car that looked to have been assembled from shrunken parts. It was twice as expensive and just as small as the last car I'd rented, a minuscule concoction from a place named Swifty's outside the airport in Minneapolis. The swiftest thing about that operation had been the speed with which they'd distanced themselves after I'd run their car into a truckload of pigs. Those seemed like golden days now. I'd only been hunting an heiress then, not someone who'd kidnapped a woman with whom I'd shared part of my life.

Hunger started abrading the nerves that were twisting in my stomach. I hadn't eaten since the handful of Cheerios I'd swallowed on the way to the airport. I pulled into a fast food place named In-N-Out, assuming that the name portended nothing of intestinal velocity but simply the speed of their service; my gut was already knotted enough. I ordered a burger and a chocolate shake. I tried to eat while I drove, but after two bites, it was no good. My nerves were more anxious than hungry.

Mindy Bennett's lawyer had offices in a low-rise stucco building three miles from the airport. It appeared to be a one-lawyer firm, but perhaps to compensate for that, it had very large furniture in its waiting room. A tidy little man sat in one of the huge chairs.

I was not asked to sit. The receptionist immediately ushered me into a large inner office. I supposed her speed could have been due to the In-N-Out onions that were most certainly in their Out mode by then, no matter the mints I'd stuffed in my mouth. More likely, her boss was anxious to buy a painting.

The soon-to-be ex–Mrs. Bennett wore a tight red dress, a blond wig that was slightly askew on her forehead, and too much real tan that had cut deep lines around her eyes and mouth. She was out of breath. She must have rushed to her lawyer's office from getting tanned somewhere.

Her lawyer, a fellow named Smilt, wore an open-collared striped shirt, a gold neck chain, and carefully sprayed-up hair that reminded me of the little hair wall that Rivertown's own Elvis Derbil, late of the Building and Zoning Department, had constructed to hide the bald patch at the back of his head.

"You've brought the painting?" he asked, as I sat down.

"Not exactly," I said. I looked over at Mrs. Bennett. She was examining her fingernails.

Her lawyer cleared his throat loudly. "As I told your partner, I'll be doing the negotiating, on behalf of Mrs. Bennett."

I turned back around. "I understand you had a satisfying conversation." It seemed like a safe thing to say.

Before he could answer, my prepaid cell phone rang. It was Mr. Bennett's lawyer, and he was nervous. "You're on your way?"

"I'm with Mrs. Bennett now," I said affably and clicked him away.

I smiled at the sprayed-up Smilt. "I'm seeing Mr. Bennett's lawyer next, of course."

His skin had gone pale beneath the tan. "I told your partner that there's no need. We're ready to close the deal now, in cash."

I snuck a glance behind me. Mrs. Bennett still hadn't looked up from her fingernails. I understood, then. The lawyer was running the deal, fronting for the sorts of investors who could deal in cash. Mindy Bennett was only along for the ride, and a commission for the use of her claim on Henny Bennett's assets.

"You'll want to inspect the painting," I said.

"The appraiser is outside," he said, meaning the little man in the big chair I'd seen on the way in. "As soon as we examine the painting, we can agree on a final amount."

"Soon," I said.

"Soon?" The sprayed-up lawyer leaned across his desk. "Let's stop this shit, shall we? As you well know, we've received calls from two individuals other than you. One said he owned the painting, that it had been stolen, and that it cannot be sold without his approval. He is not our concern. Your partner is. He called not two hours ago, stating that he is ready to complete the transaction and would get back to us. Now you're here, so very promptly. We have the cash ready. I rushed an authenticator over. Yet you've not brought the painting to be authenticated? What's going on?"

"One must be careful." I stood up. The lawyer's eyes had narrowed almost to closing. He was on the verge of realizing I'd come into his office breathing not just onions but lies.

On the sofa, Mrs. Bennett was still inspecting her nails.

I turned for the door.

"When will you contact me?" the lawyer asked.

"Soon," I said and beat it out to the car.

Someone had called, saying he was ready to complete the deal. I called Jarobi and again got routed to voice mail. "I assume you have news," I said. "Call me."

I hoped it meant the exchange was taking place, right about then. I decided to continue on anyway.

Henny Bennett's lawyer, one Mickey Gare, had offices in a considerably taller and flashier building on Wilshire Boulevard. The reception area opened to a hall with many doors, a lot of chrome and leather guest furniture, and two beautiful women. One was a stylish blond receptionist, no more than thirty, concentrating on a computer screen. The other was younger, no more than twenty-five. She, too, was blond and concentrating, on a magazine that looked to contain small pictures of big movie stars.

The blond receptionist looked up. She escorted me into a private office, where the man behind the desk stood to introduce himself. "Mickey Gare," he said, "and you are . . . ?"

"Not Mickey Gare."

The lawyer winced. The man sitting on one of the guest chairs did not. Nor did he get up. I recognized him from his Internet photos. Henny Bennett wore a suit and an open-collared shirt like his lawyer, though his was unbuttoned halfway past his heavily tanned abs.

We sat down. "I'm here to make sure your interest in the Daisy is substantial," I said.

The man on the chair nodded. The lawyer did not.

"What?" Gare had a faint smudge of white powder under his nose that reminded me of the ever-present sugar residue on Benny Fittle, Rivertown's traffic enforcement person.

"On whose behalf are you here?" Henny Bennett asked.

"Meaning do I represent the seller or the man who is attempting to block the sale?"

"That would be it exactly," Bennett said.

"I represent the person who has the painting," I said. "I believe you spoke to him just a couple of hours ago?"

"I told him we'll take our chances with a disputed title, if that's what you mean," Mickey Gare said.

"You have cash?"

"You've brought the painting?" Bennett asked.

"What?" Mickey Gare asked.

"All seems satisfactory," I said and left.

Out in the reception room, the sweet young thing on the couch looked as though she'd made little progress in the magazine she was reading, but then, pictures can sometimes take a long time. I suspected she was to be a future Mrs. Bennett, once Henny got rid of the previous, sun-damaged model.

"Don't," I said, as I headed for the outer door.

"Don't?" she asked, looking up, confused. She was gorgeous.

"Just don't," I said.

I called Jarobi's phone as soon as I got to the car. He didn't answer. I didn't leave a message.

Two hours later, I was on a plane, more nervous and confused than when I'd arrived. Perhaps the kidnapper had gotten the painting—but no one had called to say what Wendell got in return.

Forty-five

My plane landed at midnight. I hurried to an empty gate to check my phone.

Jenny had left the first voice message, suggesting dinner. Wendell Phelps left the next four. His voice was too agitated to be bearing good news. I sat down to call him.

"I need you on my payroll," he said.

I took a deep breath. I'd been sure I was going to hear worse. "Amanda; she's safe?"

"I need you on my payroll," he said again. He sounded disoriented.

"You made the exchange, right?"

Two people passing in front of me turned around. I'd shouted.

"Wendell," I said more softly. "The kidnapper called, right? You made the exchange? Amanda is safe?"

"Another call," he mumbled. ". . . you back."

I got up and started hurrying toward the garage. Something was wrong.

I called Jarobi. This time he answered.

"What's going on?" I asked.

"The king speaks to serfs only at his leisure."

"He called me four times when I was on the plane back to Chicago.

I just spoke to him. He's disoriented, doesn't seem to be making sense."

"I can do nothing, if he won't—"

"You weren't there for the exchange?"

"The man's an arrogant—"

I clicked Jarobi away; Wendell was calling.

"My people have gotten nowhere," he said. "The damned fools don't know where to start."

"Make sense, Wendell. You made the exchange, right? Amanda's OK?"

There was silence at the other end of the call.

"Wendell?" I asked, entering the garage.

"I'm here." His voice had dropped even more. He was barely whispering.

"What aren't you telling me, Wendell?"

I got to my row. Though the garage was almost empty, a tow truck had pulled up in front of my Jeep, blocking it. A man in coveralls was shining a flashlight through the side window of an Audi parked next to me. Another man, this one in a suit and presumably the Audi's owner, stood alongside, watching. He'd locked his keys in his car.

Wendell mumbled something that I couldn't hear. An awful possibility flitted into my mind.

I stopped. "Wendell, they told me in California that the kidnapper called, ready to sell the painting. Has the exchange been made?"

The two men ahead turned around at the sound of my voice.

"I didn't want some rule-abiding cop screwing things up," he said, "but I think we're still OK. I've still got the two million dollars in cash, here at home. He won't leave that on the table—"

"Where's the painting?" I asked slowly.

"I wasn't forgetful. I just wasn't," he said, his words coming now in a torrent. "He'll call again, for the two million. It must have been the stress. I've never done such a—"

"*Tell me everything.*" I looked down the empty row, only vaguely comprehending the scene ahead. The tow driver took out a flat jimmy bar, the kind cops used to pop locks for forgetful drivers.

"He called this afternoon and told me to be ready to drive to meet him on a moment's notice. I instructed Jarobi to bring the painting downtown to my office. There's public parking below ground, as you must remember. I met Jarobi by my car and put the painting in my trunk so I'd be ready instantly. Jarobi left, and I went back upstairs, to wait for the call. Damn it, that garage is patrolled."

"Then what?"

"Then nothing. I hung around my office all day, but he never called back. I left around seven, thinking he'd call my cell phone as I drove home."

The tow driver slid the jimmy bar between the Audi's outer door and the side glass, pushed down, and jerked it up. There was a loud click. The Audi driver reached for the door handle. The door opened. The Audi man smiled and reached for his wallet.

"The painting is gone, isn't it, Wendell?" I asked, my own words a torrent now that I understood. "Taken right out of your car, and now you've lost the only leverage you had to get her back?"

"I didn't think to look until I got home. My trunk was securely locked. The parking lot is monitored."

"Cameras?"

"No cameras, but guards, patrolling . . ."

I wanted to savor the man's trauma, revel in his hopelessness, but there was no time.

"You're still driving that old Mercedes, right, Wendell?"

Ahead, past my silver-taped beater of a Jeep, the tow truck pulled away. The Audi's backup lights came on.

"Thicker metal than any of the new ones," the rich, all-knowing man sputtered.

"It has a manual inside trunk release?"

"Why the hell does that matter? It's a solid automobile, no piece of tin."

The Audi drove away, leaving me alone in the garage. "When you got home, how did you unlock the trunk?"

"The mechanical release," he said, barely above a whisper.

"You gave up the damned painting without getting her back."

His silence said it all. Then he said, "That two million won't do any good, will it?"

"The painting is what he wants. It's worth tens, maybe hundreds, of millions."

I thought for a moment, and then I told him what I wanted, and where, and clicked him away.

I pulled out the business cards I'd gotten in L.A. and called the cell phone numbers. I told each lawyer the same thing: "Anybody but me that calls will be lying."

Both started to ask questions. I said I didn't have the time.

I started the Jeep, praying I wouldn't be too late.

Forty-six

Though snow was falling heavily as I left the airport, I made good time because it was past midnight and almost everyone not intent on killing was off the streets. I stopped at the turret only long enough to grab Leo's revolver before racing across town to slide to a stop down the block from the man's house.

His was a working-class block, like Leo's. The houses were dark, except for his, where a shadow moved behind a curtain. He was still home. He was in no panic to get away. I wanted to believe that was a good sign.

The nerves pulsing in my chest wanted me to act right away, to kick in the door, hunt him down, and press the gun barrel to his heart. It didn't seem physically possible to wait.

My head reasoned louder. If I was right, Amanda was in that house, and he'd not harmed her, for fear of the bounty Wendell would put on his head. He'd be thinking he didn't have to risk anything now. He'd gotten his big prize anonymously; no one would suspect him until after he left. He could be methodical, take his time to disappear perfectly so that he'd never be found.

Chances were, he'd go to work as usual and duck out at lunch to make the last calls to California, where it was still only the middle of the morning.

He'd learn, then, that a boulder had been dropped on his plan. Someone had told both lawyers only that person would have the painting. By then, I'd have grabbed Amanda, and she'd be safe.

The last light in the house snapped off. He'd gone to bed.

I sat in the cold, not daring to run the engine for heat because of the noise; shifting only to switch on the wiper to clear away the falling snow, or to seek the comfort of Leo's revolver on the seat beside me.

I went over the plan, again and again. The layout of his house would be similar, if not identical, to Leo's. I'd wait until he went to work; I'd break in; I'd grab her. It would be over.

At last the first of the dawn came, barely lightening the thick falling snow. I drove around to the alley entrance and stopped.

I called Wendell. "Your man is in place?"

"On Thompson Avenue, right where you said. Silver Honda Civic."

"Time to call a bluff," I said and went back to waiting.

Robinson drove his burgundy Escalade out of the alley at seven o'clock, his usual time. I started my engine and switched on my lights. He drove right past me but made no acknowledgment. I followed him all the way to city hall, turned around, and disappeared back into town.

He called a moment later. By then I was halfway back to his house.

"No need to follow me anymore, Elstrom. I haven't seen anyone for quite some time."

His voice was insistent and unnaturally high. He didn't want me around when he took off, come lunchtime.

He must have gone crazy, the day before, waiting for me to quit tailing him so he could head downtown to Wendell's garage, to put his plan in place. It had been a fine plan, too. He wasn't going to risk exchanging Amanda for the painting at some prearranged place; he was going to make Wendell drive around with the painting and the cash until he was absolutely sure there were no trailing police. Only then would he call him, perhaps to tell him to pull over on some random dark street.

Except Robinson got even luckier than he'd dared to hope. He'd gone to Wendell's garage downtown, to watch to make sure no GPS devices were being attached, or no cop was hanging around, set to ease down in the backseat when Wendell set off.

He was in the garage, watching, when Jarobi put the painting right into Wendell's trunk. Watching when Wendell went upstairs to his office, to wait for a call, leaving the painting behind.

To a man skilled in working a jimmy bar, it must have looked like Christmas in that garage. Like yesterday, Robinson couldn't afford to have me tailing him. Today, he was leaving town. Except now I was telling him he had a tail, offering up Wendell's man as evidence, parked on Thompson Avenue. Robinson surprised me. "Red or black?" he asked softly.

"What?" I asked, trying to keep shock out of my voice.

"The car that's tailing me: Is it red, or is it black?" Robinson was huffing, going up the stairs to a first-floor window to look out.

He really was being tailed. My mind darted back to the black Impala I'd seen along Thompson Avenue the day Jarobi had come to visit. Perhaps there'd been a red one, too. None of it made sense.

"It's silver, Bruno, a Honda Civic," I managed. "You can see it from city hall. It's parked right on Thompson Avenue."

"I see it," he said. Wendell's man was being obvious, as I'd asked. "But I don't see your Jeep."

"I'm tucked out of view."

His next words came fast and high-pitched, "All this because of that damned Snarky not being more careful, stealing the painting?"

It was a slip, a mistake. We'd never discussed a painting. None of that mattered, though. My objective was Amanda.

"I thought Snark liked jewelry," I said. "You never mentioned a painting."

"Sure, sure; jewelry," he fired back.

"Why don't you go around back, to the police department, get protection?" I asked.

Of course he wouldn't do that. He couldn't dare.

"Stay put until lunchtime," I said. "I'll manage to get between you and him when you pull onto Thompson Avenue. We'll figure something out then."

I clicked him away as I drove up his alley.

Forty-seven

Robinson had no enclosed rear porch; his back door opened out to the world, where everyone could see. It didn't matter. I smashed the glass with Leo's gun, reached in, and undid the bolt.

A wrong, faint smell hit me as soon as I stepped inside. It was gasoline. Two red five-gallon plastic jugs rested on the hall floor, and several books of matches lay on a little shelf above them. In a sick instant, I understood. Robinson had planned to come back, probably at lunchtime, to destroy every bit of evidence against him.

Especially Amanda, who could finger him as a kidnapper.

The thought chilled. I started running through the house.

The bungalow had the exact same floor plan as Leo's. The back bedroom was just off to my right. The bed was made. He'd not kept her there.

I hurried through the kitchen, to the front of the house. The dining room, the living room, and the little alcove room behind the front porch were sparsely furnished with out-of-date blond maple furniture, a sofa with a grease mark where Robinson had rested his head, and a wire magazine rack. A television sat on a black glass corner unit, directly opposite the sofa. She wasn't there.

The bedroom off the dining room was Robinson's. Unlike the front rooms, his room was a mess. Clothes lay scattered about, and the bed was unmade. He'd seen no point in neatening a room he was going to burn.

I ran into the kitchen and stopped. Next to a sink mounded up with dirty dishes, two glasses smeared with fresh milk residue sat on the counter. Two people had drunk from those glasses just that morning.

"Amanda!" I yelled. "Amanda!"

I ran down the basement stairs. Unlike Leo's, which had been simply divided into a main area and his walled-off office, Robinson's basement was divided into a rat's nest of small rooms. Each of the doors was closed.

It was the painting, though, that gave me an instant's hope. It was propped up across the washtubs. Water dripped slowly from the faucet, and a wet sponge lay dropped on the floor. Some of the lavender and green and pink had been sponged enough to smear, but not enough to reveal. The back of my neck started to tingle. There was no telling what direction his rage might have taken if he'd kept sponging and seen there was nothing underneath.

"Amanda!"

The first door hid a furnace, a water heater, and a workbench piled with tools. The second room had once been a coal bin but now held shelving jammed with old lamps, pots and pans, and an electric makeup mirror. Robinson must have been married once, to a woman who'd left him and the lamps and the pots and the pans behind.

The third door was locked. I beat on it with my fist, then stopped to listen. No noise came from within. I shouted her name and tugged on the door, but the lock was strong. I put my shoulder to it. Still the door wouldn't yield. I backed up and ran at it slightly hunched, hitting it with my right shoulder just above the lock. The door shuddered on its hinges and broke loose.

She lay on her back on a filthy camp cot. Her ankles and wrists were bound with plastic wire ties, her mouth and eyes covered with silver tape. Her hair was matted. She wore the clothes she'd worn to the turret. Blood had crusted over a small cut above the tape covering her left eye.

"Amanda," I said.

For one horrible instant she did nothing, and I thought she was dead. I touched her cheek, afraid to do more.

She made to turn her head away. She didn't want to hear or feel anything.

"Amanda," I said louder, looking around for something to cut the wire ties.

Her forehead wrinkled as she tried to shut out the sound.

I ran to the workbench in the furnace room, pushed at the pile of tools, and found a wire cutter. Hurrying back, I tore at the tape covering her eyes. She did not wince, for she did not feel the pain. Her pupils were dilated, giant black holes of fear. Leo's eyes had been like that right after he shot Wozanga, cartoon eyes of shock and horror.

I pulled the tape from her mouth, and she began gasping, sucking in the sudden new air in ragged bursts.

"You're safe," I said. "You're safe."

She saw and she did not. I cut the plastic ties at her wrists.

"You're safe," I said again.

Her chest was heaving in a fury now, desperate to breathe deeply.

I knelt to cut away the ties on her ankles. She'd fall if she stood. I rubbed her ankles, then helped her stand. I had to get her to a hospital.

"You're safe." It was all I could think to say.

She said nothing, looked nowhere except straight ahead. She was an automaton, traumatized zombielike in everything except breathing. Her lungs still heaved, fast.

"Work with me now, Amanda," I said. "A step, and another, out to the Jeep and away from here."

She took a step, and then another.

The front door creaked open above our heads.

I froze, held my breath. She did not. She kept shuffling forward, breathing fast and loud. She wasn't aware that Robinson had come home.

Frantic, I grabbed her shoulder to stop her and looked around for the revolver. I'd used it to smash the back-door glass and kept it in my hand as I'd raced to search the house, but I must have laid it down somewhere.

I raised my forefinger to my lips. "Be absolutely quiet," I whispered.

Her lungs wheezed, in and out.

His footsteps crossed above our heads. He couldn't have seen the broken back door yet.

The gun. I had to find the gun. I dropped to my knees to search the floor.

She tensed, her breathing coming in shorter, staccato bursts. She'd heard at last; she knew those footsteps. Her kidnapper had come back. I stood up and put my arm around her.

He stopped, above our heads, and in one sick instant I knew why. A cold draft of March air from the shattered back-door window had hit him.

"Son of a bitch," he shouted. His footsteps thundered toward the back of the house.

I took a last fast look. The gun was nowhere.

He pounded down the stairs.

Amanda screamed.

I grabbed the wire cutters off the cot and ran out of the tiny room. I caught him just as he stepped onto the concrete floor. He had a gun in his hand, but I'd surprised him. He was holding it low, down by his hip. I stabbed the tip of the cutters into the hard bone above his left eye. He howled, flailing at me, and fell to the floor. Something clattered out of his hand. His gun.

I kicked at it, sent it skittering across the cement. Shrieking like nothing human, Robinson got up to his knees and crawled after it, a blinded wild beast. Blood pulsed from the ripped skin above his eye, down onto the floor.

I caught up to him and kicked at his head. His elbows gave way and his forehead crashed down on the cement. He lay on his belly, howling, struggling to wrap both forearms around his head. I kicked at his ribs until he lowered his arms, and then I kicked at his ears and his cheeks until he quit howling and his arms fell lifeless alongside his body.

I grabbed Amanda's hand and dragged her past the lifeless man.

He moved. I turned to look. He'd pushed himself up to his knees, but he could not see through the bloody pulp that was his face. I tugged her up the stairs, opened the back door, and pushed her out into the cold.

"No!" he screamed from down below, and the gun fired. He'd found his gun; he'd find the stairs.

I reached down, picked up one of the red plastic jugs, and twisted off its black cap. Robinson had staggered into view at the base of the stairs, howling like nothing human. A shot rang out; something thudded on the wall behind me. He was firing blind. Surely he could not see.

I sloshed some of the foul liquid down the stairs and then threw the whole jug down at him as he moved his gun hand to shoot again.

He screamed as he heard me strike the match. *"Noooo!"* he wailed.

He fired again, but the bullet ricocheted off something in the basement.

The flame burned tiny at the tip of my fingers. I touched it to the others, and the whole packet flared. I threw it down the stairs. It landed on a wood step halfway down. For a moment it sputtered, benign. Then it found the rest of the little river of gasoline and it roared into full life, hurtling flames down into the basement. He screamed.

I kicked the other, closed jug down the stairs and ran from the hell I'd unleashed.

Forty-eight

The dawn had warmed the day enough to change the snow to freezing drizzle. Twice we nearly fell as I led Amanda around the garage to the Jeep. She moved stiff-legged, her teeth chattering, her eyes wide, oblivious to the frigid rain.

I eased her onto the passenger's seat and was about to wrap her in my coat when a house door slammed behind me. I had a horrible image of Robinson on fire, coming after us. There was no time to duck back to look, no time to cover her with my coat. I slammed her door, turned to run to the driver's side, and fell flat on the ice. I grabbed at the tail lamp, got up, and pulled myself around to the driver's side.

A shot sounded nearby. I started the Jeep but must have pressed the pedal down too hard. The wheels spun, bit, and sent us skidding across the fresh ice to crash into a garbage drum, killing the engine.

I twisted the key, certain Robinson was but a few feet away, in flames, aiming. The engine sputtered and quit. I twisted the key again. This time the motor caught and roared into life. I let out the clutch and pointed us toward the center of the alley. We half slid, half wobbled down the alley and onto the cross street.

Four-wheel drive is nice, but nothing's nice on ice. The street was worse than a skating rink. Every time I tried to nudge us beyond ten miles an hour, the wheels broke loose and I'd start to slide. I could only crawl, one long block at a time.

Behind me, high headlamps followed, the right size for a big SUV like Robinson's Escalade.

Thompson Avenue, that main drag, was littered with wrecked cars. The ice storm had come too suddenly for the town's salt truck, and early-morning drivers, passing through to jobs well away from Rivertown, were crashing everywhere, slamming catawampus into curbs and other cars inching down the street.

Yet through it all, the high headlamps stayed a hundred yards behind, almost invisible in the freezing crystal rain.

I chanced a look at Amanda. She sat stoically on the seat beside me, staring straight ahead, still wheezing deeply, desperate in her dark place to store more oxygen before someone came again with wire ties and silver tape.

I crawled west along Thompson Avenue, thinking vaguely of a hospital a few miles down the road.

I'd left my cell phone on the dash. I switched it on and called Wendell. I owed him that, and I needed help. He answered on the first ring.

"I got her, Wendell," I heard myself shout. "I got her."

"She's safe?" he yelled.

"Safe, but traumatized. Your man tailed Robinson back to his house?"

"Yes, but Robinson left again, almost right away. I've been trying to call you."

"Robinson's behind me. Call your man. See if he can get between us and Robinson."

"Let me talk to my daughter!"

I put the phone on speaker and laid it on the dash. "She's in shock," I yelled. "Call your man, get Robinson off my tail."

We came to the north-south street I wanted. I took my foot off the gas and slid more than drove into a southbound turn. Halfway through, the Jeep shuddered and broke loose on the ice. Horns began blaring as we started to skid into the oncoming lanes.

I fed the Jeep more gas and found traction enough to push us into the correct lane. Amanda's breathing began to slow, though she was nowhere nearby.

"Where the hell are you going?" Wendell shouted from the tinny phone speaker. "Robinson just turned south behind you."

"She's in deep shock. I'm taking her to DuPage General."

"Bring her to me!"

"She's not communicating. The hospital's just a few miles ahead."

"Damn it, Elstrom, she won't be protected there," he yelled. "Bring her to Lake Shore Drive."

Her condo building was heavy with security, and Wendell could make it even heavier . . . but it was so many miles east.

"Is your man behind Robinson?"

"Right on his tail, but he's driving a little crackerbox Honda, slipping all over the road. Robinson's got a big SUV."

I slowed. The big headlamps behind me did not.

I turned the wheel gently to the left. It was enough. The Jeep teetered and broke into a slide, but this one I'd anticipated. I turned the wheel a little more, pressed gently on the accelerator, and spun us just enough to head back north.

I watched the rearview. No headlamps were turning behind us.

"We're good, Wendell," I shouted at the phone. "I don't think he followed."

"I'm not hearing from my man," he said.

We drove north, then east, dodging crashed cars or other cars poking gingerly along, like us. I watched my rearview incessantly for the high headlamps, but the lights behind us were ever changing, not constant. I could only hope Robinson had slid into a ditch.

Amanda sat robotlike, staring straight ahead, but her breathing had slowed to normal.

Thirty minutes later, we crawled up onto the Eisenhower Expressway and headed toward Chicago. Wendell was an incessant chatter from the phone on the dash. Sometimes I yelled something back; mostly I ignored him. Amanda said nothing at all.

Salt trucks were moving in both directions, but they made the road more dangerous. Drivers were hitting the salted spots and thinking they could speed up with the new traction, only to lose control when they hit the next slick patch. They went into the guardrails or, worse, other cars. Somehow, a thin trickle of traffic kept moving through it all, toward Chicago.

We'd just entered the city limits when a pair of taillights ahead suddenly shot across all three lanes of the expressway, headed straight for the vertical wall of a cement overpass. The hundred taillights between us lit up like gun bursts, their drivers slipping and angling to avoid being hit. Some made it; some didn't. Cars crashed in all three lanes. The grandmother of all gridlocks was about to commence.

I couldn't risk being stopped. The Racine Avenue exit ramp was ahead, to my right. I angled across all three lanes, half driving, sometimes skidding. High-beam headlamps flashed behind me; horns blared as I followed my reckless diagonal. Then I was there. The exit ramp loomed up. I downshifted. By some miracle, the Jeep slowed without breaking loose.

A red light stopped me at Racine. I looked over at Amanda. She seemed to be barely breathing, as though she were slipping into some deeper form of shock.

"You there, Wendell?" I shouted.

Some sort of crackling came back from my phone.

"Have a doctor waiting," I yelled. "She's deeper in shock."

The phone crackled and went silent.

A pair of high headlamps was coming up behind me. The signal ahead was still red, but the headlamps behind me weren't slowing. I watched them get larger. At twenty feet I recognized the burgundy paint and the Cadillac crest on the grill.

I ground the shifter into first gear and shot out into a hole in the traffic moving slowly along Racine.

The Escalade followed.

"Wendell, where's your man?" I screamed at the phone on the dash.

". . . to voice mail . . . after . . . rings." Even though he was breaking up through the tinny speaker, I could hear the defensiveness in his voice. He must have heard the fear in mine. "Robinson?"

"He's got a gun, Wendell."

"I'll . . . police!" he shouted.

"In this ice storm? Not even your clout will get them here in time." An image flashed in my mind then, of alleys and garages. "I'm going to try to lose him," I yelled. "Make sure people are waiting with guns."

"They're already—"

"Someone is following us?" Amanda asked calmly, more startling than the sound of any gunshot.

I glanced in the rearview. The big headlamps were fifty feet back. He'd not gained on us.

"A guy named Robinson. We can talk later."

"A man was down in the basement, whistling. I could hear him through the door. Was that the man?"

"Did you see that canvas on the washtubs as we ran out?"

"I don't know."

"Robinson was beginning to sponge away the acrylics."

"Leo's."

"Not Leo's; mine. I made a copy."

She inhaled sharply and began giggling, loud and hysterical. "Now what?"

"I know tricks," I said.

Forty-nine

I didn't know tricks so much as I knew alleys, from the years when investigating hinky insurance claims was a big chunk of my business. There were good alleys in the old neighborhoods west of the city. That day, I needed to find one that was perfect.

The salters hadn't gotten north of the expressway. Hardly any cars were out. I zigzagged north on the ice-sheeted streets as fast as I dared, through gentrified blocks of dance and design studios, yupped-up fusion restaurants, and places looking to sell scarves, silk flowers, and anything else that would fetch a price greater than its utility. The sidewalks were barren, too. The young and fancy were taking an ice day off, staying indoors, sipping warm designer coffees and admiring their shoes.

I would have liked that, too, instead of being chased by a relentless lunatic with a gun.

Sometimes I gained a hundred yards and couldn't see him at all for the drizzle and the mist, only to have his headlamps charge up bright in my rearview. It would have been ludicrous, a chase done at turtle speed, except for his intent. The painting propped on the washtubs must have gone up in flames, and he needed Amanda now for the two million she'd fetch.

I turned west, into the bomb-zone old neighborhoods that would never feel the golden brush of gentrification. Many of the old gray-stones were gone, torched for insurance and pushed over. Oddly, almost all the garages remained, and that might be enough.

I swung left, then right, then darted into an alley. Loose gravel and crumbled asphalt poked up through the ice like cleats on a golf shoe, good for traction for me, but good for him, too. Cars were parked parallel to garage doors, and garbage barrels were scattered here and there, also narrowing the way.

I breezed through. So did he, so close at times I could hear his huge tires banging in the potholes. Once I chanced a look back. His head was pure white. He'd grabbed a towel for his burns.

The alley was too wide. I popped out onto the cross street no farther ahead of him than I'd been. I needed narrower.

I swung right, too fast, and skidded, barely missing a car parked at the next corner. I looked back. He'd come out skidding, too, but he was gaining ground. His Escalade was heavy and more sure-footed. Less than twenty-five yards separated us.

Crazily, I'd forgotten about Amanda. I shot a glance over. Her body was rigid; her breathing had gone back to shallow. She'd slipped back into the safety of deep shock.

There was another alley. I turned in. Again I found traction in crumbling asphalt and potholes; again I blew past garbage barrels and parked cars. Twice I heard him strike things, sending garbage barrels banging into garages and cars, but he never slowed. His big Cadillac engine thrummed above the whine of my Jeep. He was gaining even more ground.

Something sparked off a cleat on a telephone pole ahead. I looked back. His hand was out his window. He was firing, despite the potholes. If he got much closer, he wouldn't miss.

The alley continued on past the cross street. There was a vague, dark narrowing in the distance. I couldn't slow; his engine was loud behind me. I hit the cross street. My wheels broke loose, sending me into a fishtail. I pressed down on the accelerator; somehow we shot into the next alley headed straight.

I got close and recognized the darkness. Several toughs in long black leather coats and watch caps stood warming themselves around a barrel fire they'd tugged into the middle of the alley. Just behind them was a shiny blue Chevy Caprice, set to ride high on oversized wheels.

I slowed for an instant. The barrel fire was there for warmth, but it was also there as a barrier, to warn off people from the high-riding masterpiece. Right-thinking alley users were expected to back up and find another place to park until the Chevy was no longer there. Such were the rules of the thugs who controlled that alley.

The Escalade roared loudly behind me.

I pressed down on the accelerator. Hearing acceleration instead of reversal, the long-coats turned to stare slack-jawed at the breach of reason that was bearing down on them. Hands jammed into the leather coats. They weren't reaching for jellybeans.

I snuck a last glance behind me. He was close, and gaining fast.

I saw only fragments of what happened next, because I could only focus on the gap that was shrinking fast in front of me. A wrong twitch to the left and we'd slam into a garage. A wrong one to the right and we'd hit the barrel fire and be dead of gunshots by the time we crashed into the Chevy.

Their arms were raised. Their guns were out.

I twitched left, no more than a couple of inches but enough to show respect, and charged into the narrow opening. Incredibly, we were through in an instant, accompanied by no sounds of scraping metal, splintering wood, or guns. We'd gotten past clean.

Not so the Escalade. Metal hit metal, hard. Guns erupted everywhere. I slowed to look behind.

Hell was raining from the sky. Small fires were falling, burning remnants from the barrel. Others lay strewn on the asphalt and, most disrespectfully, on the black vinyl top of the shiny blue Chevy that rested, crumpled like a cheap toy, against the side of a garage.

The toughs stood surrounding the Escalade, aiming guns at its shattered windshield. Steam hissed from what was left of its grille. I could not see Robinson's towel-wrapped head.

I turned right, and left, and finally found streets that had been well salted.

"We're good, Wendell," I shouted at the phone on the dash.

He did not respond. I picked up the phone. The battery was dead. I laughed.

Thirty minutes later, I drove up the curved driveway of Amanda's high-rise.

Wendell had indeed summoned up troops. A man with a medical bag on his lap sat inside the opened door of a Mercedes. The garage attendant, an always affable, always armed fellow, stood under a huge black umbrella, out in the drizzle. As did three thickset men who had to belong to Wendell's private security force. Jarobi stood holding an umbrella, talking to two uniformed Chicago police officers sitting in a cruiser.

Wendell, the great man himself, shared an umbrella with a slick, silver-haired man. Though we'd never been introduced, because we'd never travel in the same circles, I knew him. He was a wealthy commodities trader named Richard Rudolph, and he always seemed to be at Amanda's side every time a newspaper photographer ran pictures of her at a charity event.

After I slid slightly to a stop, it was Rudolph who hurried to open Amanda's door. Her breathing had stabilized, and she appeared to have regained her focus. She looked over at me looking at the silver-maned snake. She might have given me a smile, but I don't know; Rudolph slid her out so quickly I couldn't be sure. Her father came up then, and together the six-legged creature of affluence, joined in ways I could only imagine, walked under the canopy and through the door, trailed by the doctor, security men, and cops that would keep her safe.

Not even Jarobi came over to say anything.

It was just as well. I turned around and drove back onto Lake Shore Drive. I wanted to be absolutely alone.

I drove north on Lake Shore Drive, putting more miles between Amanda and me. There was little traffic, no ice, and, despite my incessant checking, no Escalades.

My cell phone rang. It was Jarobi. "Care to share before the Rivertown police pick you up for arson?"

"There's a fire?"

"Apparently a house belonging to Rivertown's chief building inspector caught fire early this morning. Reports are sketchy, other than it appears the fire originated in the basement. There are persons of interest. A rather shabby-looking fellow and a disheveled woman were seen leaving the bungalow in a rusted red Jeep adorned with much silver tape."

"That's the problem with those eyesore Jeeps. There are hundreds of them. Too many are red, and most have been patched with silver tape."

"Mr. Phelps whisked his daughter up into her condo. She needed medical attention, so I did not intrude."

"If Robinson's basement hasn't been totally destroyed, you'll find traces of Amanda being held hostage there."

"Speaking of that painting . . . ?"

"There might be traces of it, or he might have grabbed it on his way out."

"Where is he?"

"West Side, in a bad place, likely dead of gunshot."

Suddenly, I was numb with fatigue. Other than snatches on the plane, returning from L.A., I couldn't remember when I'd last slept.

Jarobi must have heard it in my voice. "Where are you?"

"North Avenue Beach."

"Pull into the parking lot. I'll send a blue-and-white to escort you home. And Elstrom?"

"Yes?"

"Keep that Peacemaker handy until we find Robinson."

"Peacemaker?" I asked, too tired for puzzles.

"That old Colt you were waving, the first time I came to your place. It's a variation of the old single-action Colts they used in the Wild, Wild West. They called them Peacemakers. Keep it handy until we find Robinson."

"It was stolen," I managed to offer up. It was better than saying I'd dropped the gun in Robinson's basement, where someone was sure to find it, a cop or a fireman, and trace it to a man lying under loose stones.

It was a worry for a more alert man. I needed sleep.

An officer pulled up in a marked Chicago car then and followed me back to Rivertown. He settled back in the driver's seat as I walked up to my door. He was going to stay.

I supposed I should call Jarobi, to thank him for the bodyguard, but though it wasn't much past noon, the thought of trying to do anything except crawl into bed was too complicated to consider.

Fifty

In the middle of the afternoon, Henny Bennett's lawyer sent me fishing for the prepaid cell phone I'd brought to L.A. It was chirping in the pocket of my khakis, buried under a thin layer of other clothes on the chair next to my bed. I keep my duds close, so I don't have far to sprint in the cold. Also because I don't yet have a closet.

It was two thirty, Chicago time, which meant it was lunchtime in L.A.

"You were a bit cryptic yesterday," Mickey Gare said, oozing affability. Cryptic was hardly the word for the lies I'd spun, but I was too groggy to quibble.

"How's the weather out there? Sunny and around seventy-two?" I ventured my other hand from beneath the blankets to grab for the trio of sweatshirts.

"There's no need to play games. We've heard nothing from you, and Mr. Bennett remains most interested in acquiring the Daisy."

"As is the equally lovable Mrs. Bennett."

He snorted, and I remembered the slight dusting of powder I'd seen under his nose. I'd wanted to dismiss it as a bit of sugar doughnut residue, such were my sensibilities, but L.A., being a land of tight abs and loose nostrils, demanded other interpretations.

"We'd like to offer an enticement."

"A bribe? Bribes are always fun." I rubbed my legs with my free hand, to warm them.

He snorted again, and I became certain he was enjoying a lunch of power powder.

"What's that clicking sound?" he asked.

It was my teeth, chattering. "Hold, please." I set the phone down and put on the first of my sweatshirts, the XL, in gray. Then, picking up the phone, "How much of a bribe?"

"An enticement to make the final offer."

The man was a sleazy ass, and my chin was still quivering from the cold. I reached for the second sweatshirt, the plain dark blue XXL. "Last look has already been promised to Mrs. Bennett," I said, still talking as I slipped in one arm, then the other, as agile as a python.

Two snorts came this time, one loud, one more distant. Gare must have been having lunch with Henny Bennett.

"Hiya, Henny," I called out.

"No one has contacted us," Gare bleated. "Not you, not your principal. We'll pay the highest dollar."

"You already said that."

"Rudy Cassone? You do know that name, Mr. Elstrom?"

"Why do you ask?"

"I presume you know he's the one who claimed the Daisy was stolen from him and threatened to sue anyone who has possession of the picture. We did some research. So far as we can tell, no one has owned that painting since before World War II, and even then its provenance is cloudy." He paused. "And now he's dead." He took a deep sniff that sounded like a tornado sucking a tree out of hard ground.

"Why are you calling?"

"Damn it: Will this Rudy Cassone business wreck things?"

"It certainly did for Rudy Cassone," I said affably. Cradling the cell phone against my ear, I eased into my thickest jeans, made even thicker in spots by dried paint, and reached for the last of my sweatshirts. It was an XXXL in blaze orange with DEPARTMENT OF PRISONS printed on the back. Leo bought it for me, saying that although he only paid two dollars for it, the owner of the Discount Den assured him it went for more when it was new.

"What?" Gare shouted through the tiny speaker of my cell. "You sound like you're talking through a pillow."

And a cloud of cocaine, I wanted to say, but I'd had a better inspiration, born of too little sleep and too much Mickey Gare. "Things have gotten more complicated," I said.

"Speak up! I can't hear you."

I took a moment to enjoy his quickened breathing before whispering, "A third bidder."

A horrific sound, akin to an entire forest being ripped loose, came through the phone. "You—you—there'll be an enticement. Huge money for you alone."

I clicked him away. Amanda was safe, and mending. Leo was mending, too, I hoped. I had other things to resume worrying about. A worthless canvas might have been destroyed in Bruno Robinson's basement, but a gun most certainly had not—a gun that had been used to kill a man who lay under too little gravel. That gravel would have to be swept again, before the walls and the slab could be poured. Sweeping meant dislodging, and that meant discovering. Likely enough, Robert Wozanga would again see the light of day.

I walked to the window. Jarobi's guard detail was gone.

I grabbed my regular cell phone. I'd gotten no messages, especially one from Jarobi saying Robinson had been found dead.

"Oh, boy," I said to myself. Then, realizing that talking to one's self is a sign of deteriorating mental health, I went down to talk to the coffeemaker.

While I waited for Mr. Coffee to embrace the day, I switched on the little kitchen radio I keep tuned to the news. I listened for ten minutes. There was no account of a building inspector being found shot to death on the West Side.

I called Amanda's cell phone. I got jettisoned right to voice mail. Understandably, she was not taking calls.

I then tried the never effervescent Wendell Phelps at his office. His secretary said she'd have to take a message.

Finally, I called Jenny. Dinner with her seemed like the most important thing I could do, even though she'd have questions, not the least of which would be why I'd taken twelve hours to return her call. I got routed to her voice mail, too.

As I poured coffee, my phone rang.

"Good afternoon, buckaroo," Jarobi said.

"Buckaroo," I repeated, clueless.

"Buckaroos are cowboys, remember?"

"No."

"Buckaroos carried Colt Peacemakers like yours. Got it?"

"All of life is about loss."

"What?"

"Never mind," I said. "How's Amanda?"

"Her father put a wall around her. Without a complaint, I can't get a warrant issued on Robinson." He cleared his throat. "That is, if he's still alive."

I was awake now, and fully nervous. "He's got to be dead."

"You're sure it was Robinson following you?"

"I recognized his burgundy Escalade."

"And him? You recognized him?"

"I think so. He had a towel . . ."

"What are you saying?"

"He must have gotten burned in his basement and grabbed a towel to stanch the bleeding. I didn't actually see his face."

"The car, we found. The windshield was smashed in, and there was blood on the steering wheel and the front seat. No Robinson."

"What's Rivertown City Hall saying?"

"The Escalade was stolen. They don't know when."

"They're covering up," I said.

"You hope."

"You bet. I don't want Robinson alive anymore. We have issues."

"If you were sure it was Robinson chasing you, I could summon up some actionable charge, here in Chicago. If all you saw was someone holding a towel to his head . . ."

"No corpses, no Caprice in that alley, either?"

"Some fresh scrapes on a garage but that's all. Be careful, buckaroo."

I put on my coats and went out. The sun was bright; the day had warmed into the low forties. No ice glistened anywhere.

On my way to Leo's, I called Endora. "Amanda is safe," I said.

"Thank goodness," she said. Then, "It's over?"

"Not by a long shot." I braced for anger. She must have been going crazy, cooped up in some discount motel with Ma Brumsky and her own mother, sweating whether Leo would ever summon his head back to full life.

She said nothing. There was no anger, no rage.

"I'm going by his place to pick up some of his most outrageous clothes and a few CDs," I said. "They might prod some memories."

She forced a laugh that came out flat and hung up.

Leo's neighbor was on her front porch with a broom. "About time," she called out.

"For what? The snow is melting."

"About time anyway," she said.

I stepped through the slush to the back.

Grabbing clothes to bring to Leo took no time at all, because any combination of patterns and colors, no matter how unharmonious, always made him look normal. I grabbed shockingly colored shirts and pants from his closet, and a shockingly endowed Brazilian songstress's CD from the Bose system on his dresser, and went back out to the Jeep.

Before heading north, I swung past Robinson's bungalow. A Rivertown police cruiser and the fire marshal's red sedan were parked in front. No fire damage was visible on the outside. I supposed that meant little had been destroyed inside, either, especially not the fingerprints on a revolver.

I drove to the tollway. As I was about to get on, I chanced a look in the rearview and saw an older green Chrysler minivan. It had been a hundred yards behind me on Thompson Avenue and was lagging the same hundred yards now.

Paranoia, I told myself. Paranoia from a hellish few days. Still, I drove past the northbound entrance ramp and headed west.

I passed Crystal Waters just as I had the morning I'd driven to Falling Star to deliver a canvas to Rudy Cassone. Now, though, the latest snow had made the gated community's ruined grounds pristine and white. Even the enormous husks of the few houses that remained, waiting for last inspections by explosives experts before they could be torn down, looked whole and livable, as though their owners were snugged up safe inside. It was an illusion. Those houses sat on ground riddled deep with live explosives. Perhaps that's what Crystal Waters had always been, a facade, an illusion of a good life that could be exquisitely and securely lived. It had certainly been that for the months Amanda and I had been married. Until we, and it, blew up.

The minivan was still behind me, and gaining. The gap between us was less than fifty yards.

Spider feet prickled up my neck. Only one hand gripped the steering wheel. The other held a white terry towel pressed to his face. It was splotched all over with red.

The driver was leaking. He was from hell.

Fifty-one

He followed my every turn, not caring if he was noticed. Even tipped into crazy, his head a wet mess oozing red into a towel, he was Superman. He survived fire and, somehow, an alley full of guns. Now he wanted only me. He wanted revenge.

I made more turns, and so did he. I pulled onto a main highway, three lanes running north, and so did he. He had to be thinking about a big move. So was I.

We came to a forest preserve. Thick old trees lined the shoulders on both sides of the divided highway. Traffic had thinned. Timed right, he could charge up now, if I got slowed by another vehicle, and cut me into a crash. Or perhaps he was simply looking for a clear line of sight for his gun.

His green minivan still filled the same two inches in my rearview. He must have been familiar with the road and known there was a better place, farther up.

I was looking for a good place, too, a spot to do a quick U-turn, but there was too much deep slush in the median. Even in four-wheel drive, I'd sink to the tops of my wheels.

There'd been more colors; the thought slapped into my mind. I checked the rearview again. Sure enough, the green of the minivan had not been the only constant since Rivertown. Two more colors had been there as well, hanging back as precisely from the minivan as Robinson was staying behind me. That's why he'd been hanging back. He knew they were there. No bigger in the mirror than pencil erasers, one was red, the other was dark, perhaps black. Black, like that Impala I'd noticed the day Jarobi first came around.

I could evade the minivan with a U-turn, or at least swerve back into him if he tried to run me off the road. Three cars was a different deal. They were using cell phones to coordinate their moves, waiting for the right time to box me in, one car in front, one in back, to slow me enough for the third man to pull up alongside to shoot. Zigs, zags, and U-turns would buy me nothing. I could not outrun three vehicles.

Too late, I passed by an access road into the forest preserve. There might have been a chance to go off-road in there, between the trees, but not for long. The woods were too thick.

A traffic signal appeared ahead, its light green. I dropped down a gear, to slow the Jeep and to pick up the torque I'd need. The few cars behind me began catching up, but not the green minivan, and farther back, not the small shapes of red and black.

The light turned yellow. If I stopped, they'd come up behind, on foot.

I blew into the intersection just as the light turned red. The intersecting road was much narrower, only one lane in each direction. Nothing was coming from the left, but a white convertible was starting up on the right. I swung left, barely missing the ragtop. A blond woman was driving. She hit the brakes, and then she hit the horn. I didn't look back, but I supposed she got a finger up as well.

The road ahead of me was empty. Except for a couple of driveways, there was nothing. Then I saw why. In the distance, orange striped barricades dead-ended the road. There was construction. The road was closed.

I needed to ditch the Jeep and run. I looked behind me. The white convertible was turning into one of the driveways. There was no one behind her. No one had followed.

I made a U-turn and stopped, looking at the way I'd come. The traffic light remained green, stopping the northbound traffic, stopping them. Escape lay southbound on that same multilaner, if they remained stuck in the tangle of northbound cars stopped by the light.

If I was fast.

I sped back to the intersection, glancing at the congestion to my left only after I'd turned onto the wide multilane highway heading south.

They'd disappeared. All three vehicles were gone.

I didn't dare slow, but I didn't dare believe. Yet I was sure: There was no one back at the traffic light. It was like they'd been sucked into space.

I pressed down on the accelerator, watching ahead, watching behind. They had to show up somewhere.

Fifteen minutes later, I turned east, passed Crystal Waters, and got on the Tollway.

I called Jarobi. "I think Robinson's been tailing me for the last hour. I think I lost him."

"Green Chrysler minivan?"

"Yes."

"I imagined he'd be out of state by now."

"I imagined him dead," I said. "No reports of gunshot victims on the West Side?"

"There are always gunshot victims on the West Side, but no young adults like you described. No trashed burgundy Escalade, either."

"Robinson had two friends along today, in red and black cars."

"That black Impala you keep asking about?"

"I couldn't tell."

"I'll pass all this on to your county sheriff. Tell you what, Elstrom: I'll put out a bulletin, saying Robinson is wanted for questioning in an art theft."

"Think any of it will work?"

"To find a green Chrysler minivan, accompanied by two cars of unknown make and model, one red, one black?" He laughed. "Nah," he said.

Fifty-two

Dr. Feldott was puzzled by what I was carrying.

"Flags, or rags?" she asked, smiling.

"Mr. Smith's dress clothes."

She pursed her lips. "That's a shame."

"I thought they might trigger a memory or two."

"Why not? I'm afraid we've tried everything. We can only be patient. He doesn't speak much, but we hear him whispering when he's alone. Patients sometimes do that; it's a means of trying to communicate, if only to themselves. He smiles a lot, though. We think he's happy." She motioned for me to go in first.

Leo wore a white shirt and tan trousers and sat at the small desk. He swept something small into his lap.

"Do you know me?" I asked.

He gave me a nod, of sorts, but his eyes had been drawn to the magnificent songstress on the CD. I set it on the desk.

"Would you like a player for that?" the doctor asked. She'd followed his eyes.

"Oh yes," he said.

She nodded approvingly and left. It was progress.

I spilled the clothes out on the bed. Holding up one of his most atrocious Hawaiian shirts, a bright orange number decorated with red pineapples dangling from palm trees with pink fronds, I asked, "Excite you at all?"

He frowned. "Bright."

"Excellent," I said. "A lack of enthusiasm for this garment is surely a sign of a correcting mental attitude. You might become better than new."

His brow wrinkled. "Huh?"

"This is one of your favorite shirts."

He winced and turned to the CD on the desk. A leer spread across his pale features. "This is mine?"

"Yes."

"I like this," he said.

I sat on a chair next to the bed. "I came to tell you a story."

"Good."

"Once upon a time, in a crooked little village not so very far away . . ." I began. Then I stopped. "No, forget that. This isn't funny."

I began again. "Years ago, a young thief named Snark Evans worked at the Rivertown city garage for a man named Tebbins. He also worked for Tebbins after hours, helping to install residential security systems. One day, Evans stole some jewelry and a painting from a house where they were installing a system."

Leo's eyes had remained on the CD.

I cleared my throat loudly. He looked up.

"The painting belonged to a Chicago mobster named Rudy Cassone," I said.

He showed no reaction.

"OK so far?" I asked.

"OK."

"Almost immediately, Snark realized he'd stolen from a wrong guy, so he decided to get out of town quick."

"Quick?"

I nodded. "The jewelry he could take with him, to hock later. He decided to leave the painting behind, maybe because it would be difficult to fence, or maybe because he thought it wasn't worth much. He gave the picture to a friend, for safekeeping."

I watched his face. Nothing changed.

"The burglary victim, Rudy Cassone, confronted Tebbins about the theft," I went on. "Tebbins knew nothing about it. All he could tell Cassone was that Snark had taken off. So Cassone went away. Later that summer, Tebbins, or his boss, a man named Robinson, heard that Snark Evans was dead. But maybe Snark faked his own death, to throw Cassone off his trail. He could have changed his name and begun a new life somewhere far away." I paused. "Until just a few days ago."

Leo's thick eyebrows rose, like always when he was surprised. This time, though, there was no crinkling around his eyes to show that his mind was keeping up with his eyebrows.

"Enter a couple of Hollywood types named Bennett," I said.

"Types named Bennett," Leo repeated softly.

I was speaking simply. His words were even simpler, childlike . . . and chilling.

"Henny Bennett is a very successful producer of B-grade horror movies. As near as I can tell, Mindy, his wife, was successful mostly at being beautiful, at least until recently. Sadly, like us all, she's gotten older, so I think Henny started casting around for a younger model. He found one, and now he's divorcing Mindy. Each of them, Henny and Mindy, wants that painting that was stolen from Cassone so many years before. OK so far?"

"OK so far," Leo repeated in a monotone. He'd dropped his eyes back to the CD. I was losing him.

"The painting is called the Daisy, and it once belonged to a Nazi. Actually, it might still legally belong to his descendants."

"Nazi?"

"Do you know what that is?"

"OK."

"The Daisy has not been seen since before World War II. Both Henny Bennett and Mindy Bennett are willing to pay huge dollars for the Daisy because each wants it for his or her collection."

"But it's the Nazi's." His brow had wrinkled, but that could have been from squinting at the Brazilian goddess.

"Or his family's. Still, each of the Bennetts is willing to buy the painting, no matter who legally owns it, no questions asked—"

He sighed and stood up. He walked to the bed and began taking off his white shirt.

I went on, though I was now talking to myself. "Snark Evans, who's been living under another name all these years, read of the battling Bennetts in a magazine somewhere. That made him remember the painting he'd stolen and given to a co-worker that summer."

A tiny noise came from the chair where he'd been sitting. I looked at him. He hadn't heard it. He was putting on another of the shirts I'd brought, this a purple, orange, and yellow combination of trees, fruits, and birds wearing sombreros. He began buttoning the shirt.

"Snark Evans wanted that painting back, because it was so valuable, and so he called that long-ago co-worker . . ." I stopped to look at the chair. The low hum had come again.

"I've confused you?" I asked, standing up. I eased over to the chair and looked down. A cell phone lay on the seat, vibrating with a new message.

"Dr. Feldott says she hears you whispering when you're alone," I said.

He put on the orange slacks I'd brought and stepped to the mirror on the wall. His white teeth split his narrow head in two, smiling like he was breathing pure oxygen.

"Ah," he said to his image.

"Damn it," I said.

He spun into the ridiculous small dance he always used when he'd put something over on me.

"Samba," he said.

Fifty-three

He sat down, still grinning a hundred-tooth grin. "Endora," he said, glancing at the number that had set the phone to vibrating. "We mostly text."

It was why she hadn't been angry when I'd told her she had to remain away from Rivertown. She knew Leo was well and coherent.

I started with basics. "How did you get the phone?"

"Are you carrying your usual five bucks, or do you have more?"

"As a matter of fact," I said, struggling for a preen, "I've got three hundred, though my prospects have returned to being grim. The phone?"

The door opened, and the doctor came in with a boom box. "How are we doing?"

Leo smiled at her vacuously. I told her we were getting along just fine.

She set the boom box on the desk and smiled approvingly at Leo. Apparently, she saw his purple shirt and orange pants as progress toward better mental health. I could only question whether professionals like her knew anything at all.

"I asked one of the teenaged girls who helps out around here," he said, after the doctor left. "I told her I was hiding out from a gang of evil thugs. She's such a sweet young thing, all innocence. She brought me a Walmart cell phone and says she'll carry my secret to her grave."

"What nobility."

"I had to promise two hundred for the phone and the silence."

I peeled off ten of my dwindling twenties. "You texted Endora?"

"I knew she and Ma would be worried sick. Don't worry; I refused to tell her where I am, and I specifically forbade her from returning to Rivertown until you said things are safe."

"Things aren't safe. You have to remain here."

"Who's paying for this?"

"I'm paying for part; the Bohemian's covering the rest."

"Delightful. Then I'll only have to reimburse Mr. Chernek."

"Tell me what you can."

"You found out I was hiding down the block?"

I nodded.

"My memory stops when I went back to my house one night to get food." He arched his formidable eyebrows. "Do you know what set off my trauma?"

"I found you disoriented. Maybe you hit your head?"

He made a show of feeling the back of his skull. "There's no bump," he said, his eyes steady on mine.

"Tell me a story, Leo, before I inflict real trauma on that head."

He shrugged, letting it go. "Shall I talk real slow, like you just did for me?"

"Begin with Snark Evans at the garage that summer."

"You got most of it right. Snark was pinching small stuff from somewhere and peddling it out of his locker. I worked some side jobs for Mr. Tebbins at first, and you could see Snark's eyes widen when we went into a new house. It was no mystery where he was getting some of his inventory. I think he kept his grabs small, so nothing much would get noticed. Still, I worried about getting my future wrecked, so I told Mr. Tebbins that I had studying to do at home and couldn't work side jobs anymore. Mr. Tebbins knew what I was really saying. He was wise to Snark, because a couple of times, I saw him and Mr. Robinson checking Snark's locker when he wasn't around."

"Why not just quit using Snark on those installations?"

"Mr. Tebbins had a good heart and was trying to straighten Snark out with extra pay, but he'd also been too good a salesman. He'd sold more systems than he could handle. He needed Snark. He needed me, too. He never forgave me for bailing on him."

"You never heard about Cassone?"

"Today's the first day I've heard the name. I must have been gone a week from the garage when Snark stole the painting."

"Mononucleosis? Really?"

"It was the truth." He put on a mock-offended look, adding slyly, "It's the kissing disease, you know."

"Please continue."

"Snark stopped by my house early on what I now suspect was the morning after he stole from Cassone. He said he'd done a painting for his mother. The dumb thing was still wet. He said he was going to a funeral and asked me to hold on to it until he came back. He said to tell nobody about it. I didn't believe his story, but no way I figured him for hot art, so I said sure. It was an ugly picture, just grays and browns and yellows. I put it out in the garage attic to dry and forgot about it."

"You really think he planned to come back for it?"

"No, because he didn't know what it was worth. Snark wouldn't peruse art catalogs and stolen painting bulletins, and there was no Internet back then, don't forget."

"I checked. It was never reported stolen."

"I checked, too, but now I understand. Snark stole from a hood who didn't have good title. He wanted to disguise it, thinking it would buy him some more time to get away."

"And for all these years, you had no idea the painting underneath was valuable?"

"Just for three years, Dek."

"You learned it was the Daisy so soon?"

"I worked for Sotheby's right out of college, remember. One Saturday, I was up in the garage attic and came across Snark's painting. As I said, I'd forgotten all about it. I brought it down. In the sunlight, the back of the canvas looked way too old for something Snark would have. I brought it into work on Monday and examined it with their equipment. It only took the morning to learn Snark had slopped over the last of Brueghel's Four Flowers. Worse, my research showed who legally owned it."

"The descendants of the Nazi?"

"He bought it legally, though for an impossibly low price."

"The proper thing was to return it to the Nazi's heirs?"

"Properly legal, but not properly moral. The German was an engineer, suspected of helping to set up the death camps. He died at the end of the war, before he could be charged." He shook his head. "I don't know how the family lost control of it. There's no subsequent record of title, so technically it still belongs to them."

"That's what you asked Amanda to double-check, a little while ago?"

His face brightened. "You talked to Amanda?"

"Only briefly."

"I wanted fresh eyes on my research. Anyway, what I learned wasn't really helpful, because I still didn't know where Snark stole it, or who stole it before that. Nor could I sell it and give the funds to survivors' groups, because there was no way such a sale could be done quietly, or anonymously. The Nazi's heirs were sure to hear about it, assert title, and get it back."

"So you set it aside and tried to forget about it."

"No. I went looking for Snark. He'd mentioned once that he came from Center Bridge, downstate, and that his sister had a sister-in-law who still lived there."

"You hadn't heard he was dead?"

"I never ran in to Mr. Tebbins or Mr. Robinson after I left the garage."

"I went down to Center Bridge."

His eyebrows danced. "What did you learn?"

"Nothing about any sister's sister-in-law. Everybody's long gone."

"When I drove down, I did find the sister-in-law. She told me she'd heard Snark got shot in some jerkwater, fifty miles from Paducah. I called their police. They put me on to a retired cop who remembered

Snark, mostly because of his name. Snark was killed by shots to the head, just weeks after he left Rivertown."

"Hood kill?" I asked.

"Sure, now that you've told me the picture was swiped from a mobster. I figured Cassone would have noticed the theft right away and come to Mr. Tebbins. Mr. Tebbins was a decent guy, but no way he'd cover Snark on a grand theft. Mobster or no, he would have told Cassone that Snark was gone, maybe headed for Center Bridge."

"Why didn't Snark tell him you had the painting?"

"Snark was big-time dumb. He would have realized he'd left behind a very valuable picture, seeing as Cassone chased him all the way to Kentucky for it. To his last stupid breath, he must have believed he could con his way free and come back for it."

"And so things ended," I said.

"Until I got that call from someone who knew to pretend to be Snark. Right after you left, I got on the Internet and saw the news about the Bennetts and the Brueghels."

"Did you suspect it was Tebbins or Robinson who'd called?"

"Never crossed my mind. I didn't see how they could know I had the painting," he said.

"When Cassone showed up years later, to take another crack at what they might know about that painting, they realized Snark had never given it up before he got killed."

"Remember I just told you they had a master key for the lockers?" he asked, excited now. "One of them must have seen the picture before Snark painted it over. They must have turned on a computer, Googled, 'daisy painting, stolen,' and saw a picture they remembered."

"With huge dollar signs attached," I said. "That got them thinking about you and Snark having lunch together every day. It was enough to risk a whispered call to you."

"Still, stealing a picture from me, even though it was stolen goods already, doesn't sound like them. These were low-level guys, Dek, content to wash cars, tune trucks, and spread salt." He leaned back, thinking. "Besides, I told my whispering caller I'd gotten rid of the painting a long time ago."

"You've never been much of a liar, Leo."

"I suppose I knew that." He sighed. "For sure I was scared enough to send Ma and Endora away and hang back to see who'd come sniffing around. I had to figure out how to make this problem go away."

"Did you ever see anyone?" I asked, meaning the man he killed, Wozanga.

He straightened up in his chair so he could look directly at me. Usually Leo could see right into the center of my brain.

"No," he said softly. "Did you?"

"No," I lied.

"How about that man that followed you to Eustace Island? Cassone?"

Endora had told him everything she knew.

"Who else could it have been?"

"How did Cassone know to come looking for me?"

Endora would have heard about Tebbins, too. I had no option. "Cassone killed Tebbins."

"Ah, jeez." For a moment he looked off, toward the doorway. Then, "Cassone made poor Mr. Tebbins give him my name."

"For sure, he would have said you hung around with Snark, back in the day. I'm guessing he also told Cassone you lied about not having the painting." There was no need to mention Tebbins had been tortured and was begging for his life.

"Cassone then took the painting?"

"Yes, and I clubbed him in your backyard and took it back."

"Mr. Robinson then killed Cassone?" he asked.

"He was watching your house and saw me drop Cassone and take the painting. After I left, he took the bat and later used it to club Cassone, after he shot him."

"Why?"

"The shooting part was to get Cassone out of the way so he could sell the painting; the clubbing was revenge for Tebbins."

"Whoa! That's too extreme. As I said, Dek, Mr. Robinson, like Mr. Tebbins, was a garage guy, not a killer."

"The clubbing was also to get me arrested for the murder and out of the way. My prints were on that bat."

"Mr. Robinson was a decent guy. I can't see him getting that desperate." He rubbed his eyes. He was getting too much information, too fast.

I paused and asked the question that had been nagging at me the whole time we'd been talking. "You were never tempted to get the Daisy restored, quietly?"

"No point," he said after a moment.

"Because it would be recognized and returned to the Nazi's heirs?"

"Just . . . no point." His face got dark. "I need you to do something for me. I left Pa's gun in that vacant house. I want you to go get it, before someone gets hurt."

"I grabbed it with your clothes." It was true enough. I just couldn't go further and tell him I'd lost the gun, which might link him to a killing if it were ever found.

I stood up. The daylight was disappearing out the window.

"Oh no you don't," he said. "There's a lot you're not telling me."

"That's because there's a lot I don't understand. Plus, I don't have time."

"When will it be safe for me to go home?"

"Soon."

"Because Robinson's still out there?"

"Plus two others, one driving a red car, one driving a black car." I told him about them chasing me through the woods.

"You're lying about something."

I had to hurry to get back to the turret to barricade myself in before dark. "Whisper a call to me tomorrow," I said and left.

There was a Burger King a mile before the Tollway and only Cheerios at the turret. I hadn't eaten since the In-N-Out in California, over twenty-four hours earlier. Say what one would about the In-N-Out, it had done no such thing; it had gone in and stayed. I hadn't felt hunger in over a day.

Of course, my loss of appetite might have come from being chased by a killer, twice in one day.

I got two Whoppers with cheese, a large Coke, and what surely were healthy vegetables: Cheerio-shaped onion rings. Whoppers can be tough to eat one-handed while driving, so I did the prudent thing. I savored it all in the parking lot and didn't get back to Rivertown until long after dark.

The turret was too dark and foreboding, ideal for Robinson and his two friends. I drove to a supermarket for Ho Hos and Twinkies and came back to sleep on Thompson Avenue. I would not be bothered. The Rivertown police were accustomed to seeing men slumped back behind their steering wheels, eyes closed, mouths opened, along that particular patch of road.

I switched off the key and slept sporadically until the sun rose the next morning.

Fifty-four

I waited until nine o'clock before I approached the turret. No one appeared to have tampered with the door lock.

Nor had the sensor lights been tripped. I went upstairs, had coffee from previous grounds, and called Jarobi for news about Robinson and his friends.

"What's shaking?" I asked, trying to not sound like I was referring to my nerves, which would have been worse if I'd used fresh grounds, or spent the night in the turret waiting for someone to break down the door.

"A forest preserve worker found a Chrysler minivan in a storage garage, near that access road you described."

"Green?"

"With serious scrapes along the driver's side. It was Robinson's car, like I expected."

"Red scrapes or black scrapes on the minivan?"

"Black."

"From an Impala?"

"Who knows, Elstrom? Forget the Impala; we don't have the money to be CSI Chicago. There were other things, though. A revolver was found lying on the passenger's seat. Want to know what kind of revolver?"

"Oh, why not?"

"Colt Peacemaker, buckaroo. The sheriff is running it down, like there's a mystery to who owns it."

I didn't see any need to tell him it wasn't mine, but Leo's.

"What about Robinson himself?"

"Meaning was he found shot with a Peacemaker that had your fingerprints on it? He's nowhere to be found, though two blood-soaked towels were found on the passenger seat. I suppose there could have been an accident, and he wandered off to get help."

"You believe that?"

"Of course not. Robinson was already wounded, likely from that alley altercation earlier. Those cars weren't tailing you; they were tailing Robinson, to wound him further."

"Friends of Cassone's?"

"Angered by the brutal way he was shot and then clubbed post-mortem? Maybe, though I'm sensing Robinson had other issues."

"What kind of other issues?"

"Floater issues, though I suppose all sorts of folks in your charming little town might have been responsible for that."

"What about that guy?"

"It was a John Doe."

"They have no idea who it might be?"

"It's not Snark Evans, if that's what you're asking. The floater's older, a white male in his midfifties. Apparently his fingerprints aren't on file. They're going to keep him cool for another week, then bury him."

"Without knowing who he was?"

"They're dead-ended, buckaroo."

"And Robinson?"

"If he's not buried in the woods somewhere, chances are he's running from those two guys who were tailing him. Any ideas?"

I didn't know. I knew who did, though.

I called Jenny. She didn't answer. I left a message, saying I had questions and wanted to have dinner, but I didn't mean it in that order.

• • •

The cleaning service was already waiting at Leo's when I got there.

I'd asked for every person they could provide. Smelling meat, they'd sent ten. They sang in Polish as they vacuumed and scrubbed and polished. I didn't sing at all as I killed time outside, scraping the last bits of snow from Leo's walk. The glinting eyes of the next-door babushka, wondering what was going on, were too hot.

After the cleaning crew left, I took a casual, hands-in-the-pockets stroll down the alley. The excavation sat abandoned, its foundation forms upright and empty. The gravel blanket between them still appeared smooth and undisturbed, and I took that to be a small mercy until I realized that with Robinson gone, Rivertown was without a building inspector, and that meant no concrete work would be approved for quite some time. Surely Wozanga's patience, cold though it was, would run out before that.

I needed to push back at the worries, and the Twinkies and Ho Hos that had fueled them through the night. I headed to the health center.

It was still early, and no thumpers lounged about. Still, after bumping my way across the parking lot to park next to the doorless Buick, I double-checked to be sure my Jeep was unlocked before going in. Prudence dictated that anyone be able to quickly see the dash had already been plundered of its radio, lest he begin ripping at the hundred silver curls of duct tape that made my Jeep look so like an aging Shirley Temple.

The locker attendant was nowhere to be seen, though two new locks, sparkling and freshly cut, dangled from lockers. I could only suppose he'd gone off to oil his bolt cutters. Like any good craftsman, he took care of his tools.

After changing into my gym duds and pocketing my wallet and keys, I left my locker door ajar for inspection and went upstairs.

As usual, the retirees were perched on the rusted exercise machines like kids at story time, as Frankie the Bridge Inspector held forth with the day's repetition of his twelve-joke repertoire. The retirees listened not in hopes of fresh material but rather for the certainty that the old stuff would be spun up the same as every other day. In a rapidly aging world, Frankie's old jokes were forever young. There was comfort in that.

I gave the boys a wave and ran the track. Two newcomers, no doubt the unknowing owners of the clipped locks downstairs, ran more haltingly, slowed less by the rips and the tears than they soon would be by the loss of their money, credit cards, keys, and cars. I quit after a mile, gasping, took my keys and wallet down for a shower, dressed, and went outside.

Two dark-haired, middle-aged businessmen, dressed ordinarily enough in tan trench coats and brown fedoras, stepped out from the side of the building. There was nothing ordinary about the speed with which they moved up on me, one in front, one behind.

They had fast hands. The one behind, whom I now think of as Mr. Red, pinned my arms back so that Mr. Black could hit me with a fast rabbit jab to the gut. I dropped to the asphalt, certain I'd never breathe again.

It was Mr. Red who bent down to speak, bracing himself with his knee on my back and his hand next to my face. He had a small tattoo, three stars in a tight cluster, just behind his thumb. "You done with Robinson." His accent was Slavic, maybe Russian.

"Is he done with me?" I asked the crumbles of asphalt in front of my nose.

"Persistence bring pain." He straightened up, and the two men disappeared around the corner of the building, presumably to where one of their cars, either the red or the black, was parked.

"What the hell did he mean?" I asked the asphalt, when I was able to take longer breaths.

The asphalt had deteriorated too much to offer up anything. I pushed myself to my knees, then to full standing, surprised that I could. Mr. Black was fast enough to have hit me two or three more times, going down, and those would have done real damage. Instead he'd only punched once.

He was a professional. He'd meant only to drop me, and to warn. About what, I wasn't sure.

Fifty-five

I'd just balanced the little television on my lap, about to let the noon news entertain my recovering solar plexus, when Leo called.

"I'm going to take a cab if you don't come to pick me up," he said, "and I'll instruct the cabbie to bring me to your cylinder to collect the cartage charges, since I have no cash."

Lester Lance Leamington's smiling face appeared on the tiny screen, likely about to advise me to embrace my future. Without thinking, I turned the volume down.

"What about the two hundred I gave you as an unsecured loan?" I inquired.

The television screen switched to a wider shot. Lester Lance Leamington was being perp-walked in handcuffs from an office building.

It was no infomercial. "Shush," I said, dialing up the volume.

"...where today," an announcer intoned, "he was arrested and charged with multiple counts of money laundering and distributing pornography. Sources say he needed the money to cover the losses he incurred in the stock market..."

"Get me out of here," Leo yelled into my ear.

"Have you heard anything about Lester Lance Leamington?"

"Busted this morning for covering his past with dirty money and dirty movies."

"Ma and her friends aren't involved, right?"

"Right now," he yelled.

"Robinson's still loose."

"I've already checked myself out, and I have another of Pa's guns hidden at home."

There was no arguing with that, and so I drove north.

Leo was waiting inside the front door. "What's the matter with your stomach?" he asked, getting into the Jeep.

I must have been hunched over the wheel. I leaned back, with pain, and gave his outfit the fisheye. The glare was almost overwhelming. He wore an orange shirt festooned with silver and green flamingos and lime-colored pants beneath his orange traffic officer's jacket.

"Slight indigestion, though it's nothing compared to the pain in my eyes."

"You got slugged in the gut."

I drove us away, in need of something to do.

"I think I'm on the verge of remembering what sent me here," he said, watching the side of my head. When I stayed rigidly focused on the road ahead, he said, "OK, so instead tell me how you got slugged."

"I have to make a call," I said, and I did. Jenny hadn't returned the call I'd made, though it had only been a couple of hours.

Once again, I got transferred straight to her voice mail. This time I said nothing.

"The press?"

I nodded.

"Who slugged you?" he then asked.

There would be no dodging Leo. If he didn't know something, he stayed at it until he pried out the truth. "Two guys who I think are not friends of Robinson's."

"Don't obfuscate."

"Remember that little parade I led through the woods, before coming up to see you?"

"Where you so cleverly gave three cars the slip?"

"That would be the one, yes, except now I think my cunning wasn't involved."

"Makes sense."

"Robinson's van was found in a shed in those woods, with a fresh scrape indicating it may have been run off the road."

"Meaning that the drivers of those lagging two cars were anxious not to catch up with you, but rather Mr. Robinson?"

"There's more: There was an old revolver on the front seat."

"Just like Pa's?" He turned to look at me. "Or was it exactly like Pa's, right down to the fingerprints?"

"Don't worry. I'll testify you were institutionalized under a false name, loony as a bluejay, when it got stolen."

"How much are you holding back?"

"I cleverly staged a burglary," I said.

"You're talking in circles."

"Once more around and you'll be too confused to care. Those two guys tailing Robinson might be the ones that just found me at the health center. The one who spoke sounded Russian. The other was nonverbal."

"What does this have to do with Pa's gun?"

"I think Robinson had it when he was chasing me beside the woods. The Russians left it in the van."

"You're leaving too much out. This is all going right past me."

"I believe they've done him wrong, which is the only reason I'm bringing you home. I think Robinson's angered the wrong people, and he's out of the picture, for forever."

He turned to look out the window. "I don't get any of this. All I know is, Mr. Robinson was always so nice."

"Something made him desperate to get out of Rivertown."

"Something more than greed for a valuable painting?"

"Jenny tells me nasty things are percolating in Rivertown. I need to talk to her."

He gave it up, and we drove in silence until we got to his block.

"Police tape?" he asked.

He was looking at the bungalow where he'd killed Robert Wozanga.

"Cops found blood on the steps. The tape's a precaution to keep the curious out."

He shifted in the Jeep so he could look directly at me. "That's where I was hiding. How do I fit with that blood?"

"You don't."

I parked in front of his house. He made no move to get out. "You told me you had my gun. How did Robinson get it?"

"Remember that clever staged burglary I just mentioned?"

"Damn it, talk sense."

"Trust me awhile. There's a lot I don't yet understand."

"Then how about this: There's nothing going on at the new house. Is that because of the blood where I was hiding?"

"No. Our town fathers have been hassling the contractor, and that's part of what I don't understand."

I got out before he could ask more questions, and we went inside.

"Jeez Louise. What's that smell?" he asked, stopping in the tiny foyer.

I gave a theatrical sniff. "Essence of Pine-Sol."

"Ma doesn't use Pine-Sol. You had the place cleaned."

"You had intruders."

"Cassone, looking for his painting. Who else?"

"Maybe Robinson, looking for the same thing. I figured you and Ma would feel better if any traces of them were washed away."

"What else?" he asked. He used to say that all the time, when we were kids. He was relentless then, and he would be relentless now. He was going to bombard me with questions until he understood exactly what had sent him to a clinic with amnesia.

We walked into the kitchen. "They even ran the dishwasher," he said.

"Actually, I needed the practice. I aspire to owning one myself someday."

"You'd need dishes that won't dissolve in hot water." He continued down the hall. Just inside his room, he bent over. "Odd," he said.

"What?"

He dropped to his knees and sniffed the carpet. "There was a stain here, but it's been shampooed away."

"The cleaning service was most thorough."

"It wasn't just a simple cleaning. You had this place scrubbed," he said, standing up.

"I told you: I thought it would make Ma feel better."

His eyes were unblinking. "Ma said she and Endora cleaned the place before you made them go away again."

"I told you that Rudy Cassone was in here. Likely Robinson, too."

"And the bat with yours and Robinson's fingerprints on it, along with Cassone's blood, is where?"

I beamed, as though to a dull child. "A police lockup. I'm hoping that since Cassone was killed by gunshot, and not clubbing, no one will think to print the bat. Even if they do, thanks to clever me, there will always be that burglary I reported, to explain away a missing gun and bat. "

"Want to know what I think?"

"No."

"I think you're worried there were even more fingerprints in this house, fingerprints that would implicate me in something I can't remember."

Like Wozanga's death, but I hoped to spend the rest of my life never having to say that.

We walked down the basement stairs.

"You even cleaned the mound of things Brumsky?" he asked, pointing at the orderly pile against the wall.

"Top to bottom, professionally wiped. No telling where Cassone was."

We went into his office. Everything sparkled in the light from his desk lamp and, like the rest of the house, stank sickeningly of Pine-Sol. I took the green overstuffed chair; he sat behind his desk.

He pulled a pencil out of the cup and began walking it between his fingers as he looked around the comforting familiarity of his office. Surprise lit his face in a half-smile when he got to the space above the mismatched file cabinets. He got up and went to finger the lavender barn. "You really left it here?"

Perhaps later, on a summer night, sipping a Czech beer, I'd give him more partial answers.

For now, I said, "No one dangerous knows its history. Cassone's dead; Robinson's missing, likely dead; and the Bennetts don't know about you at all, or where I came from. It's yours to do with what you want, with impunity."

His face had gone sly, an expression I'd seen plenty of times, right before he pulled a figurative ace from his sleeve. "I so love impunity," he said.

"What are you thinking?" I asked.

"Perhaps one last step, to be sure," he said.

"Sure of what?"

"Sure of that last step."

Then he laughed.

Fifty-six

Driving back to the turret, I watched the rearview as much as the road ahead. It was a new habit that had gotten old.

I called Jarobi. "I have news, I think, about the drivers of the cars that tailed Robinson. Two guys in trench coats slugged me earlier today. One of them told me to quit poking around about Robinson. He had a Slavic accent and a tight cluster of three stars tattooed at the base of his thumb."

"Three stars and a Slavic accent?"

"They mean something to you?"

"Why do you think they warned you to stay away from Robinson?"

"You're the cop. You tell me."

"Are you at your castle?"

"Turret, but yes."

"Walk your cell phone out to the river and look west."

I went down to the water. Blue police lights flashed down by the dam, just like the night they fished out John Doe.

"See me waving?" he asked.

"Of course not; you're too far away. What's going on?"

"Robinson."

"Drowned?"

"Two shots behind the ear, plus he'd been burned pretty badly."

"What kind of gun?"

"It wasn't your Peacemaker, buckaroo, but I have other interesting news. I called your county ME this morning. He was surprised he hadn't heard anything on the identity of the John Doe, so I called your cops and offered them the use of my own people to assist in their investigation."

"Our cops are turtles."

"Not this morning. They called me back within a half hour, with the miraculous news that they'd just identified the floater. He was Dimitri Kostanov, age fifty-three, a midlevel player who moved from a Russian gang in New York to fashion a new life in Chicago. They're becoming influential here, into all sorts of nasty things."

"As I said, our cops are turtles."

"Your cops are liars. Kostanov's prints were in the system, which meant your cops had him identified right away. Plus, Kostanov had another distinguishing characteristic. Want to know what it was?"

"A tight cluster of three stars tattooed at the base of his thumb, just like the man who slugged me."

"Rivertown is suffering an infestation of Russians, and that's making your cops nervous. For some reason, they've wanted to keep the floater anonymous. When I forced them to give up the ID, they tried explaining it away by saying Kostanov was simply the victim of a gang rivalry, spilled downriver from Chicago. They also said they were done with the case—and that, buckaroo, is where things get real wrong. It's an unsolved homicide. They're supposed to be telling everybody that they're sifting through leads, putting the word out to the community, the usual nonsense we puke out when we're utterly nowhere on a case. You're following me, Elstrom? They don't want me nosing around. Those Russians who accosted you don't want you sniffing around, either."

"Robinson was killed in retaliation for Kostanov?" I guessed Jenny would make perfect sense of it, when she finally called.

"Tit for tat. What's for sure is my boss is pulling me away from all this, now that Mr. Phelps has shipped his daughter off to Europe."

When I said nothing, he asked, "You knew that, right? That Amanda Phelps is now in Europe?"

"No, but that explains why she didn't answer my call."

"Without her, there will never even be a complaint of kidnapping, and therefore no official file."

"So Robinson's case will die like Robinson?"

"I'm not so sure. There's press interest. Your county ME told me some reporter is hot on the floater. He referred her to the Rivertown PD, probably with a laugh."

"Her?" I asked, like I didn't know who she was.

"Some woman. Why? Is there a woman reporter in your life?"

"Go on," I said, but I said it too slow.

"Be careful, Elstrom. Your crooked little town has always been small-time, right? Stolen cars, hookers, backroom dollar slots, but never murder. Things might be changing. You've had a tattooed Russian and now one of your own building inspectors bob up in your river. Another building inspector got shot in his home. Throw in a dead mob boss last seen alive in Rivertown, and you've got a crooked little town that's suddenly gotten quite lively."

He paused, then said, "Here's the worry: I can think of only one person who has links to both Robinson and tattooed Russians. Want me to spell out why each side might be angry with him?"

"I suppose not."

"Keep your eyes open, Elstrom. Dig a moat. Start boiling oil to throw out your skinny windows in case you're attacked."

He hung up. He'd meant it well, but he'd been wrong.

I wasn't the only person who had links to both Robinson and the Russians.

Fifty-seven

I called Jenny again, and again got sent to her voice mail. By now it was the eighth time.

I had two other calls to make. Demons were demanding to be let into the light.

I phoned Amanda's office first. "Any word from the tycoon?" I asked Vicki, her assistant.

Vicki and I had always gotten along on a superficial level. Used to be, Amanda always took my calls, and that meant it was OK for Vicki to laugh, a little.

Not today. "She's out of the office, Dek."

"Out of the country," I said, as though I hadn't learned it from a cop instead of the woman I'd once loved. "I was just calling to see how she was."

She softened, a little. "She's been working awfully hard. She needs a rest. Taking some time off will do her loads of good."

"Absolutely," I said to the vagueness.

"I'll tell her you called, when she phones in?"

"That would be swell," I said and hung up.

I had to make the second call, even though it made me smaller.

"Rudolph and Associates," the receptionist said.

"Mr. Rudolph's office, please."

"Mr. Rudolph's office," his secretary, presumably, said.

"I'm calling, really, to leave a message. He's in Europe, right? Vacationing?"

"Well yes, but—"

I hung up. Richard Rudolph, the silver-haired and no doubt silver-tongued commodities broker who'd been waiting so solicitously when I drove her back to her condo, hadn't just been Amanda's social escort. He'd been there waiting, right with her father. Now he was escorting her to Europe.

Oddly, I did not feel anger, or hurt. Mostly, I felt relief, though I wasn't ready to probe at that.

I called Jenny again, thinking to leave a ninth message.

"Yes?" she asked abruptly, whispering.

"I'm wondering—"

"Yes. Dinner. Next week?"

"I'd like that, but let's also talk now. I've got questions about a tattooed Russian man, maybe three."

I was expecting a laugh, as a mask, but what I got was a curt "Can't talk" before she hung up.

It might have been nothing; it might have been more.

I sat down in the La-Z-Boy to watch a Chicago news show and promptly fell asleep. I didn't wake up until after eleven. I was famished. I slipped into my peacoat and went out. Even though it was late, the night was unseasonably warm. The last of the drab dirty snow had melted, revealing a drab brown tinged green by the sickly yellow of my outdoor lamp. The glory of spring was on its way.

A drive to the Hamburgers was in order. A late-night, venerable fast food location on Thompson Avenue, it routinely changed owners and offerings, from hot dogs to Chinese, tacos, southern barbecue, and even once to fried fish, though images of things snagged whiskered and weeping from the Willahock killed that incarnation even quicker than the others. Never, though, had any of the owners been confident enough to gamble good money on a new rooftop sign, and so the place remained the Hamburgers.

Leo would be fine company, if he were home. He'd be up for

grease and whatever laughs might be needed to settle unsettled thoughts about what was going down in Rivertown.

I'd just turned onto his block when a tiny white light flickered in a window next door to the excavation. There was no power in the empty bungalow. Someone was inside.

I drove on. A lamp was on in Leo's front room, but there were no reflected images from the big-screen television. Ma and her friends must have been putting in bingo time at the church to salve their consciences about the movies that were soon to be flaring up again.

I edged forward a little to see down the gangway. There were no lights coming from Leo's basement office either. He must have been at Endora's, putting in bingo time of a different nature.

I continued to the end of the block, bothered by the flicker I'd seen in the empty bungalow. I was bothered, too, by Jenny's abruptness on the phone.

I turned the corners. Sure enough, Jenny had parked on the next block over. I parked twenty feet behind and got out, pulling up the collar of my peacoat, tugging down my watch cap, and looking, I supposed, like a thug out for an evening stroll.

I continued around the block to the excavation and ducked behind a stack of extra forms that hadn't been needed for the still-unpoured basement walls. After a moment, I snuck a look at the bedroom window across the hole. No tiny white light flickered from it now.

What I'd seen might have been a faint reflection of my own headlights or a lamp in a house nearby. I decided to give it ten minutes before taking my misfiring, suspicious mind down to the Hamburgers and feeding it something besides unfounded fantasies.

I only had to wait for half of those ten minutes before a van coasted silently to the curb, fifteen feet from where I was hiding. It had pulled up like a ghost ship, without headlamps or even brake lamps. Somebody had worked to make it run invisibly in the dark.

A door creaked open, and another, and then both were softly closed. Another set of doors opened. I eased up to look around the pile of forms. Two figures, one tall, one shorter, stood at the back of the van, silently sliding out an aluminum extension ladder. They carried it to the edge of the excavation and set it down gently. The shorter of them hurried back to the van and returned with a long-handled shovel and laid it next to the ladder. Both then walked back to the van and, together, tugged something out of the back.

It looked like a roll of carpet, wrapped in plastic. They each took an end and began lugging it to the excavation. By the way they struggled, it was heavier than carpet.

A woman's voice softly counted out, "One, two, three," and they heaved the bundle into the hole. It hit the gravel with a soft thud.

And perhaps a last gasp of outrage, though that was likely my imagination.

I tucked back behind the forms. They'd see me if they looked around.

The soft creak of aluminum against aluminum came next, as the ladder was extended past the forms. It rattled as it was set down into the hole and hard-soled boots began climbing down.

"Hurry, damn it," the counting voice called softly. I'd heard that voice before.

From down in the hole came the faint sound of metal scraping at stones. I'd made those same sounds, the night I buried Wozanga. The person in the hole began grunting as the digging got harder, into the frozen clay. Several times the shovel clanked against rocks, and finally the person in the hole swore at the noise. I was sure of his voice, too.

Then, in less time than I'd taken, the sound of gravel being shoveled came again as the hole was being covered up. He'd not dug as deep.

Footfalls climbed the ladder. It was pulled from the hole. They took it to the van, and slid it inside. The woman hurried back for the shovel and put it in the van, and they were gone. Only at the corner did they switch on their headlights.

I stayed low, waiting. Less than a minute later, footsteps hurried down the front steps of the bungalow next door, growing louder as the woman's shape came toward me. It could only be Jenny.

She stopped at the far side of the hole. Bright light from her video camera flashed into the excavation for an instant, and then she was done. She hurried down the block.

It was no time for a reunion. I waited until she got to the haze of light at the corner before I straightened up. I'd let her drive away before I headed to the Jeep.

She disappeared around the corner, and I stepped onto the sidewalk . . . and froze. A man had emerged from between two parked cars and was following Jenny from the street. He, too, was backlit by the streetlamp when he got to the corner. He wore a fedora. Few men wore them anymore. Except for two, outside the Rivertown Health Center.

I moved into the street, staying low and close to the cars like he was doing. He turned at the corner, toward where Jenny had parked her Prius.

I got there just as lights flashed briefly halfway up the block. Jenny was in the street, using a remote to unlock her car.

He was beside her in an instant. She stiffened. I could only stop, three cars behind them.

He reached around her, opened the driver's door, and pushed her into the bright light of the interior. He gestured with something in his left hand; no doubt he had a gun. She scrambled onto the passenger's seat, and he got in behind the wheel. The interior went dark.

I was only fifteen feet away but would be powerless against a gun.

He switched on the headlights. The Prius moved silently from the curb.

I slipped into the Jeep, waited until they got to the next corner, and started my engine.

Fifty-eight

I ran without lights, two blocks behind, as they drove east through the bungalow neighborhoods. Then, abruptly, they turned onto the dark old road that led to the factory district.

Old-timers at the health center still talked about how that narrow old road used to jam up tight with factory workers, three shifts, six days a week. They said the big-ton stamping and molding presses used to pound the road so hard that cars shook clear up through their steering wheels, and a man couldn't hold his beer right until he'd been home fifteen minutes and the shakes went away.

No more. Now it was pitch black nighttimes, because there was no sense replacing burned-out bulbs on a road that went nowhere. The asphalt had crumbled, giving in to years of the brown husks of weeds, some as tall as late-summer corn, that ran in arrogant abundance down the center of that nowhere road. Mr. Black, or Mr. Red, pushed Jenny's headlamps through them like he was bulldozing used-up crops, filling the night with the gunshot sounds of dry stalks snapping fast beneath the Prius's front bumper.

Only a killer would have need for such a road.

The Prius flashed its brake lights, lighting the night red. I cut my engine and coasted to a stop a hundred yards behind, careful not to tap out any red of my own.

He'd stopped in front of the old wood bridge crossing a bend in the Willahock and switched off the headlamps. The Prius faded into the darkness, and for an instant, the night went silent. It was March; it was cold.

The Prius's interior light snapped on as the passenger door flew open. Jenny lunged out of the car, hugging something. A gunshot sounded loud as the man in the fedora fired through her open door. She disappeared into the darkness. Running, or down.

Mr. Black, or Mr. Red, twisted toward his door, to get out and finish his kill.

I turned the key and gunned the Jeep forward, switching on my high beams.

He rolled out of the Prius, throwing up his left arm to shield his eyes, and raised his gun with his right to fire into the blinding light.

He was too slow. My bumper hit his knees, slamming him back against the Prius's open door. He went down like the dry stalks he'd just mowed over. I threw the Jeep into reverse, spinning my wheels backward to see how bad I'd hit him.

He was flat on his back, unmoving in the light of my headlamps. Blood ran from his nostrils, gashes on both arms, and one leg. His gun arm was extended at crazy angles, broken at least twice. His automatic had flown out of his hand and lay on the crumbled asphalt a yard away. He was Mr. Black, the man who'd dropped me with one punch at the health center. I killed my engine, but left my lights on, and got out.

"Jenny!" I yelled into the night.

A twig snapped past the shoulder of the road, and she came up on skittish legs to stand trembling beside me. "Is he . . . is . . . ?"

I kicked his gun well off the road and knelt to feel his neck. There was a pulse. It was faint. He might live.

He might wake up.

"Let's get to the Jeep," I said, straightening up.

"I have to find my camera."

"In a minute." I grabbed her arm and tugged her to the Jeep.

"The camera's all I have," she said.

I fished behind the seat for a roll of silver tape, grateful that every financially challenged Jeep owner must carry at least one, for those moments when previously taped tears in the vinyl roof open up to greet the sun. Or more usually, the rain.

"The key's in the ignition," I said, bringing out the roll. "Take off if he wakes up."

"I threw it down the bank," she said, making no move to get behind the wheel.

"So someone would find it, after you were found dead?"

"Brilliant, right?" Her voice was shaky, no matter the cool of her words.

"Let me take care of Mr. Black, then we'll look."

The Russian still lay motionless, but broken arm or not, I figured him for having more in killer instinct than I had in ingenuity. I worked feverishly, winding tape from his good wrist up to his neck for a once-around, then down to finish it off around his broken arm. One yank with either arm would send him to the moon in pain, if it didn't choke him.

I taped his ankles together, and his knees. I wrapped his eyes and his mouth, reasoning that if he couldn't see and couldn't yell, he wouldn't try to hobble off, and he'd stay put long enough for the sheriff to get there. When I was done, I did it all again, until I'd trussed him into something that looked mummified in shiny silver linen. By then, I'd run out of rational. I walked back to the Jeep only when I ran out of tape.

I took out my cell phone to call the sheriff.

"They'll be here any minute," she said, heading toward the Prius. "I need a flashlight."

"Who'll be here?"

"The Rivertown police, of course." She stopped, noticing the look on my face. "Dek, what's—?"

"I was at the excavation, too, Jenny. I saw, same as you."

"OK; good," she said, like it was no problem.

"No, not good. I recognized the bray, Jenny, and I recognized the sister's voice."

"What are you talking about?"

"When you called, did you give your name?"

"Some kid answered. His mouth was full. I told him there was a killer bound up at a bridge on a dark road and hung up."

We'd gotten lucky, at least for a few minutes. Benny Fittle had pulled night duty. He'd have to call somebody. That would take time.

"They can't have witnesses, Jenny. We've got to get out of here."

She stared at me for a moment, wanting to ask a hundred questions, but then she ran toward the Prius. "Not without the camera," she yelled.

She grabbed a flashlight from the glove box and disappeared down the embankment.

The road toward town was still black, but they wouldn't come with their lights on.

Please, Benny Fittle: Be confused. Be slow to call.

I ran after her. By now, she was halfway down the embankment, moving her flashlight beam side to side through the weeds.

She stopped. The camera lay on the mud, five feet from the ice at the edge of the river. It was small, almost pocket sized, and I was surprised she'd found it.

The bank of the Willahock was still dotted with slippery splotches of frozen snow, and it took too many minutes to reach the camera. It was light and didn't rattle when I picked it up.

She turned to look up toward the road. "No one's coming."

"They won't use their headlamps."

"No witnesses?" she asked, suddenly shivering.

"We've got to get out of here."

We scrambled up the embankment.

Mr. Black lay immobile. I couldn't tell if he was breathing, decided it didn't much matter.

"Your fingerprints are on the silver tape," she said, looking at him.

"They might not worry about that," I said, thinking of the speedy digging job earlier, at the excavation.

I ran to the Prius and tried to pull back the ruined driver's side door. It was bent back flat against the front fender and wouldn't budge.

I slipped behind the wheel. "Follow me."

She didn't protest. She ran to the Jeep.

We ran without lights, seeing only by the moon. I hugged the right side of the road; odds of a head-on collision between two cars running dark were good, if they didn't find us first by the sound of the Prius's ruined door. It banged against the front fender like a big steel drum at every ripple and heave in the road.

Luck rode with us. We got to the neighborhoods without passing anyone. I stopped so she could pull up alongside.

She reached over to roll down the Jeep's window. "What now?" Her voice was high, but she was in control.

"Is there anything in this car you want to keep?"

Her face froze, and then she understood about the blood that must be smeared all over the front bumper, a concern for any body-and-fender shop. She got out. "My damned camera, Dek. My notebook, and my purse." She came around to the other side, swept papers from the glove box into her purse, and grabbed her notebook and camera.

She ran back to the Jeep. "Do not pull in behind me," I called out.

I drove to the health center. This time I stopped right in the middle of the parking lot and got out holding the last of the cash from my wallet. After a moment, two of them sauntered over, zippered in black leather and smelling opportunity like wild things sniffing meat.

I handed them the money. It was a little more than a hundred and fifty dollars. "There will be no report of a theft for a week," I said.

I walked out to the curb and got in the passenger's side.

She tried for a smile. "My car's been stolen?"

"In a week, no sooner, though I expect it will become parts to-night. Let's get you home."

For an instant, she stared straight ahead, out the windshield. Then she drove to the turret.

The sensor lamps switched on the moment we stepped inside,

lighting the two white plastic chairs, my table saw, and all the fears and promises in the world on her lovely face.

Once before we'd had such a moment, supercharged, as hot as the sun. Though it had been July, it had been cold from fear and horror, just like now. We'd let that moment go; our ghosts were too close.

Now she moved a few miles closer to me and looked up. A fine grin spread wide across her face. "You've got wood?"

I nodded. For sure I had wood.

"Then let's have a great fire," she said.

Fifty-nine

The sun had not yet risen when my cell phone rang from someplace cold, under the bed.

"You've got to get over here," Leo said, when I fumbled the ringing thing on.

"Why?" I whispered, rolling over. Surely I'd been dreaming.

It had been no dream. Jenny was sitting up in bed, watching me, impervious to the cold on so much of her skin.

I took the phone from my ear, but not her from my eyes. I was not at all impervious to the cold on so much of her skin.

The phone display said it was four thirty. We'd only been asleep for two hours.

"I'm always amazed at what can happen in Rivertown," Leo said.

"I'm certainly thinking that way, too," I said, agreeably.

"I was coming home from Endora's," Leo chattered on, "and, well, jeez, you're not going to believe it. You've got to get over here."

There were heavy diesel noises in his background. "There's construction at this time of night?"

"A backhoe and a bulldozer, hoeing and dozing like it was the middle of the day." The diesels had gotten louder; he'd gotten closer to them. He shouted something unintelligible, and then the connection went away. He'd hung up.

I've always trusted Leo's instincts, but there, in my bed, in the middle of the night, embers still smoldering in the fireplace across the room, and so much closer . . . Jenny and I hadn't so much sought to banish the memory of what had happened at the excavation and the bridge as we'd lunged to claim what we'd let slip away the previous July.

"That was Leo?" Jenny, ever the newswoman, asked. "You've never told me the whole story about Leo."

"You never told me how tattooed Russians fit on his block," I countered, warming even more beneath the covers.

"Why would Leo call in the middle of the night?" she asked. The cold had finally touched her consciousness. She reached to pull the blanket up.

"Oh, don't," I said, a man of immediate need.

She grinned and let the blanket drop, knowing the cold would only improve the view. "Tell me why Leo called."

"Something's going on by the excavation."

"What?"

"Bulldozing."

Her face froze, remembering what she recorded. "Oh, no," she said, scrambling out from beneath the covers.

I remembered Robert Wozanga. I scrambled, too.

"You can't take your camera," I said needlessly, opening the timbered door. The camera wasn't in her hand anyway. "No one from city hall can ever think you might have been filming at the excavation."

"Understood," she said.

We had to park beyond the cross street. Rivertown police cruisers had blocked off both ends of Leo's block. Their lights flashed blue across the furious faces of two hundred people, rousted from their sleep by the noise of the diesels and the glare from the enormous construction lights.

They'd worked fast. The backhoe had already demolished the vacant bungalow and its foundation, dumping the debris into the new hole and on top of the splintered forms that lay ruined in the excavation next door. The bulldozer hovered attentively behind it, pushing in dirt from the mounds piled at the back of the lot.

Dozens of the neighbors shouted from behind the cordon of cops, demanding to know why things had to be smashed in the middle of the night. I doubted the rank-and-file cops had been allowed to know.

The original plan must have been to wait until first light for the demolition and filling. Little scrutiny would be attracted that early, and their first shallow burial would have lasted well until then.

That was before Jenny's anonymous phone call about another man, at the bridge. There wasn't time to scrape more gravel, dig more clay. People would be headed off to work soon.

Worse, no one knew who'd made the call, or what the anonymous woman knew. No one knew if she'd called the sheriff.

Things couldn't wait until dawn now. The plan was moved up.

"Where is city hall?" one of the bravest of the neighbors shouted. Nothing in Rivertown was allowed without the approval of city hall.

Nothing indeed, I thought. It was brazen, quite lizardly. It was perfect.

Jenny moved forward, mercifully without her camera. I stayed at the back of the crowd, resisting the thought that I should break into song and dance. Rest at last, Mr. Wozanga.

Leo found me a moment later. In the bright of the lights from the construction lamps, his hat, traffic jacket, and pants were a blur of muddy greens and oranges, except for the purple pom that now looked black and appropriately funereal on the top of his knitted hat.

"Why are you grinning so broadly?" he asked.

"I'm merely reveling in the spectacle that is Rivertown."

"You and the press arrived together," he said, struggling to produce as much of a leer as his clownish outfit would allow.

"The press is everywhere."

"If it satisfies you, then I find it deserved, and delightful. What's going on here?"

"I told you: I just arrived."

Four large haulers rumbled up, loaded with extra dirt, and everyone in the street had to back away to let them in.

"Obfuscate if you must," he shouted above the new engine noises. He pointed to a man stomping through the crowd. "He's the general contractor. He's going crazy."

I put on one of my dumb faces. I have several. "Trying to find the person in charge here?"

He tilted his pommed head back in mock concentration. "Let's see. Mr. Tebbins, the building inspector, is dead. His boss, Mr. Robinson, is dead. That leaves . . ."

"Yes? Yes?" I taunted, laughing at his antics, sure, but more in final relief that he was there at all, prancing, clowning, the old Leo, close enough to being as good as new.

"Our newest building and zoning commissioner, soon to be our mayor!" he pronounced, raising his arms like a boxer victorious in the ring. People nearby looked and, despite the chaos, smiled. They loved Leo; they were his neighbors.

"Interestingly, she's not here, enraged at what's obviously a violation of Rivertown working-hour statutes and instructing our inert police force to stop these goings-on."

"I still don't get it," he said, suddenly serious. "Why a demolition?"

"This isn't a demolition," I said. "This is a burial."

Sixty

Jenny was in a dark mood as we drove back to the turret. She didn't speak until I pulled up in front.

"Can I use your car? I want to check what I've got on professional equipment." I assumed she was talking about what she'd recorded earlier at the excavation but figured, too, that she wanted to get far away from Rivertown.

"Of course," I said. "I'll run in and get your camera."

I started to get out but sat back when she didn't move to come around to the driver's seat.

"Did I get a man killed tonight, Dek? Should I have known not to call the Rivertown police from the bridge?"

"You mean to protect the man who abducted you and took you to that bridge to kill you and dump you in the river, for what he thought you knew? You think you should have protected that man, Jenny, so he could try to kill you again?"

"I should have known to call the sheriff, not the Rivertown cops."

"That was my instinct, too, until I realized they'd simply have passed it on to Rivertown. That's why we're lucky you called anonymously. Rivertown's city hall will do anything to hush this up, including bringing in dirt movers in the middle of the night. They'd kill you, Jenny, for what you know about what's been going on."

"You're sure of the voices at the excavation?"

"J. J. Derbil and brother Elvis, dumping Mr. Red."

"And it was J. J. and Elvis who went to the bridge tonight, not the cops?"

"You'd never be able to prove it, because no one will ever get permission to dig at that excavation site again."

"I'll see you later," she said.

"I'll get your camera," I said.

She managed a small smile as she patted the pocket of her coat. "I kept it low so no one would see."

A clatter outside woke me at noon.

The Jeep had been returned. A stake truck was parked behind it. Two men were off-loading firewood and carrying it around to stack in back.

I dressed, went down, and, thinking that everything in life was temporary, used fresh grounds for the coffee. By the time I had two cups the truck was gone.

I went outside. The day was gray with the promise of new snow, perhaps lots of it. I was cheered by the hope that Jenny had seen brightness in so much gloom, and by the prospect of so much new wood.

I drove to Leo's neighborhood, anxious to see amazements. Which I did. The excavation and the bungalow were no more. The entire three-lot property had been overfilled with new dirt swept into gentle mounds.

Leo answered the door wearing a bright yellow sweatshirt adorned by a SpongeBob SquarePants holding a surfboard.

"Come in. We're having coffee and apricot Danish," he said.

I followed him into the kitchen. Two Rivertown lieutenants, still wearing their tan trench coats, sat perched on Ma's gold-flecked vinyl chairs.

Pa's revolver lay in the middle of the table, next to the Danish.

"I love impromptu parties," Leo said, pouring coffee into another of the scratched porcelain Walgreens mugs Ma had liberated, back when she'd been a full-time working girl and part-time lunch counter thief. He set a matching Walgreens plate, like the ones the officers had, on the table next to it. Ma liked everything on her table to match.

"I was just telling my friends here that they ought to go over to your place and arrest you, for your fingerprints are surely on Pa's revolver, along with mine," he said.

One of the bruisers smiled as he brought the last of a four-inch slice of Danish to his mouth.

"That true?" his partner asked me, because he could. His mouth had cleared.

"I've held that gun several times since I was a kid. You're aware I reported a burglary here, while Leo was on vacation?"

The partner nodded, but it might have been in anticipation. His eyes had drifted to the remainder of the Danish.

They were big men. Quick as lightning, I cut off two inches and dropped it on my plate.

"You got my fingerprints from the index?" I asked. My fingerprints had been on file since the Evangeline Wilts trial.

The first cop raised his eyebrows, surprised. "No," he managed, chewing.

The partner's plate still held only crumbs. He looked at Leo. Leo nodded. The second man cut off another wide slice of Danish. There was but an inch left. Wide slices can kill a Danish in no time.

"Any other prints on the gun?" I asked.

The first cop reached over and stabbed the last inch with his fork. "This is really good Danish," he said.

"Where'd you find the gun?" I asked, as though Jarobi hadn't already told me it had been in Robinson's minivan. I wanted to know what Rivertown's cops knew

"In some woods, I heard." That was the way it would go down: A gun with nobody's prints was found in nobody's car in nobody's woods. The two bruisers came to return it, so nobody would think to wonder what nobody had been up to. Robinson needed to be erased.

They finished their Danish and stood up. They left the Colt on the table.

Leo walked them out and came back. "Pa registered the thing, can you believe it? All I can think is a cop must have lifted his head off the bar one of the nights Pa brought it in. He liked to wave it around the tavern. It was a real antique."

"A Peacemaker," I said.

"A what?"

"A Colt Peacemaker, the gun that won the West," I said slowly, savoring the fact that I knew an irrelevant bit of minutiae that he did not.

Standing, his eyes were at the same level as mine, though I was seated. His didn't blink.

"So far as anyone need know, it was stolen in the supposed robbery here?"

"Sure," I said.

"How did Robinson get the Colt, Dek?"

It was time to give him another installment. "He kidnapped Amanda."

His face got stricken. "She's all right?"

"She's fine, off on a vacation, actually," I said quickly. I told him everything about the kidnapping.

"How could you drop the gun in Mr. Robinson's basement?" he asked when I was done.

"It was a time of some nervousness. Now, thanks to Robinson getting pushed off that highway alongside the woods, you got your gun back. I'm so tired of being chased."

"Where he was abducted by those two hoods?"

"Russian hoods, exports from New York."

"Why?"

"It has to do with that excavation that just got filled in, and a floater they found in the Willahock. To understand that, I need to talk to Jenny."

"Those Rivertown lieutenants said nothing when you asked about other prints on Pa's revolver."

"Robinson's were all over that gun. By wiping it down, they distanced city hall from anything he'd been up to, on their behalf or his own. They brought it back and blew you off. Now it's something stolen in a robbery, nothing more," I said.

"I think you want me to forget about that gun, too."

He was right, of course. I never wanted him to wonder about that gun either.

"I know you, Leo," I said.

"Yes?" he asked, about to be victorious.

"I know you never buy just one Danish."

He sighed and went to a cabinet, coming back with a long white bag. Opening it to reveal a second Danish, truly a miracle of golden crust, bright orange apricot, and sweet white drizzle, he said, "There are so many holes in the stories you're telling me."

I cut a fine wide slice of the Danish.

"My second night at the clinic," he said, "I had a vague dream about someone chasing me into that empty bungalow. I shot him with Pa's gun. I've had the same dream four more times since then."

"You should fantasize about better things," I said, raising the Danish to my mouth.

"You know what they say about dreams," he said.

"What?" I stuffed the tip of the Danish into my mouth so nothing unnecessary would come out.

"Ultimately, they tell the truth."

Sixty-one

That evening, Jenny answered on the first ring.

"I've been thinking about you," I said.

"More than our friend by the bridge?" she asked.

"Lustful thoughts pushed him away."

"I'm batting my eyelashes furiously, trying not to blush." Her voice was high, tight, working at trying to be funny.

"Want to have dinner?"

"Oh, be still, my beating lashes," she said, still tight.

"I could pick you up, wherever you live."

"I'm closer to you."

"How close?"

"I'm just turning off Thompson Avenue."

I ran upstairs, found a reasonably unwrinkled shirt and an un-stained pair of khakis, and was out the door in no time flat. She was waiting in a black Ford Edge.

"You look . . ." she began.

"The same?"

"Always." She laughed. This time it was genuine.

"Since you're driving, I'll give the directions?"

She agreed, and we took off in silence, both of us edgy, I thought,

planning responses and defenses to the terrors and the wonders of
the previous night.

"Where are we headed?" she asked, after several turns and fifteen
minutes.

"A medium-fancy place I know."

"What's that mean, medium-fancy?"

"Unstained tablecloths and uncrusted silverware, but still affordable."

"It's got logs on the outside," she said when we arrived.

"But, one hopes, no wood-boring beetles."

She laughed, but only a little.

We ordered unfashionable Rob Roys and food that didn't matter:
fish for her, a small steak for me.

"Your camera?" I began, in lieu of small talk.

"The camera's fine enough, but what I got at the excavation is too
dark. You can't recognize anyone. So the last of it, the bulldozing, is
meaningless."

"You'll just have to stay close to Rivertown, waiting for the next
chapter," I said, trying for light and serious at the same time

Our food came, and we talked of the corruption in Illinois and the
mop-headed former governor who, just a few days before, had flown to
Colorado to begin a fourteen-year stretch in a federal prison for being
a mop-headed greedy jackass, and how he'd driven right past the gates
so he could stop at a hamburger place to do one more meet-and-greet
by the soda machine with people who had no idea who he was. Things
like that kept us in Illinois from becoming excessively prideful.

"Speaking of confluence," I said, when we were done eating. It
was the word I'd tried out on Leo, what now seemed like light-years
before.

"Confluence?"

"A joining together of two or more—"

"I know what confluence means, you naughty man. This morning
was lovely."

"I was referring to the not so happy confluence of Russians and
lizards in Rivertown, which is your cue to answer questions."

"Does medium-fancy mean we can order tiny after-dinner drinks?"

"Oh, absolutely."

I only had to raise my hand an inch before the waiter who'd been eyeballing her all night raced over.

"Double Scotches, no ice, please," she said.

He was back with them in an instant.

"Pray ask away," she said, taking a small sip. "I'm enthralled."

I went for the unanswerable first. "It was Elvis Derbil who called you in San Francisco?"

"Nice try. An unnamed source tipped me that something odd was afoot in Rivertown. A Chicago lawyer, representing an anonymous owner, had purchased three houses in your bungalow belt, all in a row, and had applied for permits for their demolition. More mystifying, the lawyer applied for only one building permit, to construct an enormous pillared Greek Revival mansion of some nine thousand square feet. My unnamed source was quite concerned, because such temples are never built in Rivertown. I thought it intriguing enough to ask for a short leave."

"So it was that, and not the thought of a certain heartbroken eccentric, hopelessly fluttering his handkerchief out his turret, that enticed you back?"

She mock-slapped a giggle. "That's the Scotch, not me. Anyway, I worked backward from the lawyer and found he was representing a New York lawyer, who was involved with Russian mobsters, both there and here in Chicago."

"Complicated."

"Tortuous, designed to obscure."

"Too complicated for your source to be Elvis Derbil?"

"Have you read your Capone?" she asked, by way of not answering.

With that, I began to understand. "You mean when reformers made Chicago too hot for the Scarface, he moved his operation to Cicero because it was cheesy and small and he could take control of the whole town quickly?"

"Yes."

"Russians coming to take over Rivertown?" I almost laughed—it sounded like a bad play on an old Alan Arkin movie—except her expression was serious.

"They were going to go Capone one better," she said. "They knew no one in town would welcome a foreign gang. On the other hand, so many people in Rivertown were out of work, they might welcome the devil himself if he could raise home prices, create any kind of new jobs, and otherwise bring boom times. To calm the natives about their arrival, perhaps even enthuse them, they decided on a very big and visible first step."

"Build a mansion in Rivertown that everyone in town would see as signaling a coming prosperity," I said.

"A nifty plan, yes?"

It was starting to sound brilliant. "Still, Rivertown's such a cheesy place. Our crime is so tawdry."

"That's what represented the opportunity. Let me tell you about a friend of mine, a weatherman out east. He liked to go down to Miami to blow off steam. The first night, he goes into one of their grubbier little bars, meets two girls who only have eyes for him. They drink, and drink some more. It's a happy place; people are singing; the bartender is snapping pictures; everyone's having a great time. My weatherman blacks out, something he's never done before, and wakes up in his room the next morning with a small memory and a big hangover."

"His money and credit cards are gone?"

"Wrong. His wallet is intact, alongside his Cartier watch on the nightstand. His sport jacket is hung neatly in the closet, his shoes placed at the foot of the bed. All that's missing is his glasses.

"Now get this, Dek: There's a message on his phone. One of the girls has left her number, apologizing about those glasses. Apparently, he'd set them down on the bar, and she was afraid they'd get broken. So she put them in her purse and forgot to leave them with his other things, when she and her friend brought him safely back to his room. These girls are wonderful, right? He calls her, and suggests they meet up again that night. She's thrilled, tells him they'll be at the same bar at eight o'clock."

She took another sip of the Scotch. "Guess what? Things go swimmingly that night, too, though the girls did say they were leaving town early the next morning. Again there is much drink; again our hero passes out and wakes up the next morning with a huge hangover and an equally large gap in his memory. No bother. His wallet, watch, and glasses are safely resting on his nightstand. He never sees the girls again, drinks his way through the rest of his vacation, and heads home. A month later, his credit card bill arrives."

"He's had an expensive time?"

"Forty-five thousand dollars at that one bar alone."

"What?"

"Obviously, there's been a mistake, right? Who can spend that much on booze in a grubby small bar, two nights? He contacts his credit card company. They investigate and report back that it's no mistake. They've got credit card receipts for Dom Perignon and other very, very fine champagnes. Fifteen hundred, two grand per bottle. Not only that, but because that grubby little place prided itself on its hospitality, the bar owner produced photos of the glassy-eyed weathercaster holding aloft all sorts of different bottles of that very, very fine champagne. According to the owner, the weatherman bought for the house."

"Bottles with fake labels."

"The photos were a little blurry."

"And his tongue was too thick to taste fine champagne, even if he did know good stuff?"

"They made sure he wasn't wearing his glasses the second night either, just in case. Very smart, very clever; they thought of everything."

"He got stuck for the whole forty-five thousand?"

"He threatened to sue. There was a settlement. He didn't tell me much more, because he was embarrassed about getting so fleeced. He only told me as much as he did because we go way back."

"The girls would have been part of a rotating team, working with ever-changing owners of that bar," I said. It was a marvelous scam.

"Want to guess what kind of accents everyone had?"

"Slavic."

"They're creative, Dek. Rivertown is close enough to O'Hare and Chicago for conventioneers to find good times. Your infrastructure is already in place; you've got many little bars. My weatherman's champagne story is just one example of how creative the new gangs can be."

"That new house on Leo's block was big for both sides," I said.

"For the Russians, the propaganda would be their best first toe-hold. For Rivertown's rulers, it was something to be stopped quickly, before they lost control of their town. An epic battle was brewing."

"With your unnamed source stuck right in the middle of it."

"He cared about Rivertown."

"Now it's my turn to admire your loyalty," I said.

She drank the last of her Scotch. "I told him I couldn't do much, but I was too late anyway."

"There was absolutely nothing you could have done."

Her eyes had filled with tears. "These are me, not the Scotch," she said, trying for a smile.

"You got it wrong," I said.

"What?"

"Your man wasn't killed by Russians," I said.

Sixty-two

"I should have figured it, by the way he tried to help Snark," I said. "Your source was Tebbins, not Elvis Derbil."

"He was a decent guy. He believed so long as the crime in Rivertown stayed small-time, the town could make a comeback."

I signaled for two more Scotches, singles.

"Trying to get a lady drunk?" she asked.

"Trying to get a lady to understand how a painting could salve desperation."

"Finally we get to talk about Leo?"

"So long as neither he nor Amanda appears in any of your accounts."

The waiter came with the Scotch. After he left, I walked her through as much of the story as I'd ever admit.

I raised my drink, a third Scotch on top of the Rob Roy with dinner, and set it back down. The boundary had been tested enough for one night.

"You have questions at this point?" I asked.

"We're agreed Robinson and Tebbins saw an epic war brewing in Rivertown," she said, "and that's why Tebbins contacted me in San Francisco. They saw themselves as the first foot soldiers in a war Rivertown wasn't going to win."

I nodded. "They were desperate; they wanted to stay alive. Then, by a stroke of what they could only think was good fortune, Cassone shows up, asking about that old painting Snark Evans stole. Tebbins and Robinson do some research, find out the painting they saw in Snark's locker is now worth millions. Best of all, it might still be in Rivertown; Snark's old buddy from the garage might still have it. Pretending to be Snark, they call Leo and hear him obviously lying."

"Desperate times demand desperate measures, these two good men tell each other; they're going to steal that painting, save their own lives, and leave town rich men in the bargain." She shook her head softly, marveling.

"Then Leo goes into hiding, and I come around, out of the blue, asking about Snark Evans. Surely they thought I was on the trail of the painting, too."

"Adding urgency to their mission," she said, "but then Tebbins gets killed."

"By Russians, Robinson and the rest of city hall naturally think, as pushback for stopping their construction. Someone at city hall, maybe Robinson, maybe someone else, retaliates by killing Kostanov and dumping him in the Willahock."

"Now Robinson has to get out of town, fast," she said. "He starts watching Leo's house, maybe waiting for Leo to return, maybe just trying to determine the best way to break in."

"He's scared of the constant vigilance of that nosy neighbor," I said.

"And who comes around? Rudy Cassone. Only one way Cassone could have known about Leo."

"Cassone tortured it out of Tebbins."

"He then sees you club Cassone and take something that's wrapped like a painting back to your place, but you leave behind a bat that Robinson thinks may be useful later on," she said.

"He grabs the bat, yes."

"Now he switches to watching the turret, because that's where the painting is now. Then, much later that same day, up drives Amanda Phelps?"

I nodded.

"She stayed the night?" Jenny's eyes took on an intensity that didn't have much to do with the story I was telling. Of course, that might have been the Scotch, setting me to thinking wishfully.

"A couple of hours," I said, "just enough to examine the painting, but long enough for Robinson to think she fit into my life somehow. He grabbed her when she left and took her back to his place."

"Hitting even more pay dirt when he went through her purse?"

"His original intent would have been to ransom her directly to me, for the painting. When he found out she was the daughter of one of the richest men in Chicago, he contacted Wendell Phelps instead, demanding not only that Wendell get the painting from me but that he throw in two million dollars as well. Then he continued watching me to make sure I turned over the painting to Wendell. I didn't, though, because I didn't yet know anything about the kidnapping. Instead, I met Cassone in a bar, and Robinson assumed I was about to turn over the painting to the mobster. He had to stop that. While I was buying painting supplies at the craft store, he followed Cassone from the bar, shot him, and then clubbed his corpse with the bat I'd left at Leo's. It was perfect; I'd be the suspect."

"The next morning, he sees you carry out a painting, tails you to Cassone's place, and then watches you emerge some time later. He sees you give that painting to someone who he assumes is Wendell Phelps's agent."

"Jarobi; yes. Now all he has to do is get the painting from Wendell. Robinson then made up a story about his being followed."

"Are you sure he made it up?"

"I thought he was trying to make himself appear as an innocent, perhaps even about to be a victim, so I wouldn't look too closely at him. Now I think he might have been telling the truth. I think Mr. Red and Mr. Black were following him. Anyway," I went on, "I messed up his plan. I started following him, thinking the tail might lead me to catching Amanda's kidnapper."

"Those pesky tattooed Russians again," she said.

"Plus me, all of us intimidating, all of us on his tail at one point or another, though I think the Russians were only at it sporadically, just enough to make him nervous now and again."

"Confluence all to hell," she said. "He couldn't arrange to exchange Amanda for the painting and the two million with you watching his every move."

"Until I told him I was going out of town. That solved his biggest problem: me watching him. As soon as I headed to the airport, he called Wendell, probably from Wendell's office garage, and told him to get the painting and the money ready immediately. Soon enough, Jarobi arrived with the painting, and Wendell put it in his trunk. Then, amazingly, Jarobi left and Wendell, ever the believer in his fortresslike Mercedes, went up to his office, leaving the painting untended in his trunk. Christmas had come. All Robinson had to do was jimmy the lock on Wendell's car, press the trunk release, and grab the picture. He'd gladly forgo the two million if he could avoid the risk of getting caught at the exchange. The painting was what he really wanted."

She'd finished her Scotch and reached for mine. "You messed that up, too?"

"I told him that somebody was watching him that morning and that I was back and on his tail. It must have been too much; people were watching him all the time. Instead of keeping him penned in his office, at least long enough for me to grab Amanda, it triggered him to flee. He raced home to grab the painting."

"And discovered you escaping with Amanda? Why didn't he just run at that point?" she asked. "Why take off after you and Amanda?"

"I can only assume that the gasoline I was sloshing down the stairs got onto the painting as well, and it caught fire. Now the two million, waiting at Wendell's, mattered. He took off after us to get Amanda back."

"Why paint a fake in the first place, Dek?"

"It wasn't my place to hand over something Leo had hung on to all those years."

"Speaking of loyalty," she interrupted, "Amanda Phelps is appreciative?"

"Very. She went to Europe."

"Ah?"

"No; not an 'ah?' as in a question. Amanda has moved on. I have moved on."

"A man of free will," she said.

"Totally unencumbered," I said, answering what she hadn't quite asked, adding, "Especially these past few hours."

"Ah," she said again, though this time without the lilt of a question.

There didn't seem to be anything more to say, and we left. She decided I'd drive, since she'd finished my Scotch as well as her own. It would be some time before she'd get past her guilt over Mr. Black.

When we got to the outskirts of Rivertown, she asked me to drive down Leo's block and stop in front of the excavation site.

"Leo heard it's to be a park," I said.

"I suppose that's fitting," she said. "Two men are buried there."

I saw no need to correct her.

Sixty-three

"What's next?" I asked, as I slowed to turn off Thompson Avenue.

"For the story?"

"OK," I said.

"It isn't a San Francisco story, and I'm no longer tethered to any station here, but that doesn't mean I can't get traction from this."

"A book deal?"

"Or better, a career-enhancing hour of true crime television. The story's got the right ingredients."

"Once it's out there, they can't do anything to you. In the meantime, be careful." Then I said, "The Russians will give up on Rivertown?"

"They may retreat for a time, but they won't give up."

"Neither will the lizards."

"Good deal. More news from Rivertown."

"Thank goodness I've got all that new wood."

We'd both started to laugh at the cheesy double entrendre, giddy as kids, when I slammed on the brakes.

"What's wrong?" she asked. "Why are you stopping so far away?"

A light I'd never owned was shining dimly from my second-floor windows.

"Stay here," I said, reaching for the door handle.

"Are you nuts?" she asked, getting out.

We went up on foot. The timbered door was locked, but that didn't mean someone hadn't picked it. I pulled out the key, twisted it in the lock, and eased the door open.

The kitchen light I'd left on was off. Now only the new light cascaded faintly down the wrought-iron stairs.

"Go back out," I whispered. "If you hear anything, call the police."

She followed me up the stairs.

The new light, very dim, spilled out from opposite the kitchen. I tiptoed up the last few steps, stepped carefully onto the second-floor landing, and looked through the doorway.

It was small, brass, and battery operated. It was a gallery light, mounted at the top of a framed painting that hung, wrapped in a wide neon green ribbon, on the wall above the fireplace.

"It's even uglier than you described," Jenny said. She stepped close and moved the ribbon to see the artist's signature. Then she laughed loudly. Of course, that might have been the Scotch.

My cell phone rang.

"You're nearby, are you?" I asked. "Watching me?"

"Having a giggle in a bar on Thompson Avenue, imagining your consternation," Leo said.

"I am indeed consterned," I said, not caring that it wasn't a word. "I don't want it here, even for the night."

"Nobody knows you've got it, except me, and I don't want it either," he said. I could hear Endora laughing in his background.

"I'm not babysitting it."

"I went into the city today. A friend I know has equipment that sees through paint. He confirmed that it's the perfect gift for the next chapter in your life."

"What next chapter?"

"Are you alone?"

"I'm with the press."

"I rest my case. Swear her to secrecy."

I motioned Jenny to lean close as I switched on the cell's speaker.

"There's one little detail I neglected to mention," he said. "You'll recall, our man Snark painted over the Daisy?"

Jenny's perfume was light, lilac scented, perhaps.

"Of course," I managed. She and I were breathing in perfect unison.

"Old Snark used the heavy-duty oil-based stuff that we had lying around the garage. The city used it for pavement, park benches, light poles, and signage before the state outlawed it as being too toxic."

"Toxic, you say?" I said, between our breaths.

"That old paint will eat through all sorts of things, though, strangely, not canvas."

"The Velvet Brueghel was dissolved?"

"It's no longer the Velvet Brueghel; truly it's now . . ."

"The Velvet Brumsky," I said, but by then, it was to myself. I'd clicked Leo away.

Jenny left my side to pick up an armload of wood. At the base of the stairs going up, she turned to arch an eyebrow. She had but to mouth the word.

"Confluence."